Fallen Souls

The Fallen Favorites, Volume 3

Amelia Rose

Published by Amelia Rose, 2024.

• • • •

First paperback edition October 2024
First eBook edition October 2024
ISBN: 9798990211735 (eBook)
ISBN: 9798-990211742 (Paperback)
Written by Amelia Rose
Cover design by Amelia Rose
Book typeset by Draft 2 Digital

A Brief Content Warning

Hello reader, there are certain themes and elements within this book that might not be suitable for certain readers. Previous books had plenty of graphic violence, torture, and some self-harm ideation.

However, this book delves into some more personal traumatic themes. So, prepare yourself accordingly, read the list of warnings below, and decide whether or not to continue.

~ Semi-graphic violence, and body horror

~ Swear words during heated moments.

~ Conversations about, and recollections of SA trauma.

~ A brief on-the-page SA attempt (with consequences immediately doled out, I promise).

~ Multiple instances of being touched without consent.

~ Implied mass death.

~ Some explosions.

Your mental state and health are important, so please take care of yourself first.

But if you have made it this far and aren't perturbed, then you will enjoy Fallen Souls, its characters, and all the books in my series, whether released, or yet-to-be-released.

*All depictions of souls and soullessness are purely creative, and do not reflect any kind of religious belief or conjecture.

CHAPTER 1

JEB

Great choice, Jeb. Real great choice. Tension snaked down my spine while I tracked his movement across the bar, my fingers twitching toward my jacket pocket. *I really don't want a fight tonight.*

My teeth were already burning from hunger, but now they were sharpening in anticipation of a fight. *Easy boys,* I told them, reeling in the reflexes and running my tongue over them to ensure they were back to normal.

I was hungrier than I thought. Sure, skipping a meal in favor of an X-Files marathon on TV hadn't seemed like a big deal last night, but my cravings would grow uncomfortable if I didn't get blood soon. I'd thought the venue I'd chosen was a poor decision before, but now my chances of feeding on any of the brewhouse's patrons had evaporated because of the Lapsus crossing the bar.

My kind had always had a natural aversion to each other, and though that part of the curse might be gone, we're creatures of habit. Some of us float, not caring about turf or location for feeding purposes, while others lay claim to certain areas.

Me, I floated, and tonight my hunger had led me straight into this one's turf. I'd seen him before several years back, though his name escaped me. He had a natural cruel tilt to his brows, bright red hair, and a hunched gait that made him appear shorter than his true six-foot height.

I remained still as he approached. Despite the tension in my shoulders, it was apathy that kept me from moving toward or away from him—the furthest thing from fear or true concern.

But he walked right past me.

The hell? One eyebrow twitched. My hunger had distracted me from sensing him when I walked in, and he hadn't noticed me at first because I was warded. But my wards just muted my Lapsi aura, making me less detectable. They weren't that good. He'd walked within feet of me; there was no way he didn't feel or see me.

At the door, Ol' Ginge stopped for a second to greet someone—another Lapsus, of all people—and the pair left the bar together.

My brows twitched and my head tilted. Curiosity piqued, I followed.

I cast one last look behind me at the brewhouse. It'd been a poor choice for my meal. While in my time as a human, it would have been the most happening den of depravity—I should mention that would have been Puritan New England—it wasn't the most happening place tonight. It was a simple brewhouse that mainly sold beer and IPAs and was located a few blocks away from the truly hopping nightlife of downtown Portland, Oregon. I'd chosen it for the nostalgic vibe, but now I chased a different lure.

Not just because a particularly aggressive and volatile Lapsus ignored me, but because now there were *two*. *Two*

Lapsi that didn't deem me a worthy threat—which, fair, but ouch. And two Lapsi that didn't think it strange that there were *three* Lapsi in a fifty-yard radius. Because it *was* strange. Very strange.

My kind isn't as numerous as popular fiction suggests. There are *maybe* a few hundred in a single state. The odds of me running into another on any given day are slim, especially since I avoided the densely populated nighttime attractions. But here in a single bar were two. And me made three.

We weren't loners just because we're predators. It was part of the whole deal. We were the Fallen, the Fallen Favorites, or Lapsi Venti in Latin. We're descendants of Cain, the first murderer, whose punishment was to live forever, sustained by mortal blood, and to forever be shunned. Desperate to escape the loneliness, he made more Lapsi, but he underestimated the curse. His descendants didn't just shun him—we shunned ourselves.

My kind could stay together for a while, sure. But we'd never succeeded in staying in a cluster long enough to build a house or a town. This kind of nerve-itch made us more irritable and aggressive over time.

Or, rather, it used to.

Technically the curse was altered a few years ago when a young Lapsus named Danielle killed Cain. We retained everything that made us badasses: immortality, strength, and rapid healing powers. But that unbearable nerve-itch that drove us into self-imposed exile *supposedly* no longer existed.

Habits were hard to break, though. We'd been adverse to making more of our kind for millennia, and that wasn't going to change just because we could live together happily now. At the core of our being, we're predators, and predators don't like competing for resources.

The Lapsi I followed were the perfect example of our predatory nature. A human wouldn't notice, but I could tell in the way they both eyed every attractive human with a *hunger*, like wolves. But they didn't attack any of them, as if they were out tonight for more than just a tag-teaming hunt.

Dismay spread down to my fingertips as they met a *third* Lapsus at the mouth of an alley. I carefully angled myself into a shop's doorframe to avoid suspicion. I strained to listen, but whatever words they exchanged were done so telepathically. A moment later, they disappeared down the alley.

I quickened my stride so I wouldn't lose them and passed the alley as casually as I could, just in time to see the trio vanish through a nondescript door. I could feel the wards all the way from the mouth of the alley. That explained why the Lapsi had *walked* to this location rather than shifted: those wards couldn't be shifted through, and if I took one step into the alley, the wards would broadcast my presence.

Why would they need wards? My curiosity morphed into incredulity—bordering dangerously close to true concern. Because this wasn't weird anymore: it was bizarre.

CHAPTER 2

HANNAH

I had a date that night. Sorry, I'm just jumping right in. But that's the only way I can think to start off my part of the story. I had a date.

Mind you, I wasn't exactly looking forward to this date. Dating as an adult isn't the way it was in your teens. There's no giddy, butterfly-tummy, jumping up and down excitement before a date. Like when your eighth grade crush asks if he and his mom can pick you up and take you to a crappy movie. Where you rush home to tell your mom and spend the next several days mulling over what you're going to wear. Not that I ever had that kind of *normal*, but that's beside the point.

No, when you're an adult, the most you feel before and after a date is *dread*. Though perhaps it's just me.

I still don't know why I said yes in the first place. He was a fellow nursing student, and I'd spoken to him only a handful of times. But when he asked me out, instead of saying, "No, I really should study for our midterm that's next week," I said, "Sounds great!" I might have even giggled. To my never-ending shame, yes, I definitely *giggled*.

I nearly canceled twice but chickened out both times. Because I keep my word, and when I say I'm going to do something, I do it. But damn it, I should have canceled.

Instead, I found myself meeting this fellow student in downtown Portland for drinks. I fretted over my outfit for exactly ten minutes and ended up walking out of the house in a loose-fitting green tank top tucked into a short, *short* black skirt, and a black pleather jacket. My eyeliner perfectly ringed my brown eyes. And my long blonde hair was fluffed and styled to look effortless. All I can say, looking back on the outfit, is that I'm thankful I wore sneakers that night.

I said goodbye to my roommate on the way out the door. She was in the living room, putting on a movie. Her textbooks and notes were spread out on the coffee table in front of her. I wished I was joining her in her studyfest instead, but I didn't say it.

She and I didn't know each other well, and our rooming situation was as uncomplicated as it could get. She loved my record player and stereo. And I loved that the second floor was graciously mine and that it had a wall-to-wall mirror and a ballet barre.

I feel bad about disappearing on her like I did. It wasn't my choice or anything, but I *am* sorry I couldn't reach out to her, and I'm sorry for the worry it caused her. Though I genuinely hope she got lots of use out of my stereo system.

I only had to wait a moment on the porch for my Uber to pull up. My date had offered to pick me up, but I wanted to err on the side of caution—I didn't want him to know where I lived—just in case. He didn't press the matter, thankfully, and was going to Uber also. That way we could both drink *and* we could leave separately.

The Uber drive was uneventful and almost completely silent. As we approached downtown from the suburbs, we passed a brewhouse that didn't look too busy. *That would have been a better place for a first date.* But, alas, we'd settled on drinks in a much more crowded part of downtown, close to the river.

We arrived at the bar my date had chosen—or, rather, the Uber driver got as close as he could get, which wasn't very, and I got out. I dodged puddles of concerning viscosity and unknown depth and waited outside the bar for my date—he was five minutes late, but seeing how much trouble my Uber'd had getting close, I didn't fault my date.

During those five minutes when I was outside alone, I was approached three times by older men, but only one called me a bitch when I politely and firmly dismissed him. I let myself believe that was a good omen. Maybe the night wouldn't be as bad as I was dreading.

CHAPTER 3

I watched the door in the alley from the roof. It was a safe place outside the wards and a good vantage point in case more unfriendly Lapsi approached. I hoped no more showed up. I was already feeling more unease than I'd had in fifty years, and I wasn't sure how much more I had left in my reserves.

Almost an hour had passed since I left the brewhouse, and the hunger was growing more intense by the minute. But I didn't dare leave my post to find my fix.

Instead, I passed the time by people watching and silently lauding humanity's progress in the fashion department since I'd died in 1631. For those first few years of my existence, the peak of fashion in my humble village had been tight pants and loose, billowy white shirts crammed into tighter over-layers. Why did that ever make sense? Our shirts were knee-length, and we tucked them into breeches. Unbelievable. And an unnecessary waste of good fabric.

And women had it worse. I only had to worry about my tucked-in shirt giving me a lumpy backside, but women had so many layers. Underclothing, corsets, petty skirts, then yards and yards of fabric. I saw more women die of heatstroke in those days than died in childbirth.

Over the centuries, I rejoiced as their clothes got less restrictive, less voluminous, and less controlled. I loved the flapper days. I enjoyed the sundresses of the '50s and '60s. And I applauded when pants became universally accepted for all.

I made it through the phase of obscene neon triangles and shoulder pads of the 1980s by living in Miami and donning fitted pastel suits. I wasn't the biggest fan of the pastels—seriously, what is wrong with black?—but it beat the alternatives of tight leather pants or amorphous dad jeans. But, truly, I preferred the '80s to the '90s.

Thankfully, fashion made men's pants looser over the decades, and they no longer hugged everything our fathers gave us. It went a little too far though in the '90s, with those grotesquely baggy pants. Combined with the lingering love of Cosby sweaters, 90s fashion was obscene.

Things started looking grim again in the early 2000s when skinny jeans returned in emo fashion—or was it the '80s nostalgia? But then again, there might have been a method to that madness. Maybe the skinny jeans trend was started by ecologists after they traced the exponential population growth down to its true root cause: pants tightness. The looser men's pants, the bigger the baby boom.

I smelled a conspiracy. I made a mental note to cross check the population growth of the late '80s against that of the early 2000s as soon as I got home.

This musing was mostly to distract myself from the itching hunger growing stronger as the night stretched on.

What a Lapsus feels when it needs blood isn't exactly a hunger or a thirst: it's a *craving*. Your teeth itch, wanting to grow into their pointed fangs. Your insides start to burn, like you're holding your breath—even though we don't breathe. Anxiety builds until all you can hear is a pulse in your ears, but it isn't your pulse you're hearing: it's everyone else's. It gets worse until you get your fix. And I *hate* it. I hate feeling like nothing more than an addict.

I'd never gone more than a few days without it. The older the Lapsus, the longer they can push it, but I didn't like going longer than two days. After that long, I felt more like an animal than a powerful, immortal man.

Finally, there was movement in the alley. Though what I saw file out into the alley didn't make me feel any better.

Ten Lapsi walked out of whatever little meeting had taken place. I assumed this state had only a couple hundred Lapsi. And right there below me were *ten*.

What the hell is going on?

I gently probed their auras with telepathic feelers, like I'd been doing earlier while following the first two Lapsi. Not all of them gave me the heebie-jeebies: two hunched their shoulders and shoved their hands in their pockets as they walked away shaking their heads. Like me, they seemed unpleasantly puzzled—bewildered, even.

The majority walked back into the alley, arrogant as ever, but somehow looking even more needlessly hungry than before. These headed toward the busier street and disappeared. The wards had been lifted apparently—or they were only one-way wards. The other two walked the other way down the alley, toward the outskirts of downtown, before it turned into a residential area.

At first, I'd allowed myself to think this was something innocent—as innocent as things could be for blood-suckers. Maybe they were forming a softball club for Tuesday nights. That wouldn't be bad. Would I have wanted to join them? Hell no. But it would've satisfied my curiosity, and I'd have gone along with my existence.

But the majority of the Lapsi down there were the bad sort. The kind that kills just for fun, not caring about the risk or hiding the unexplainable evidence. And they'd left this meeting looking almost *hyped*. Being in the minority here was unsettling.

I was about to turn from my post and disappear when someone else stepped through the door. I leaned forward over the ledge to see better.

She was tall and willowy with long fiery red hair that fell down her back in loose curls. I couldn't see her face or gauge how old she appeared. But she was young—most Lapsi were, but not as a rule. She wore a long white skirt and a fitted peacoat. She followed the two retreating Lapsi.

"Oh, boys," she called softly as she approached.

The two Lapsi stopped and turned around. One looked like he was sixteen and the other no more than twenty-five—though their true ages were anyone's guess. They eyed her warily.

"I couldn't help but notice your frowns back there. You weren't as sold as the others, were you?" the woman said.

"You made some valid points." The older-appearing of the two Lapsi placed himself between her and the younger one. "We're still considering."

"I understand." Her voice was practically a purr. She sounded pleasant enough, but my eyes narrowed. She took another step toward them and stopped. "It's a lot to absorb. But you see, I already know what your decision will be."

Silver flashed by her side an instant before she plunged the blade into his chest.

"Michael!" the younger Lapsus exclaimed as the older—Michael—collapsed. Only he didn't collapse: he crumpled and then simply, well, he dusted.

Shit. It was all I could really think. I was too surprised.

Youngster let out a lamenting moan and lunged at the woman. Before he made it more than a step, he was thrown back against the wall of the alley, though not by the female Lapsus.

The figure that'd appeared by her side was humanoid in shape, but it wasn't anything close to human—I knew better than most. The bald head and large, pointed ears gave it away. His bare torso and arms were covered in dark, interlocking tattoos. I was on the roof above them as he crouched over the fallen Lapsus, but I *knew* his face had vertical slits where his mouth should be and black gaping holes the size of baseballs where eyes would be on a human face.

Soul Eater. I took a step back in revulsion.

While I'd seen a Soul Eater before, the younger Lapsus hadn't, but he was perceptive enough to be unnerved. Demons are uncommon; the most common were Kryrie, but they 'd been officially banished. I'd encountered only one Soul Eater in my entire existence, and it'd cost me dearly.

The creature placed a hand over Youngster's mouth—a hand that contained a horrifying sucking vortex in its palm, like a vacuum—before he could jerk his head away. His scream was snuffed out as the hand pressed over his mouth.

It was over in two seconds. Youngster blacked out and slumped backward against the wall. The Soul Eater disappeared, guzzling hungrily at its vacuum-hand. *Creepy fucking bastard.*

The woman kicked dismissively at the dust on the alley floor. Most of it had either blown away or formed a kind of mud on the damp alley floor. Without another glance at the slumped, now-soulless Youngster, she continued down the alley, toward the quiet streets beyond.

My mind was firing through thoughts faster than I could entirely process. I'd just witnessed an atrocity. But *why* had it occurred? Clearly, something bad was afoot, and Red was a key component, if not the ringleader herself. She'd killed the one Lapsus without hesitating, but for what reason? And what nagged at me most was that she hadn't killed the other one. What was the point of stealing his soul instead of killing him?

For the second time that night, I followed someone when I should have turned the other way.

CHAPTER 4

JEB

Before, I'd been following someone out of curiosity. But why the hell was I following this one? To join her? Hell no, I wasn't going to do that. And I'd seen what she did to those who refused her. Was I following her so I could stop her? I theoretically *could*.

The other Lapsi hadn't been expecting it. Lapsi-on-Lapsi violence rarely resulted in death, and they hadn't been armed. I, however, had multiple silver weapons concealed on my person that would be fatal if used in the right context. I didn't make a habit of it, but I'd killed Lapsi before. And call me paranoid, but I liked to be prepared.

It didn't mean I was gung ho about killing Red, even after seeing her destroy two Lapsi, unprovoked.

I stayed on the rooftops, shifting from one to the other and keeping a safe distance from her so I wasn't detected. This worked well until we reached the definitive end of the downtown area. The buildings gave way to a wider street and, several hundred feet farther, a freeway interchange. Across the wide street were some one-story failed businesses and a seedy paycheck advance office. Beyond that were houses.

The city block ended in a small courtyard with a decorative memorial arch of some distinction. I reached the end of the last roof before the courtyard and halted. Red crossed the courtyard, into the open, but she stopped when she reached the sidewalk.

"Are you going to stay up there all night, or are you going to ask me to dance?" She turned and looked directly up at me.

Shit. I was caught. I'd been wondering why she was walking away instead of shifting. Now I had my answer. She'd been luring me.

I could have disappeared right there—and probably should have. But that was the move of a coward. I had to go down there and confront her. But how? I thought of the Lapsi I'd seen leaving the meeting. The majority of them gave me the creeps, but they were the ones who'd gotten out of it alive. I had to pretend to be like them and lean into my sociopathy that I usually tried to mask.

I shifted from my spot on the roof and reappeared behind her—a power move.

"I was only wondering why I wasn't invited to the party," I said in a low, not-quite growl.

She turned smoothly toward me, and at last, I could see her face clearly. She was exceedingly pretty with a regal, aquiline nose, rosebud lips, and dark brown eyes. Her curly red hair was pulled partially back and away from her face, though ringlets hung from her temples.

And it wasn't a skirt she was wearing, but a long white linen dress with simple gold embroidery around its empire waist and a deep V neckline. It was reminiscent of classical

Grecian dress, and strangely anachronistic when paired with the long black peacoat.

"My apologies," she cooed, her rosebud lips turning slightly downward into a kind of pout.

Her appraising gaze traveled from my head to my feet. Surely, just as I found her exceedingly pretty, she found me rather attractive as well. I've no reason to deny I was attractive. It's not a boast, it's just how it is. The pretty are more alluring and attract the most prey—and envy. Attracting and repelling simultaneously was Cain's curse.

When we're changed, our best youthful features are accentuated and frozen in time. Bones and cuts heal, and acne clears up, like we died at the peak of health, though not many of us actually did.

I'd been a goat farmer on the outskirts of a Puritan village. I grew up lean due to the modest, meager wages—but with strong bones from the milk. Popular fiction paints us as fair, with nearly translucent skin, but it really all depends on where and how we're changed. I spent much of my life outside, walking and tending goats. My skin was tanned when I died, so tanned I remain. My medium-dark brown hair had been the same length and texture for nearly 400 years: not short-cropped, but not touching my collar, with a kind of attractive but not overpowering wave to it, which I styled, or at least tamed, when I was so inclined.

When her gaze returned to my face, her smirk had turned teasing.

"We didn't mean to be so exclusive, but unfortunately secrecy is kind of a must at this stage of the game."

"But not too much of a secret that I wasn't able to smell that something was happening," I said, still keeping my voice low and menacing. I turned one lip upward into a sneer. "But those pesky wards kept me from attending. I'm sure it was informative."

"So you follow a helpless woman through alleyways to voice your annoyance at being locked out?" She challenged me pleasantly, but I could sense the irritation in the words. A woman calling out a man for his creepy behavior. It was fair, but I had a part to play.

"I was *over* the alleyways, technically," I corrected her, deepening my sneer. I chanced a step toward her, challengingly. Asserting more predatory dominance, I circled her. "And from what I saw, you're hardly helpless. Sorry I didn't offer my assistance, but you seemed to have it well in hand."

Cutting down two unarmed Lapsi in cold blood. Yeah, you had it very well in hand.

"Yes, just a slight disagreement, that was," she said, her voice low like mine. She didn't bother turning to follow me with her eyes as I circled her: she waited until I was facing her again. Her eyes narrowed slightly, but her smirk reappeared. "I appreciate a man who doesn't interfere with a woman's affairs."

I could sense the double edge in her voice. She was lauding me for not interfering earlier, but I could hear the warning in her words too. Challenging her would be unwise, but backing down completely would show weakness. Ultimately, my inner sociopath decided to stick my hand into the fire.

"You got a name to go with those sultry lips and devastating curves?" I asked, raking my eyes down her figure again.

"Cassandra," she said, her smile widening to show some of her white teeth. "Cassandra of Troy."

I've never met anyone from the real Troy. I fought to hide my interest and retain my bored expression.

"Cassandra, really?" The only evidence of my surprise was a shift of my eyebrows. "But your hair is rather reddish..."

"Yes, it's extremely rare, but it is all natural," she said. Her eyes flashed dangerously for a second. "Rare and coveted for its beauty. I was abducted from my home for it."

She didn't elaborate, but I knew the gist of her fate in the fictionalized epic. She had been kidnapped by Ajax and taken to Agamenon, where it goes without saying, she was raped. Numerous times. Like the fate of Troy, her tale was not a happy one.

"Sounds rough," I said with an ambivalent shrug. I gave her a bored eyeroll, then hunched my shoulders and continued in a low growl. "Everyone's got a sad past. If you think that makes you special, you're mistaken, girly."

She didn't rise to the bait like I expected her to. The changes in her facial expression were minuscule, but I was experienced in reading them in others. Her eyes flashed with seething anger—I'd struck a nerve—then they narrowed in a subtle look of incredulity. Good. I wanted under her skin. The more she talked, the easier it was for me to play the aggressor. Then she looked almost smug.

"I suppose," she said in agreement, her mouth curling back into a smirk. "Such is our lot in existence, isn't it?"

Before I could retort with something sarcastic, she plowed on.

"My life is only one example of what we all have to endure. I was abducted from my people, then I was changed into something that could never have a people. Not only were my people—my beautiful city—destroyed, leaving nothing for me to return to when I was free, but I couldn't ever belong anywhere."

"It's a lonely gig," I said, but I rolled my eyes in disinterest. "But that's not how it is anymore."

"Exactly," she said emphatically. "We've been prevented from community, from loving our neighbor, for millennia. But things have changed, as you said. The worst part of Cain's curse has been lifted, and we are no longer barred from having what humans have."

I would argue that the worst part of Cain's curse was feeling like an addict every time we needed blood, but I was willing to concede this one point to her. To each their own.

"Ah, so you're...organizing," I said, satisfied at last to be getting to the point. I realized that I sounded displeased, but every plan needed some skepticism to spur it forward. I had a feeling Cassandra would take that bait. "Making a little club?"

"Oh, far more than that," she said, shaking her head and pouting.

"A commune then," I said, narrowing my eyes. This had *cult* written all over it. I hated cults, but I buried my disdain for the purpose of prying further. "That's going to be a little difficult, don't you think? We're scattered across the globe.

Not a lot of people to join the little town you're thinking of constructing."

She looked annoyed, like I was missing a big piece. What big piece though?

"Not yet, but there will be," she protested with a cunning grin. "Sure, the older Lapsi might still have a few qualms about making more Lapsi, but that will change over time. The younger ones though ... those who haven't spent so many years feeling the torturous burn when trying to stay with someone they love. They will—and are—making new Lapsi. Think about it. A boy is changed. Shortly after that, he changes the girl he loves. She then changes all her girlfriends. It will snowball before too long.

"Just imagine: so many new Lapsi suddenly released from the laws of man. Not to mention the strain on resources that until now hasn't existed. And the unwanted attention that, say, fighting over resources will bring down on us." She shook her head in disgust. But she didn't pause long enough for me to jump in with an argument—had I had an argument. "We will need order. And structure. Otherwise, it will be chaos. Chaos is such a *human* thing, and we're not human. All I'm doing is laying down the groundwork for the beginnings of a community. Somewhere we could live and not be challenged. Somewhere we could undeniably belong."

Yes, definitely a cult. And, like with all cult leaders, I found I couldn't disagree with her points. If the population of Lapsi grew too big, too fast, some kind of infrastructure *would* be needed so there wasn't a death-spree every other week. But something was off: something my brain was tripping over itself to figure out.

She'd cut down two Lapsi who might have been the kind who wanted community. The way the older had put himself between Cassandra and the younger wasn't lost on me. They had the lovesick vibe.

But the Lapsi she hadn't attacked weren't exactly the type to want that order. More like, they would want a new world order, with Lapsi on top.

Oh. Oh no. A sick feeling spread in my gut as I followed this train of thought. *Shit.* But I couldn't let her know what I was realizing. She was warming me to the idea by telling me the small details first, to see how I would take them.

"Sounds lovely," I said, but I added in a grimace to show my disdain. "But peace, love, and sharing space with other Lapsi isn't something I'm interested in. I'm better off on my own." That part at least wasn't a lie.

"Are you so sure? It's something that has been denied us since the beginning. It's the one thing that humans had that we couldn't. For too long we've been living on the outskirts of humanity, denied feeling like we belonged or feeling that we owned anything. We've been overlooked and turned into a sparkly laughingstock. Denied community. Denied love. Denied a feeling of permanence, despite being very, *very* permanent. Denied a seat at *any* table."

I couldn't help it. I had such muted emotions that feeling anything but boredom and annoyance was rare. But as she spoke, my mouth split into a genuine grin. This was ridiculous. When she finished, I burst into derisive laughter that wasn't fake. She probably wasn't expecting it, but I didn't see her expression. I was too busy rolling my eyes.

"That's what you think?" I said after my brief laughter died away. "That we're a kind of second-class citizen, beneath *mortals*? If that's how you've been living and seeing the world, you've had a truly sad existence. We're stronger, faster than them, and guaranteed to survive. We were gifted powers a human only wishes they had. Humans are fragile, mewling infants playing a board game that they don't know the rules to. They're messy and stupid, they have such short, pointless lives. If you've been bowing down to that—if you've felt second-rate to that—then they aren't the issue. You are."

I meant these things, but I also liked humanity. They invent gods to bring them comfort and devils to punish their enemies. They have such short lives that they live for the moment. They're adorable and beautiful in their flaws. They're optimistic to a fault and never stop hoping things will improve. They adapt so things *can* improve, and that's what I envy and respect the most. They adapt and innovate, while we just ... exist. We observe but never really take part.

But I held all this back because it wasn't what Cassandra would want to hear.

A sly, cunning smile was spreading across her lips while her eyes narrowed, as if she knew something. Had I walked into something she was setting me up for? Instead of postering at me, she'd led me to defend my race. I thought I'd been playing her well enough to garner information from her, but she'd been playing me. She was good. *Shit.*

"My, my, I could sure use you and your rhetoric on my side," she said in a purr. She took a small sauntering step toward me. I wanted to move away, but I held my ground. I knew she was armed, which made me wary, but after falling for her play, I needed to hold onto whatever ground remained. "I admit I find you so interesting. You and your lack of soul could be so useful to me. But unfortunately, you aren't all you want me to think, are you?"

I said nothing. I kept my gaze narrowed, on guard and aggressive. *Give nothing away, Jeb*, I told myself needlessly.

"A soulless Lapsus with so much passion for his race? Very intriguing, I'm not ashamed to admit," she continued. I should have sensed where she was going, but her prowess—and those lips—were distracting. "But, unfortunately, with still half a soul, you aren't as useful to me as I would like."

"I don't—"

The Soul Eater appeared behind her, and my reaction to the sight of those gaping eye sockets and thin tattoos covering its exposed skin was involuntary. My lips curled back into an animalistic snarl, and I took a step back, onto the edge of the curb.

A deep, throaty laugh bubbled up out of Cassandra.

"You see?" she cooed. "You wouldn't be afraid of him if you didn't still have remnants of a soul to lose."

I glared, recovering some of my composure. The Soul Eater hadn't advanced, but my skin itched with wariness.

"Cute," I said spitefully, making my shoulders relax and standing to my full height. "Tell me, how did you get one of those as a pet?"

"I could tell you, but I won't," she said, unfazed by my oppressive, menacing presence staring down at her. "You see, I want you on my side. I would love that very much. But I've seen myself triumphant, in front of my city. And I didn't see you there, Jebediah."

The hateful, angry sneer that spread across my face at the sound of my full name was an instant, knee-jerk reaction. It outweighed my surprise—I'd never told her my name.

Cassandra smirked at having riled me.

"Yes, you're far too interesting. I don't want to kill you, Jeb." Her eyes unfocused for a second and flashed back into focus. A wide grin spread across her face. "Thankfully, I have something to distract you with so you don't waste any more of my time."

She moved so quickly that I had only an instant to prepare myself for the sharp sting of a silver blade to my non-beating heart. At least it would be quick.

But instead, she pressed her hands to my chest and shoved with a strength three times that of a mortal. Unbalanced, I stumbled off the curb and into the street.

CHAPTER 5

HANNAH

I t was a very bad date. I knew it would be, but it didn't make it any better knowing it. It wasn't the worst date, but *still*. Pretty bad.

It was a mix of poor choice of venue, poor conversation, and a general lack of shared interests. I downed two strong drinks in the hopes of improving things, but it didn't. I think he'd heard down the grapevine that I was a dancer and asked me out because he thought it would be more interesting than it was. Or he just wanted a piece of "dancer" ass. Most likely the latter.

Anyway, I don't want to talk about it. Even after all that's happened since then, I still think the date was the worst part. Which is hyperbole, mind you, and unfair to the guy, but still. I don't want to talk about it.

Instead, I'd rather talk about my Uber driver who picked me up from this bad date. He seemed like a decent man. I wish I could have known him better.

Oh. I used the past tense, didn't I? That's foreshadowing, isn't it? I'm sorry. But for the small part he has in this story, I feel he deserves a full description. It's only fair.

By some act of providence, some of my date's friends showed up after an hour and a half of awkwardness. Normally that would be horrifying, but for me, it was a way out. They talked him into joining them for the rest of the night, and I managed to disentangle myself from the group with minimal difficulty.

It was late in the evening—about midnight, maybe a little later—but the streets were still hustling and busy, and I had enough alcohol in my system to make me fearless and confident. I walked a few blocks northwest to somewhere where the streets were more maneuverable with a car and dipped into an uncrowded by-the-slice pizza place.

I bought a can of soda and sat in a booth to call an Uber. I eyed the pizza on the heated racks and thought seriously about purchasing a slice. I'm thankful I resisted: with everything that happened later, I would have vomited pepperoni if I'd eaten.

I waited approximately four minutes to hear from the driver. He called me instead of texting his location.

"Hello, this is Gerry from Uber. Are you ready to be picked up?"

"Yes. Please. And. Thank you," I said, enunciating each word.

"All right, just letting you know that I am still about two minutes out. Are you alone, miss?" Normally this question would raise flags, but it didn't. He sounded like a good, genuine guy. And trust me, he was. There's no twist here, but damn that past tense.

"Yes. Thank the stars! Yes, I am alone," I responded emphatically. I was drunk. Not terribly so, but drunk enough to be silly.

"All right," Gerry said again. I could hear the good-natured amusement in his voice. "I will be at your location in a bit. I am in a green Chevy Spark. You stay inside until I pull up, okay? Be safe."

I agreed and we hung up. Precisely one minute and forty-five seconds later, the green Chevy pulled up to the curb.

"Hello, Gerry from Uber," I said as I slid as modestly as I could into the back seat and closed the door behind me.

"Hi there. How's your evening going?"

"It could be better, Gerry," I said, closing my knees primly—short skirt, remember?—and buckled up. I slumped back in the seat, suddenly so tired. "But I don't want to talk about it."

"I won't ask, then," he said with good humor. He glanced at me through the rearview mirror. He was maybe my dad's age. I wish I could give a detailed account of what he looked like, but I can't. I just remember sandy hair, crow's-feet around the eyes, and sleek wire glasses. "You been drinking, hun?"

"Just a little. But I'm legal," I said, winking at no one.

"I wasn't questioning that, I promise," Gerry said as he pulled slowly away from the curb. "But there is a small cooler on the floor back there. It has water in there if you want it. Help yourself."

"Thank you, Gerry," I said, perking up. I couldn't stop saying his name. I liked the sound of it. There was something comforting in it. It sounded so mundane and safe.

True to his word, a little cooler sat on the floor. I opened it and pulled out two chilled water bottles. I downed half of the first one before we made it a block.

"Are you married, Gerry?" I asked conversationally as we cruised to a gentle stop at a redlight. His turn signal flashed rhythmically and soothingly.

"I am! Married with two girls. One about as old as you." Another glance in the rearview mirror.

Called it, I thought, smiling to myself. I looked out the side window as the light turned green and we started forward again. The lights looked so pretty.

"I don't know if I want to get married," I said randomly. "It is so...expected. So...appealing, though. But, ugh. Dating. Dating sucks, Gerry."

"Are you a student, miss?"

"Yes. Nursing student. I'm on year two of an intense, accelerated program," I said proudly.

"Well, I'm going to sound like a dad here." He glanced back at me again. The crow's-feet were crinkled further—he was smiling at me. "But love and getting married is nothing to rush. Focus on your studies and your career first."

"Didn't sound too dad-like to me," I said after a giggle. "My dad would have said to stop being such a sloppy drunk, you're embarrassing yourself. Okay, maybe he wouldn't say that. But he would say I should be studying instead of being out."

"Well, I can't argue with that last part," he joked. "But it's Friday night. You're allowed to live a little."

Another red light, and I looked back out the window. We were almost out of downtown.

"Are you a Gerry with a G? Or with a J?" I asked as the light turned green. I couldn't remember what the app had said.

"It's Gerry with a G," he replied nonchalantly.

I giggled uncontrollably for a second. I couldn't tell you why I found it so funny.

"Well, that's good. You know why?" I said after I stopped giggling. "Because you are a G. You hear? I know people don't say that anymore, but you are a G, Gerry."

He chuckled, and I chose to believe it was a genuine laugh and not just humoring me. Actually, I take it back. I think he enjoyed the joke. Because Gerry was a sweet, kind man. For the five minutes I was in his car, he was nothing but kind.

My head lolled on the back of the seat, but I righted myself as I felt our speed increasing. I looked out the window at the signs. We were at the edge of the downtown area. The freeway onramp was ahead of us.

Gerry was glancing in the rearview mirror at me because of my movement. In the split second his eyes were off the road, mine were on it. I saw the man stumble into the street in front of us before Gerry did, but I didn't have time to draw a breath to warn Gerry.

It didn't feel like we hit a man, though. It felt like we hit a wall.

CHAPTER 6

I woke to a rhythmic pressure on my chest. A pair of small hands was pressing over my breastbone in short bursts of five, pausing, and then doing another five compressions. And someone was muttering "please live" each time she pressed into my chest. *What the hell?*

The scent of human blood was strong in the air, and I groaned with hunger before batting the hands away from my chest. A gasp sounded above me, and she—whoever she was—shifted her weight painfully onto my groin. I stifled another groan—this one in agony rather than hunger—and unconsciously grabbed her sides to lift her off before finally forcing my eyes open.

"Holy shit, you're alive!" she blurted, staring at me with huge dark hazel eyes.

She was a young blonde, around my frozen age, straddling my hips. She was rather underdressed in a...very...short skirt and a tank top. Blood was smeared across her forehead and in her hair, and she was bleeding profusely from her hand. My hands still clutched her sides, and as I sat up, I guided her off me. She didn't protest and moved almost like a posable doll until she was kneeling on the street next to me. She stared at me incredulously the whole time, but my eyes were elsewhere, already taking in my other surroundings. I couldn't remember what had happened or why I was in a street.

"Thank god! You had no pulse...I was so scared—"

"You bled on me," I said, turning from her and looking around. My mind was still trying to recalibrate. It usually took a moment after scrambling, but this was rough. *What even happened? It takes a lot to knock me out. It takes...*

About twenty feet from where we were both crouched was a car—or what was left of it. *Oh. Right.*

"Yeah, I–I'm sorry. I cut my wrist, I think," the girl said, holding it close to her chest in her nervousness. "The door didn't work. I had to climb out..."

My eyes went back to the car. It must have thrown me. The car itself was crumpled beyond recognition. The hood was torn open and flared out from the center. It didn't make sense how this girl was even still alive.

"Were you driving?" I asked, still staring at the wreckage.

"No, I...was Ubering. The driver...he's...he's dead," she said.

Now I could see the top of a sandy head leaning over the steering wheel and dashboard. The sandy hair was glistening with blood.

"I'm sorry," I said flatly. My mind was still catching up, and I couldn't gather up any of my few emotions to put sympathy into any words. "This is my fault."

Lapsi aren't impervious, but we're hearty. Getting hit by a car won't kill us, but it will do a number on the car. I would say it's like hitting a deer, but it's even more than that. More like a tree. That car hadn't been going more than forty miles per hour, but if you hit a wall at that speed, you're going to die. This girl was in the backseat, so she had a higher chance of survival, but she was lucky to be alive. Very, very lucky.

"You—you didn't have a pulse," she said warily, as if apologizing for trying to do CPR on me. I would have laughed if I my thoughts weren't so sluggish.

"Yeah, that happens sometimes," I mumbled vaguely, not thinking. The girl kind of nodded in acceptance and fell silent.

I couldn't think clearly. Had Cassandra done something to me before I got hit? Who was Cassandra? Oh, right. Big baddie with a Soul Eater pet. Red, I'd nicknamed her. I had to stop her, right? Why was I in a street? Oh, right. Car. Dead human over there, bleeding human behind me. I think I'm craving. Why is she bleeding? Did I do that?

"I—How are you alive?" she asked, watching me carefully as I stood up without any injury.

"Just very lucky, I guess," I said, still not really paying attention to what I was saying. "As are you."

Something was bothering me about my surroundings, but I couldn't put a finger on it. I couldn't hear anything suspicious or much of anything at all. The night was quiet, but wait—wasn't *that* suspicious?

"How long was I out?" I asked her. She didn't respond immediately. I turned back to face her, stepping toward her. She stood, swaying and started to stumble. I cupped her elbow to steady her but still eyed the street and the wreck warily. "How long were you doing CPR on me?"

"I–I don't know. It took me a few minutes to get out of the car. I don't know how long I was out," she said, looking anywhere but at the car and the glistening sandy hair in the driver's seat.

"Why is no one here?" I voiced aloud, though I didn't expect an answer. I stepped back from her and turned, looking all around us.

Where was everyone else? We were away from the busy, gridlocked streets of downtown nightlife, but we were close to the freeway interchange. Cars should be passing from either direction, even if it was an odd time of night. Someone would have called an ambulance or the police. But this street was as empty as if it were three a.m. on a Tuesday. Surely someone had wandered or driven by in the five or more minutes since the accident and called for help? So then where were the sirens?

I turned from the street and back to the girl. She was looking around wildly, also seeming to notice the lack of any cars or sounds of sirens. Her hands were shaking, and her chest was moving rapidly.

"Hey, hey, it's okay. They're coming. I promise they're coming," I said, closing the distance between us. I put my hands to either side of her jaw to keep her focused on me and only me.

I reached out to her mind with my own and exerted some mental pressure—just a tiny bit—to calm her. I shouldn't have. She might be in shock or concussed. Sedating her, even to keep her calm while I thought things through, couldn't be good for her. But I needed her calm.

The mesmerism worked immediately. Her breathing relaxed, and her eyes focused on mine. I silently promised her I wouldn't mesmerize her again, though I didn't know why I cared. I could only think of one thing at a time, and right then it was the girl in front of me.

"What's your name?" I asked her quietly. I wanted to keep her talking while I assessed the damage on her.

"Hannah," she answered automatically but slightly warily.

She was pretty. Slim and small-chested with long blonde hair and deep hazel eyes that were almost brown—something uncommon in blondes. Her eyes were unclouded and alert but a bit dilated. I could smell liquor on her breath. If she was drunk, it would explain the slow reactions, and it would explain how she was alive. She would've rag-dolled in the crash, which probably saved her life.

"Hannah," I repeated. "Mine's Jeb."

"Jeb?" she parroted. I didn't blame her. It's not a common name.

"Yes. Please don't ask me what it is short for," I said. "How old are you?"

"Twenty-two." Hannah replied, still automatically.

Young, so young. I moved my attention from her eyes to the rest of her face. The blood on her forehead and in her hair didn't seem to be from a headwound. She must have run her bleeding hand over her forehead and through her hair. A gnarly bruise had formed from her shoulder across her chest—seatbelt. I wondered if she had any worse injuries.

"Does anything feel broken?" I asked. It was a stupid question, but I wasn't entirely focused on what I was saying. She shook her head. "Okay. Can I look at your hand?"

She nodded and held her injured hand out to me. I was apprehensive of touching her blood, because I was still unfed. I was in control and still had some time before it became concerning, but the scent was so intoxicating already. I forced down my apprehension and took her wounded hand gently in mine.

It wasn't just one cut, it was several. She'd done quite the number on it. Her palm was open in a few places, and a long, deep gash ran up her wrist—not near any important veins, thankfully. I couldn't tell quite how many cuts there were or how deep because of the mess of blood all over her hand. I imagined her climbing out of the car, crawling to the driver's window, and scraping her clumsy arm along the broken window so she could feel for the driver's pulse.

"Okay. Help is coming," I assured her. *Surely help is coming.* "But I think I should wrap this...or at least clean it, somehow."

"I have water," she said, almost absentmindedly.

She took her hand back and turned away from me. She crouched a few feet away and retrieved an unopened water bottle from the street. I looked her over as she stood back up. She wore a lose-fitting tank top tucked into a short black skirt and nothing else. No jacket, no purse, no phone. She'd grabbed a water bottle from the wreckage before grabbing her phone. *What an exceptionally puzzling human.*

"All right, uh, let's get out of the street first," I said when she held the bottle out to me. I put a hand gently to her back to guide her over to the sidewalk—twenty feet down from where I'd just been talking with Cassandra. I pushed those thoughts aside. *Prioritize.*

I set the water bottle down for a moment and removed my denim outer jacket. I set it down carefully on the pavement so it didn't make any noise. I was—as I mentioned before—armed for a threat. Actually, I was armed for a number of threats, and it wasn't just knives, so I didn't want the heavy clank of my pockets to alarm Hannah.

Taking off the flannel shirt I'd been wearing open over my T-shirt and turning away from her, I extended a fang to help me tear the fabric. I ripped a chunk of fabric from the torso section and tore it into strips. I opened the water bottle and poured a sparing amount over Hannah's hand and wrist. She winced as the chilled water hit her skin and gritted her teeth as I gently worked the damaged skin to help the blood wash off, but she didn't complain. She stared at me the whole time, as if trying to figure me out. That was good: at least she was alert and not catatonic.

I gently pressed the large torn section from my shirt over her hand and wrist and patted the area dry. Some of the cuts were already clotting, which was good. The deeper ones were still seeping, though. My teeth throbbed, but I did my best to ignore it and keep working. When her hand was relatively washed—I could only do so much without making things worse—I wrapped the strips tightly around her palm and wrist. It wasn't great, and she'd lost a healthy portion of blood, but she probably wouldn't bleed out before she got to a hospital.

I handed her a damp section of fabric so she could wipe down her forehead and used the remaining portion of water to clean my hands as best I could. The blood on them was distracting. I couldn't get it all off, but it would have to do.

She was still staring at me when I glanced her way again, but now she was shivering. She sat on the curb with her knees together, but I could still see...so much skin. I instead looked at her face. My brain connected the dots that she was barely wearing anything and must be freezing seconds after it should have.

"You look cold," I said lamely, mentally kicking myself.

"I had a jacket," she said, nodding toward the car. "But it...got shredded."

I could only nod in response. I handed her the remains of the button-down shirt, the top portion and the sleeves still intact. I helped her arms through it. It looked like an intentionally cropped overshirt on her. It wasn't much, but it was a thicker flannel material, so it would provide some warmth. I picked up my jacket and put it on myself.

Did I feel like a dick not giving her my jacket? Yeah. But *weapons*, remember? With all I'd seen that night, like hell I was going to go unarmed.

It finally occurred to me to call authorities for help. Surely there was a logical explanation for help not arriving sooner—a game downtown or something—but it didn't seem likely. However, my thoughts were still a little muddied by the crash, so the alarm bells were duller than they should've been.

I took a seat on the curb next to her and tucked her carefully into my stiff arms to provide her with a little more warmth. I tried to will some compassion into my limbs, to loosen them and provide comfort rather than just body heat, but my reserves were drier than usual.

I could've made her forget me and left her there to wait for the ambulance. I had more important things to worry about than one human girl. Help was on its way now, so she wouldn't be alone for long.

I toyed with the idea for another moment, but ultimately, I couldn't do it. Even soulless as I was, there was something innately wrong about leaving her alone, bleeding, and vulnerable on a street corner downtown. I would stay with her until help came. I owed her that much at least. Then I would determine what to do about Cassandra, if anything.

CHAPTER 7

O ddly, it wasn't an ambulance that arrived first but a squad car. Its lights were going but still no sirens and no real urgency. What the hell was going on?

I stood up from Hannah's side on the curb and approached the car as it came to a stop and parked. As soon as the cop got out, though, I froze in my steps, figurative hackles already raised.

Lapsus.

He sensed me like I sensed him, and he stopped too on his way around his squad car.

He was young for a Lapsus. I could tell it in the wariness in his eyes upon seeing and sensing me. In frozen years, he looked maybe thirty years old. His hair was dark brown and cropped close but longer on top, with silver just starting at his temples. He was stocky and broad-chested.

A Lapsus being a cop. It made no sense. We're dead. We're untethered and have no need for a job. I didn't know whether to laugh or rub my eyes to see if the image disappeared. I straightened and squared my shoulders, though, when I remembered Hannah behind me.

I smoothly shifted my weight, angling myself so I mostly blocked her from his initial view. I had about a foot in height on him, and I used it to my advantage, like I had with Cassandra.

We stood for a second, sizing each other up. He was my thirteenth Lapsi that evening, and I was over the novelty of it. I wasn't going to let my guard down again.

"Howdy," the cop said, fake-cheerful. "What have we got here?" He motioned to the car wreck to his right.

"An accident, sir," I said flatly, adding the *sir* only for the charade.

"I'd say that," he agreed. He studied the car wreckage, aiming his flashlight at it even though he didn't need it. He turned back to me with a knowing sneer. "It hit you?"

"No. A deer," I said.

"Some deer," the cop said, smirking.

"It was."

"And where is the deer now?"

"It got up and ran away. Deer are hearty. Cars aren't."

Hannah could hear us, and she knew it hadn't been a deer. I wasn't trying to mislead her; I was trying to guide this smirking Lapsi in what he should put in his official report—even though I had a feeling there wouldn't a report of any kind. I also was persisting to reinforce my power over him as his elder. He was young—less than a year changed—and I outweighed him in strength by four hundred years.

The cop nodded, his eyes still narrowed. But he smiled a cocky grin a second later.

"And...?" He shifted his weight to his right and looked around me. He was eyeing Hannah.

I moved again to block his view and keep his attention on me.

"We need medical attention," I said.

"She yours, I take it?" The cop had lowered his voice.

This cop Lapsus was so green, he didn't even think to use telepathy if he didn't want Hannah to hear. I swallowed my annoyance and kept my expression the same: intense and unamused.

"She needs a hospital," I said.

The cop glanced at Hannah again, no doubt taking in her bandaged hand and forearm, where blood was already seeping through the makeshift bandage. He returned his gaze to me, an eyebrow raised.

"Why?" he asked quietly with a little snort. His smirk widened.

And there we have it, ladies and gents. Any residual amusement melted away as he confirmed the sinking suspicion in my gut. I inhaled sharply through my clenched teeth but managed to keep my lips from curling in my disdain. *That* was why there weren't any sirens. If I weren't here, Hannah would be dead. And because I'd claimed her in his eyes, he automatically assumed I was going to kill her—and he didn't blink. *Bad Lapsus.*

I regained my composure, trusting that the idiot would take my sharp inhale as impatience rather than me deciding I was going to murder him before the night ended.

"I want her to feel like she's somewhere safe first," I said, lowering my voice even more to make sure there was no chance Hannah would hear. I wouldn't use telepathy with this prick. I wasn't about to give him that idea.

I remained motionless, waiting for him to process my words. Tension coiled further in my muscles, ready in case he moved to fight me for her. *All the better if we do.* I slowly curled my fingers into a fist. If we fought, I'd win. If he didn't fight me, I'd let him think I was going to kill her. But I knew for certain I wasn't leaving her side until she was safely deposited in an ER. And as soon as her back was turned, I was going to kill this cop.

"All right, all right," the cop said with a laugh. "It isn't my place to kink shame anyone. To each his own." He laughed again.

"Help me get her somewhere safe, and I might even share," I said quietly, swallowing my annoyance and turning up one side of my mouth, mimicking his sneer from earlier.

In truth, I could've shifted me and her out of there, but I'd already decided not to mesmerize her again, which meant I'd have to explain our sudden change in location, which I'd never had to do before. No, I needed him to play his part as well.

The cop's leer stretched into a wide, greedy grin, as I expected. He wiped it from his face a second later, however, and approached Hannah on the curb. She was still sitting, huddling over her knees that she pressed together as modestly as she could. Her cheeks were glistening with fresh tears—she hadn't been crying moments earlier when I'd been sitting with her. The cop eyed me with an eyebrow cocked upward, as if to say "you do this?" about her tears.

I stood behind her, facing the cop. My hands were in the pockets of my jean jacket, my right hand fingering a switchblade. Ready, just in case.

"Hey, sweetie," the cop said, putting on his sweetest you-can-trust-me-I'm-a-cop voice.

From where I stood directly behind her, my calf touched her back, near her shoulder. She'd been shaking before, but when the cop put on his fake voice, a distinct shudder vibrated up her spine through my leg. *Perceptive girl.*

"I hear you're cut up pretty bad," the cop continued, still using his friendly voice. "Is that right? May I have a quick look?"

She nodded once and held out her bandaged right hand for him to see. The cop looked it over, but he didn't touch her.

"I see, I see. Are you injured anywhere else?" the cop asked, sounding genuine in his sympathy and concern. Hannah shook her head and the cop nodded. "All right. I tell you what. You don't really need an ambulance. That would be an unnecessary expense, I think. How about I take you to the hospital myself instead? We'd get there just as fast, and I don't charge out the ass for it." He paused a second for her to respond, but she didn't. "How's that sound, love? I'll take you and your friend to the hospital?"

Finally, she nodded once and looked down at her knees again. The cop, while still crouching, raised his eyes up to me. He fixed me with a sly "our-little-secret" expression, but something else was in his look: savage lust.

He stood and held his hand out to Hannah. She took it with her uninjured hand, and he helped her to her feet. She swayed a little bit, and I caught her by the elbow and slipped my other arm around her waist. I again inserted myself between her and the cop while he led the way to the squad car.

"What about him?" Hannah said suddenly, pausing in her stride. She was glancing at the wreckage. I knew she didn't mean that the driver needed to be saved. But he would need to be cut out of the car and taken somewhere regardless. That was her concern: she cared more about the driver's body than her own.

"More help is on the way, I promise. I want to get you out of here before that, though," the cop explained. He opened the back door on his side of the car and helped her get seated inside. "You don't want to see that."

She already has, dickwad. She'd checked him to see if he was alive before she checked on me. Somehow, I knew that was why she'd been crying when I left her alone to talk to the cop. She'd been crying for a man she'd known for five minutes.

Hannah fell asleep shortly after the squad car peeled away from the scene of the accident. Her head was lolling against the backrest. I watched her through the rearview mirror, making sure she was still breathing, concerned about blood loss and concussion. Really, I should have been back there with her, keeping her awake until we reached the hospital, but I hadn't been thinking.

"Man, oh man, friend," the cop said as he drove. He too was glancing back at Hannah in the mirror. "That is one sweet-looking girl, there."

"Yes, yes, she is," I agreed in a low growl that was really a warning.

"No worries here, pal, she's yours. I respect it. Just—wow," he said with a soft little chuckle. "She just said 'clean it up.' If I'd known what I was cleaning up, I'd have gotten there faster. Might've beat you there, even."

I wanted to stab him every time he said "friend" or "pal" like a chump. But what he said distracted me from my stabbing fantasies. Ice formed in my stomach.

"She," I said.

"Yeah, *she*, you know who," the cop said unhelpfully. "Now *that* is a beautiful woman."

"Yeah. Yeah, she is," I agreed flatly. I looked again in the rearview mirror. Hannah was still passed out. And still breathing. "And she's planning something impressive. I'll give her that."

"Hell yes, she is," the cop said. "You've heard, then. About the things she's laying down?"

Cassandra had used a similar verbiage. *All I'm doing is laying down the groundwork for a community*, she'd said. The word choice couldn't be coincidence.

"Yes, I have. And I'm picking them up." It was a lame colloquialism, but it also felt more like a code for Cassandra followers.

"Marvelous, really." The cop gave me a conspiratorial look. "I wasn't going to stay a cop after I was changed, but I'm finishing up a few things. Some of my more recent cases are going to court and such. But my boys are doing a great job with things."

"Your boys?" I repeated.

"Yeah," he said with a sly grin. "We're doing good work right now, cleaning up the city a bit, before. The crime rate's way down, too, if you get my meaning. And waaay less paperwork."

Oh. Oh, no. Very, very, no. This sergeant had changed some of his team. It was like Cassandra had said about the chain of new Lapsi but *so much worse.* A bad cop had made worse cops, and they were out...killing their perps? One could argue that my own moral compass dipped, shook, and danced, never really pointing due north, but this...fuck this man. My hand slipped inside my jacket pocket again.

"Speaking of my boys," the cop said after only a short pause. He glanced back at Hannah again in the backseat. "Don't take too long once we get there. I can't guarantee my boys'll be able to control themselves when they see her...and smell her."

"Your boys are going to be at the hospital?"

The cop pulled an as-if face at me, and the ice returned to the pit of my stomach.

"Why waste a doctor's time when you're just going to kill her?" The cop shrugged. "You wanted safe. My precinct is safe. At least as far as she's aware. And we can clean it up in there with no one the wiser."

Son of a bitch. My basic plan was to arrive at the hospital, see Hannah safely inside, kill this cop, and be done with this night and all its bullshit. But we weren't being driven to the hospital where I could see her to safety and never worry about it ever again. We were being driven directly into a hell's nest of evil Lapsi, and it would be exponentially harder to get her out of this alive.

I glanced back at her in the rearview mirror. She'd cut her own arm to ribbons to check the pulse of a stranger.

She'd spent precious minutes doing CPR on pulseless roadkill instead of worrying about her own bleeding hand. And she'd grabbed a bottle of water while climbing out of a wrecked car, rather than her phone or purse, on the off chance she'd need it to clean a wound or something. She deserved more than to die in a precinct and be disposed of.

I would get her out of there alive. I owed her that much. But I couldn't only save her; I also had to take as many of these abominations down as I could. I'd killed Lapsi before, if they pissed me off, and I'd killed humans before, for a lot less, but these fake cops had pissed me off far more than any of the others I'd killed.

I had the beginnings of a plan as I fiddled with my jacket pocket. It wasn't a great one. And it involved risking Hannah as bait, but it was the only plan I had. I steeled myself to sink into my inner sociopath for the second time that night.

Staring at Hannah in the mirror, I allowed myself to get lost in the scent of her and her blood. It wasn't hard; my shirt was covered in it from her silly chest compressions. Even though it was dried, it still smelled heavenly, and I was *craving*. I'd been ignoring it, but now that I embraced it, my god, was it strong. As I watched her in the mirror, I noticed her bandages were seeping again. The blood on them was shiny and glistening.

This was torture, and I hated feeling like this animalistic junkie. But in this moment, I needed to lean into it. I just hoped I'd be able to regain control when it came down to it. Because Hannah smelled so good and she was so, so helpless...

HANNAH

Never in a million years would I have believed it if someone had told me my night would lead to me being in the back of a cop car. How the hell does a crummy date end that way? Drunk—but quickly sobering up—bleeding—bleeding a lot—and in a cop car. How was this my life? But that's something you say after a crazy, wild story that ends on a happy note. Not a crazy, wild story that ends with a dead Uber driver weighing you down with guilt.

Jeb told me help was coming, but they were taking a bafflingly long time in getting to the accident. I couldn't understand it. I could've been bleeding out if Jeb hadn't wrapped my arm. And I don't care how miraculously uninjured he appeared, Jeb needed medical attention too.

At last, someone did show up, but it was a cop. Not an ambulance. Where was the ambulance?

Jeb went to talk to the cop, and I stayed on the curb mulling over the billions of thoughts in my head. The shock from the accident was wearing off, but thankfully my panic from earlier didn't return. I still felt the slightly tottering effect from the drinks, but I was rapidly sobering.

I was cold, woozy, scared, and very exposed, there on the curb. Stupid short skirt. It had been a stupid kind of power move to prove to myself that I *wanted* to trust men again. And in a way, I'd been trying to will this night to go better than I expected it to. *But now look at your night, idiot. You're half-dressed and bleeding on a curb with a stranger and a cop just a few feet away.*

Cops always made me nervous. Maybe it was the fact that it was a mostly male profession and that it had a kind of arrogance around the profession itself. These figures that say they are helping the people but really they're just intimidating them.

I felt the cop's gaze and shivered automatically. I pulled Jeb's shirt tighter around me and hugged my knees harder. As Jeb talked to the cop, I watched the pavement in front of me and willed an ambulance to show up.

The cop laughed, and I grew irrationally angry. How could he laugh when someone was dead? Someone whose body didn't deserve to be ignored in his wreck of a car. Someone who'd been nothing but kind and gentlemanly to me. Tears stung my eyes and I closed them tightly, but they still leaked out.

The cop approached and knelt in front of me, and Jeb stood directly behind me, his shins brushing against my back. The man was young for a cop—maybe thirty or so. He spoke sickly sweet to me, and though he thinks he hid it well, I could see the arrogant, hungry look in his eye as he looked me over. He asked to see my hand, but he made a point of not touching any part of the bandage. *What, a squeamish cop? Prick.*

Warning bells were going off in my head when the cop said he'd take me to the hospital, not an ambulance. Even if he was right—an ambulance would be expensive—cops *do not* escort injured people. They just don't.

But it'd taken so long for even one cop to show up to the scene of this accident, I didn't dare risk waiting even longer for an ambulance. I needed a hospital, or I might lose the use of my hand.

As we walked to the cop car, I paused to ask about Gerry. The cop barely glanced over at the car and dismissed it. He said once again that more help was on the way. *Prick.*

Once inside the car, I was so grateful for the warmth, I didn't even mind the wire grate between the backseat and the front seat making a cage. My eyelids drooped even before the cruiser was out of park.

I woke to the car door opening on my left. Jeb glanced briefly inside at me, but he didn't make eye contact. He opened the door wide and turned around. He kept his back to me and placed himself between me and the cop as I got out of the back seat—blocking the sight of my mostly bare legs from him. *How did he know I was so uncomfortable?* I wondered in awe.

The awe died immediately, though, when I looked around. We weren't outside an ER. We were in a parking garage, with dozens of other cop cars parked around us.

"Why aren't we at the hospital?" I was surprised to hear my voice come out demanding, rather than the squeak I'd expected.

"We talked about it, and we want to get your statement first. Then we'll get you right to the hospital," the cop said, waving an arm airily out to his side, as if to say *after you*.

"Why couldn't you get my statement when we were still on the street?" I asked, not moving from my spot. Jeb closed the door of the car and came up behind me.

"Hannah—" Jeb started to say, his voice kind of husky, but I cut him off with a shake of my head.

"It's standard protocol, isn't it?" I said, glaring at the cop. Jeb thought I was meek because I'd been so quiet and small on the street. But I'd been in shock then, and the shock had worn off. Now I was scared, tired, in pain, and angry. "You get the statements before leaving the scene. If you can't, then you follow to the hospital and get it there. You *don't escort*."

The cop shot the briefest of glances over my head to Jeb. When his eyes returned to me, I could read the annoyance he was trying to keep in check.

"As I said, more were coming to clean everything up," the cop said pointedly.

I felt the same stab of grief when I thought about Gerry. But this time anger bubbled up with it.

"I didn't want you to have to see that," the cop said when I didn't say anything.

I already did see it. I glared at him. *I'd checked on him, taken his pulse, and mourned this stranger. You hadn't even looked.*

"Besides, you aren't that injured. You don't even need a hospital. It would be a waste of time at this point."

"The hell it is," I snapped. "You barely even glanced at my arm. I need a hospital before I start bleeding again." *Too late.* I could feel the dampness of the shirt-bandage.

"Look, if it would make you feel better, we have all the supplies to take care of your arm here at the precinct," the cop assured me. But I saw the eyeroll—minute as it was. "We can take care of you here."

"Oh, *can* you? Really? With all your medical knowledge?" I scoffed angrily, putting emphasis on every other word. "Tell me, are you a doctor? Can you suture? Because I will need *at least* thirty stitches."

The cop looked more annoyed than ever, but I felt triumphant, if not still livid.

A kind of familiar pressure entered my mind, smoothing the tension a fraction. The anger and spite were still there but were somehow just out of my reach.

Jeb moved forward, into my peripheral, and put an arm protectively around my shoulders.

"The faster we get this over with, the faster we can get to the hospital," he said, though whether it was to me or the cop, I couldn't tell. I shot him an incredulous glare, but he wouldn't look at me.

The cop seemed pleased that my protestation had run its course. His gaze traveled the length of my body briefly. I willed myself to stand tall, even though I was jumping out of my skin. When his gaze returned to my eyes, the annoyance was back on his face. I could almost hear what he was thinking: *It's only because you're pretty that you're worth this much trouble.* I barely resisted recoiling with a shudder.

FALLEN SOULS

He turned and walked toward an elevator a short distance away, motioning in a "let's go already" way. Jeb moved to follow, but I paused. I pulled off the shirt he'd given me and tied it around my waist. He'd torn a good chunk off the bottom, but there was still enough that, when tied around me, it gave my legs a little more coverage than my black skirt. My arms and shoulders were bare, but I somehow felt less exposed. Besides, maybe the fact that I had blood all over my arms and shirt would get me a little more sympathy inside than I was being shown out here.

Jeb watched me do this, but his face was unreadable. His eyes were dark and had a weird kind of—I could only describe it as *hunger*—to them. Not like the cop, though. No, Jeb seemed to be holding something at bay. He wouldn't look directly at me.

As we entered the elevator with the cop, Jeb's arm returned around my shoulders, and I let myself feel safe there on the uncomfortable ride up the elevator.

It was dumb, because I didn't know him at all, but I trusted Jeb. Call it what you will, be it imprinting on him after the accident or transference. But I'd felt nothing but safe near him that evening. He was young, maybe twenty-four, but something about his deadpan expressions and mannerisms felt much older. Or in the way he seemed to command and take charge out of duty. And he didn't just leave me to wait for authorities alone. He bandaged my arm when he didn't have to. He stayed when he didn't have to.

The elevator doors opened, and we were guided down several hallways and through a large processing annex full of cops, desks, and computers. Jeb was looking around at everything but acting like he wasn't. Like he was learning the exits. *So he feels like a caged animal, too, I guess.*

All the way through that large room, I felt eyes crawling over me. Jeb's grip on my upper arm tightened possessively, but not painfully, like he felt it too. I kept my eyes lowered, not meeting anyone's gaze, and begrudgingly followed the cop to the other end of the room. I cradled my arm with my uninjured one. It was starting to shake. I couldn't tell what color the fabric used to be.

The cop led us into a room at the end of the annex. This new room was smaller, with longer desks and simple folding chairs, like a classroom. *Briefing room*, I realized. In this room were maybe four other cops, not including our escort. Jeb tensed as we walked through the door. The cop entered after us and closed the door behind him, then walked over to the other cops. This seemed wrong, but I didn't know why.

Jeb's arm dropped from around me, and he drew up even taller and tenser, somehow. He stepped forward, farther into the room, but his hand gently brushed my arm—the slightest little reassuring touch. I might have imagined it. I thought I heard his voice in my head telling me to stay where I was. I sure as hell wasn't going any farther into this room, I wanted to tell him. So many alarm bells were going off in my head.

Jeb approached the cops, and they conversed in low voices. I couldn't hear them, but I watched Jeb. His whole posture had changed from earlier this evening. He stood taller yet hunched, with his head inclined forward, like a hunting animal. Why did I suddenly feel like I was caught in some trap?

After a moment of them saying heaven knew what, all of them turned eyes that I could only describe as lustful and *hungry* toward me. Though their faces weren't familiar, I recognized the expressions. It reminded me of the one party I'd attended the year after high school—a frat party, full of hungry, predatory boys who'd never been told *no* before.

Jeb stepped forward and continued approaching. His expression mirrored the cops' and all the blind trust I'd poured into him evaporated. Suddenly I was *afraid* of him. Afraid like I'd been of those frat boys. And I stood just as frozen and paralyzed as I had that night. I was barely breathing.

"Jeb, what—" I started, but I didn't even know what I was about to say. My voice came out breathy and small, like a child's.

Jeb put a finger to his lips. His lips behind his finger tilted into a humorless, leering sneer. Was my heart even beating anymore? *My heart, my constant beating companion my whole life, has abandoned me.* I was scared to the point of lunacy, apparently. All that was left to me were Jeb's eyes, holding me hostage, and I was terrified.

Do you trust me?

It was the strangest thing. I heard his voice, clear as a bell, but his lips didn't move. I'd imagined it, surely. In my fear, I'd imagined it. I felt and heard my heart pounding in my ears—it hadn't abandoned me after all. It had just leapt into my ears instead!

Jeb's expression hadn't changed. He was directly in front of me, and I was still paralyzed. *Move you idiot*, I heard my little thought-voice screaming, but it was far away. Jeb took my injured hand in his. The gentleness in his touch was at such odds with the menace in his face. He was unwrapping the bandage. The fabric had partially adhered to my clotting wounds, and when it was pulled away, piecing pain shot through me. I gasped and almost whimpered, but something stopped me. The pain dulled too, almost as fast as it came. Weird.

You don't need to trust me, but you do need to run. Okay? His voice again. I knew I heard it that time, but his face still hadn't changed. *Run when I tell you, okay? Straight back. Go through this door and keep going straight. Only straight. Okay? And I am so sorry.*

There was something there just then. A little flicker in his eyes—a wink. Too quick to even register.

NOW, his voice yelled in my head, at the same time as his menacing expression split into a garish snarl. I swear, four of his teeth had grown long and sharp. He had fangs. *No way. No way,* I thought distantly.

Run! His thought-voice yelled at me as he snarled.

And, oh boy, I did.

I slammed my uninjured arm into the door release and was through it before I even knew what I was doing. I sprinted back across the room, not looking at anyone. Just trusting that anyone in my way would jump out of my path. Terror was controlling me now. Careening me forward because it was all I could do.

Straight, he'd said. Straight, I went. I reached the end of the room and kept going. There was a short hallway at the end of the processing annex, and at the end of the hallway, a door. A door to stairs or—maybe—outside. I don't know why I was so convinced it led outside, but I seized on this hope and kept going toward the door.

This one wasn't a push-door, though. I threw myself against it, then had to pull it open and run through it. I was barely through the door, when a hand struck me on the back and sent me sprawling. I caught myself on one hand on the floor and sprang back to my feet. But I'd messed up.

The door didn't lead to stairs or an exit of any kind. I was in a small, empty room about ten square feet. I spun around, panicked, to face the door. The man who'd shoved me wasn't Jeb but the escort cop. And behind him were maybe ten others—all of them cops.

I backed up as the others piled into the room around him, a scream welling up in my throat. The first cop lunged at me before the scream broke free of my lungs. Hands, hard and strong as iron, gripped my shoulders, and one of them snarled in my ear. Then, the grip on my shoulders vanished. My eyes flew open—I hadn't realized I'd closed them—in time to see the first cop thrown aside by another cop, who fixed me with hungry eyes. But then someone else threw him against the wall.

Then, Jeb. His eyes were hungry but determined in a way different from the cops. He'd fought his way through the throng and flung his arm around me. Somehow, he pulled me with him toward the door, fighting off the others' sprawling, clawing hands. As he backed us up against the door, he dug into his jacket pocket with his free hand. He pulled something out and threw it into the center of the room. It was a knife—a switchblade that shone brighter than most knives. It stabbed into the linoleum floor in the center of the group of vampires. They all froze and stared at it, confused, then back at us.

Jeb unceremoniously grabbed the side of my head and forced my face into his chest while he dug something else from his pocket.

"Abracadabra, boys," he growled and threw a small glass vial directly at the knife.

The room and hallway vanished. The last thing I saw of that precinct were the faces of the eleven cops. Their faces...they reminded me of wolves. Hungry, bloodthirsty wolves.

CHAPTER 9

My secret weapon was basic chemistry—well, alchemy—well, chemistry with a little help from a witch. It was an explosive silver compound called silver fulminate, commonly used in minute amounts in novelty Fourth of July pop-its. The substance is highly reactive to friction, even with itself—much like us Lapsi used to be. It was packed tightly into a small glass vial, about the size of my pinky, with the help of a witch's stabilizing spell. It used to be a potent weapon for witches long ago when they hunted us. This weapon was more of a relic than anything else, but combined with even more silver creates an even bigger *boom*. Basically, it was a silver frag grenade.

Why did I have it in the first place? I honestly couldn't tell you. I'd had it for what felt like forever and never thought I'd have a use for it. It was more than enough for one Lapsus, and before that night, seeing more than one Lapsus was a rarity. It'd been like carrying a grenade with me on a deserted island. Regardless, I was glad I'd had it with me.

With luck, it had killed every Lapsus in that room, but I shifted Hannah and myself far, far away just as the glass shattered against the silver knife.

I expected her to yell. A lot. I accounted for that and shifted us to a place that I knew was empty and not patrolled by any kind of security. It was a basement classroom in the school across the street from my apartment building—a few thousand miles from Portland, Oregon.

What I didn't account for, though, was how close I'd been to losing control. In the precinct, I'd had one arm on Hannah. Now, I had both around her, and I was holding her tightly to my chest. The blood in her hair was dried and crispy, but it still smelled...

She beat her good hand against my side, her yell muffled into my chest, but I heard my name. With an inhuman snarl, I gathered enough sense of mind and pushed her away from me. She stumbled and fell against a desk, nearly toppling it over as she fought for her footing. She left a bloody handprint on the desk's surface as she steadied herself. She turned back to me when I wished she wouldn't.

"What the hell just happened?" she demanded. She took a step toward me, but I growled and stepped back.

"Hannah—"

"What the fuck was that!?" She yelled more—mostly expletives. I appreciate a woman with as dirty a mouth as mine. Really, I do. And I'd tell her so later, but right then I couldn't do it. Not when my self-control was holding the crazed animal back with a single ragged fingernail.

"Hannah, shut up!" I shouted when I couldn't hold it in anymore. Or at least that's what I thought I said, but for some reason I heard a roar come out of me. Regardless, she did shut up.

I spun around and put a hand against the wall. I first meant to flip the light switches, which I did. But as the lights turned on—for her benefit only—I stayed with both hands on the wall, hunched over and trying to get a better grip on myself.

I'd leaned further into my savagery than I ever liked to do, and I never imagined how hard it would be to reel it back in. I can only describe it as an animalistic sense of blue balls. It was like bringing yourself all the way to the point of giving into an addiction—needle already in the arm—but pulling back at the absolute last second.

My fangs were still extended, and I focused on them, willing them back into their harmless forms. For a full, terrible moment, they didn't budge. I let out a pained moan as I finally felt them return to normal.

This kind of horrifying experience was not usual. Feeding isn't anything like this usually. It's sensual and intimate—sexual even. There's a reason why popular fiction sexualizes it and makes it romantic: because it is. But embracing the bloodlust, and the violence and savagery of the past few moments, had reduced me to an animal. It was temporary though, if I could just get myself under control.

Slowly, my thoughts returned, and the pounding of her blood in my ears quieted a few decibels. I released a ragged breath, letting the tension flow out of me, along with the stale air. My shoulders sagged forward as my muscles relaxed. I didn't turn around immediately. Instead, I stayed where I was and leaned my forehead against the cool wall.

I was in control now but still hungry. My teeth throbbed, and my veins were starting to burn. I needed to get blood, and soon.

It wouldn't be Hannah's blood. Even though it would be so easy—she was right there, and she was already bleeding. But I couldn't do it. Somehow, after everything that night, it seemed cheap for her to end up as my snack. I'd already used her as bait. I wouldn't use her as *food*, too.

I had to give Hannah all the credit she was due. I'd needed her scared. I'd needed her to run her heart out, and I'd needed her to blindly trust me with her life. And she'd accomplished all of that beautifully.

The plan had nearly derailed in the parking lot when she was losing her temper and berating our escort. I regrettably had to mesmerize her into shutting up, even after I'd promised her I wouldn't do that again. But she didn't know I'd promised that, so...no harm done? Oh, whatever, my conscience was clear because she was alive.

I'd known she was bleeding again—every Lapsi had known it. But I'd unwrapped her makeshift bandage to further draw everyone to her—at the expense of my own cravings. When she took off running, so did everyone else—as expected. What I hadn't expected was to be outrun by the other Lapsi. The cops were faster, and their leader almost killed Hannah before I could get there.

At last, gritting my pulsing teeth, I turned toward her.

She was seated across the room at a desk, gripping her wounded wrist tightly and holding it above her head. She was staring at me with an expression that was a perfect blend of anger and perplexity.

"What are you?"

"A Fallen Favorite," I said, sitting down heavily at the desk next to her. There was no point in lying. "A Lapsus. A Descendant of Cain. What drab society likes to call a vampire."

She didn't say anything in response. She lowered her wrist from above her head and set it on the desk in front of her. I expected more of a reaction. Instead, she gave me a look that told me to go on.

"Cain was the first Lapsus. He was cursed for drawing the first human blood, or whatever, and his punishment was being forced to live off of it. He passed it on to others, and they passed it on to other ...but we aren't as numerous as that makes it sound." *Or we didn't used to be...*

"And the cops were Lapsi, too," she said, only half a question. She surprised me by using the proper plural form of the term without being told.

"Yes. But I've never seen so many in one place..." I said, though I didn't mean to say the last part out loud.

"Okay," she said, in complete ambivalent acceptance.

"Okay? You just accept it, just like that?"

"What? You think that after everything I've seen tonight, I'm going to call bullshit?" She shrugged. "You're a vampire. Great. So were those cops. Great. And now we're away from them. So can we *please* go to the hospital?"

I almost smiled at her stubborn moxie, but then logic caught up to me and I realized I couldn't take her to a hospital.

"Jeb, *please*," she pleaded, her voice desperate. She slumped in frustration. "I need—"

"Just let me think for a minute," I interrupted her. I willed my mind to think quickly.

My goal had been to get her to a hospital in Portland and go on my merry way after that, knowing she was safe. But now...now I'd just killed a dozen Lapsi and used her in the process. I'd gained so many enemies tonight, and so had she. I made her a part of all of this without ever meaning to. There was no leaving her safely at a hospital near her home now. There was no *safe* in that city.

"We can't. I can't take you home," I said. I rubbed my hands roughly over my face and through my hair.

"Okay, that's it." She slid out of her chair and stood up, a little wobbly. "I don't know why I'm just sitting around waiting for someone to take me there. I can figure it out. So, thank you very much, but I can find my way to a damn hospital from here."

I almost let her leave without saying anything. It would have been so easy, really, and if she left, she was no longer my problem. I could get back to the bigger problem at hand. But still, it seemed stupid to have gotten her this far and have her stroll to her death now.

"You can try that, but I'm telling you now, if you do, you'll be killed." I stood from my seat at the desk, but I didn't follow her.

I was exaggerating a little. She could get to a hospital here fine—we were halfway across the country. Really, the danger was in her returning to Portland, but my heavy words were enough to make her stop halfway to the door. Her shoulders were set in annoyance, and she looked up at the ceiling without turning around.

"Look, earlier tonight, I stumbled onto something. And that something seems to keep getting bigger." I spoke quickly, deciding that from here out, it was pointless to lie to her. "That cop was a part of it. He made several of his colleagues a part of it. And I stupidly killed them, bringing down a lot of heat on...both of us. And I don't know how deep all of this runs."

Hannah moved to the wall by the door and slumped against it. She looked so tired.

"So now I'm caught up in all of it too?" she said, rolling her eyes to the ceiling.

"I didn't mean for this, I promise," I told her honestly, but it sounded deadpan. My reserves of emotions were all but dried up from the efforts of the past hour. "I'll get you out of this. I just don't know how yet. Until then, I promise to try to keep you safe."

"So, it's more blind trust you want?" she said.

"Hey, it's only blind trust because I'm blind. I'm as blind in this as you."

"But, Jeb..." She looked at me pleadingly. She didn't have to finish her sentence. I knew she was tired and in pain and just wanted to *not* be there.

"I know. I know," I assured her, trying to think. "Okay. We need three things: medical help, protection, and a plan. I can get the first two...and work on the third thing later. Help me think through the first thing. If we forgo the hospital, what is it you need?"

She sighed and looked away, but I could see her working through the problem. She looked down at her hand. Dark blood was still bubbling up from the deepest wounds in her wrist.

"I need to get this clean so I can see how bad it is and prevent infection. And I need to get it to stop bleeding. It hasn't stopped bleeding since the accident."

"Okay. We can do that much," I said, thankful for somewhere to start.

"But, Jeb, I can tell you right now...I'm going to need stitches for this to heal correctly and to keep the wound from opening again." Her voice was so calm, but it was just exhaustion. "And stitches mean I need a doctor."

I nodded but didn't say anything. I had an idea forming in my head of a way to avoid doctors altogether. I knew someone who could help, potentially.

"But theoretically, if we get it cleaned and bandaged, could stitches wait at least until morning?"

"I guess...but why?" she said, slightly exasperated.

"Because I have someone in mind that we can trust. But they aren't a doctor...and they aren't nocturnal."

CHAPTER 10

HANNAH

At the start of the night, I knew the date would be terrible. I never once even flirted with the idea that it would end up back at his place. And even further from my mind was going back to a *different* guy's place after the aforementioned crappy date.

The circumstances were even more bonkers than that. I'd been in an accident. I was bleeding profusely from a number of cuts on my right hand and arm—my right one! What would I do if I couldn't use my right hand?

I'd been taken against protocol to a police station, where I was stared at by numerous hungry predatory eyes. I still shuddered remembering the feeling of their eyes on me. It was too familiar, too reminiscent of another traumatic event. Then I 'd been chased and cornered in this police station, nearly killed—again—and then whisked away at the last second, while about twelve cops perished.

They were bad cops, though. And vampires—or Lapsi. They were going to kill me...but the looks in their eyes hadn't only been hunger. It had been *lust*. I was almost certain that, though they wanted my blood, there was something more sexual about it. I might have almost been raped and killed. Or bitten, then raped, then killed.

I couldn't think too much about it: I just couldn't. I was too tired, and my nerves were too frayed. If I let myself think about everything that had happened tonight, and all the dark ramifications, I'd lose it. I'd think about it all tomorrow in the light of day, when everything is less scary.

Tomorrow, I'd get angry that I'd once again found myself in such a situation. Tomorrow, I'd cry that I had frozen, *again*, and didn't fight when I thought I was going to be assaulted. Tomorrow, I'd begin again the uphill battle to be stronger than my trauma.

But not tonight.

Instead, I thought about all of the bones in the hand and recited them in my head as we walked. They'd be on my midterm on Monday—which I probably wasn't going to make it to.

"Proximal, middle, distal..."

"What?" Jeb said, cutting through my thoughts.

I hadn't realized I'd started reciting them aloud, but rather than explain what I'd been doing, I shook my head. We were nearing the entrance to the apartment building Jeb said he lived in. It was across the street from the school he'd transported us to from the police station.

"So, vampires are real. And vampires are called Lapsi. And Lapsi can teleport..."

"Don't call it teleport," he said with a shudder. "You make me sound like a mutant from Marvel. We don't teleport. We...shift."

"You *shift*, then," I said in a fake snobbish voice. I stumbled up the front steps—my feet didn't want to work well anymore. "Then why are we walking? Why can't we shift straight into your apartment?"

"Because I put wards up to keep others away." He held the door open for me.

"And the wards were put up...before you discovered this scary plot?" I meant it to sound teasing and bitter, but I also did kind of wonder. If I hadn't seen what I'd seen that night, I would've loved to think he was just a paranoid loon.

"I just like my privacy." He led the way to a stairwell off to the right. He paused at the bottom. "Unfortunately, I'm on the third floor."

"Ugh." I slumped against the stair railing. "Can't you just carry me?"

I'd been kidding, but he closed the few feet between us and had me in his arms before I could protest, one arm under my legs, the other supporting my back. I was grateful I still had the shirt tied around my waist—it helped cover my ass as he carried me.

"I was kidding, you know...but thank you." I wrapped my good arm behind his neck and kept my bleeding one away from us both. I found my head uncontrollably leaning against his chest, and my eyes closed briefly.

He had no pulse. I'd been doing chest compressions on him for a minute or two, trying to get his heart pumping, when it probably hadn't been beating for years. The thought made my chest tremble as I suppressed a nervous giggle.

"How old are you, Jeb?" I asked quietly as we climbed the stairs.

"Almost four hundred years. Born, bred, and dead on American soil," he said.

"New England, I take it?" I didn't know why I was asking. I just wanted to keep talking so I could stay awake.

"Yup. Puritan New England."

"So, what is your full name? What is Jeb short for?"

"Jebediah. Jebediah Endecott of hearty New England stock," he said, looking down at me with a grimace.

"That's a rich-sounding name," I commented, smirking at the old-fashioned name. It fit his old-fashioned vibe that he tried to downplay.

"I was a goat farmer," he said cheerfully yet still deadpan. He winked, but his smile didn't reach his eyes and seemed faked. A lot about Jeb seemed fake, but not in a distrustful way. More, like, he was doing things and *acting* for the benefit of others rather than actually *feeling* things.

We were passing doorways in the hall, and I was suddenly acutely aware that it was well past one in the morning, so I didn't ask any more questions. We stopped at a door, and Jeb put me down so he could fish out a small set of keys from his jeans. He said his place was warded—implying magic. Apparently on top of vampires—Lapsi—magic was also real. I didn't feel anything, however, when we walked through the doorway. *I must be too human.*

"What...what the..." I said as I stepped into the entryway of his apartment. "Why does it look like Fox Mulder and the Lone Gunmen's office in here?"

It did. Foil was taped up over the glass of his windows above a bookcase filled with case files, newspapers, model UFOs, and weird radio-looking things. On the wall between the two windows was the very same poster from Mulder's office of a UFO with the words "I Want to Believe" printed on the bottom. A wall adjacent to the windows was covered in newspaper clippings and photos, with an amorphous web of red yarn connecting them all.

"For the record, Mulder and the Lone Gunmen never shared an office. Mulder worked in the FBI in Quantico, and the LGs worked out of a garage," Jeb corrected me. He winked again, then closed the door and locked it. "A neighbor comes to my door to borrow an egg, they get one look inside at this—" he waved a hand at the scene in the living room "—and they can't get away from me fast enough. I also subscribe to a lot of conspiracy theory magazines. The looks I get in the mail room are pretty funny."

He wanted so desperately to be left alone, and he went to extreme—theatrical—measures. But then why live in an apartment? Why not a house? *He wants to be left alone, but he doesn't want to be far from humanity.* It was hard to bite back my smirk. *He probably doesn't even realize that's what he's doing.*

"All right, so what supplies do you need?" he asked, his face serious again.

"What do you have?"

"I have...nothing. At all. But I can get whatever you need."

He didn't say where or how he was going to get the things. After everything tonight, was he going to perform a conjuring act?

"Rubbing alcohol, iodine, gauze, bandage tape, *pain killers*. Liquid stitches if possible," I listed off, as I looked at my hand. "And...before too long, food."

"I'll see what I can find. Please. Don't leave." He waited until I nodded before he went back out his front door.

As soon as he was gone, I realized I desperately needed to pee. Thankfully, bathrooms were easy to find. What wasn't easy to find, however, was toilet paper in a Lapsi's bathroom, apparently. No matter. I washed off and dried down there as best I could with soap and water. I managed to find a small clean towel, which I wet with warm water and washed the blood off both hands and arms.

It was probably poor form, getting blood all over a stranger's hand towel. But who cared at this point? The guy had used me as bait to kill ten to twelve cops less than an hour ago. I was allowed to bleed on his things.

Yes, I knew Jeb had used me to lure all those Lapsi cops into one location. He thought I didn't realize it, but I wasn't stupid. I knew he'd gambled with my life while trying to save it. Maybe I could forgive him for that, but I couldn't easily forgive his façade beforehand. He'd worn the face of a rapist and expected me to trust him. He made me feel small and helpless again, and he didn't even realize it.

I couldn't think about that, though, or I might shatter and cry. So instead I compartmentalized and focused on wiping blood off my arm, rinsing the towel, and repeating. And I took a little bit of petty pleasure in ruining something of Jeb's. I rinsed the towel one last time and wrung it out as much as I could. I pressed it to my wrist as I left the bathroom.

Jeb was standing at his kitchen island, staring down at the armload of medical supplies on the counter in front of him. Two rolls of gauze, medical tape, iodine, a handful of Advil, and even liquid stitches. None of it was new or wrapped, though, meaning he didn't buy these things.

"Where did you get all of this?" I asked, stepping up to the counter opposite him.

"Next door neighbor. He's a heavy sleeper and a bit of a hypochondriac." His medium-length hair was falling forward over his forehead, obscuring his eyes.

"You stole these from your neighbor?"

"I can't exactly travel far from here, leaving you alone," he said. "I also coerced the passwords to his streaming services when I moved in. I have all the good stuff." At my dubious face, he added, "But I pay him handsomely for it. He just doesn't know that I pay him handsomely for it. Let's just say he finds a twenty dollar bill he forgot about in his jacket pocket...more often than most people do."

"A genuine gentleman thief. How chaotically neutral of you," I quipped with a smirk. It was a joke, but it fit him.

One side of his mouth turned up, and I caught sight of just one tooth through his lips—a perfectly normal canine tooth, when earlier tonight it had been long and pointed.

It struck me suddenly how attractive he was. Sure, I'd noticed it throughout the evening—like when I was resuscitating him or when he was telling me silently to run—but it hardly registered during the shock. He was tall and lean with tanned skin. His face was unblemished and had a strong jaw, a straight nose, and—I hated to admit it—incredibly kissable lips. I remembered his eyes were a stony gray, but I couldn't see them through his mid-length, slightly wavy, brown hair.

I wondered if that's what I'd look like if I were a Lapsus—like I was frozen at my prettiest—and that was how people would see me from then on. It sounded good but also a bit like being stuck up on a pedestal, apart from and above everyone normal.

I distracted myself from his alluring good looks by getting to work on bandaging myself. Now that the wound was clean, I could see the damage properly. My palm was covered in cuts, but most were superficial. Two deep ones lay in the meatiest parts of my palm, one beneath my thumb, and the other along the pinky-metacarpal. Those had mostly stopped bleeding. The long, jagged lines along my inner wrist were deeper, more concerning, and still bleeding. I wiped everything down with hydrogen peroxide, which bubbled and fizzed and helped remove debris and germs from the cuts. I then dried them with another of his towels—this guy didn't believe in paper products, apparently. I applied liquid stiches to the gashes on my hands, which coated and sealed the wounds like waterproof spiderwebs. My wrist, I wrapped tightly in gauze to keep pressure on the wound and encourage clotting. Blood dotted the first layers of gauze immediately, but I hoped it wouldn't soak through when I was done wrapping.

When I was finished and looked up, Jeb wasn't there anymore. He'd retreated and was leaning with his back to me against the arm of his couch, clear across the apartment and in the dark.

"All clean and bandaged," I said cheerfully as I approached. I looked for a light switch but settled for turning the knob on a lamp by the TV.

Jeb looked over at me as the light came on. He smiled his fake, for-my-benefit smile. His hair was pushed back from his face again, no longer in his eyes. He looked still more beautiful than was fair—but more haggard than he had moments earlier. I imagined I had more than a little haggardness in my own face.

His gaze fell on the bandage. "You're good at that. Not afraid of the sight of blood or digging into wounds."

"I'd have to be. I'm studying to be a nurse." I shrugged and slumped into an armchair across the living room from him. I stretched my arms and back, overwhelmed with fatigue suddenly. I ran my hands through my hair and shuddered at the crisp dried blood in the strands. "I could do with a shower..."

"You can," he said tonelessly, shrugging. He seemed so distant and ambivalent—more than he'd been all night, that was. "We aren't going anywhere until morning. But, I mean, you just got that all dried and bandaged."

I tossed the idea around in my head for a moment. The idea of being naked in a stranger's apartment was simultaneously thrilling and scary for me, but at the same time, it was just a shower. And bathroom doors lock. I could resist the urge to get clean, but I wanted out of my bloody, ruined clothes.

In the end I decided on a shower. At my request, Jeb stole a plastic bag from his neighbor, which I taped around my bandages with medical tape. Then I retreated into the bathroom for a shower. Every muscle relaxed in the hot water, and I focused only the luxury of a hot, cathartic shower. No thinking allowed.

It wasn't until I got out and was toweling off that I realized my folly. I had nothing to change into. I looked at the small pile of clothes on the floor: black skirt, bloodied green tank top, underwear, bra, and socks. I didn't want to put anything on, ever again. *No matter*, I thought, fixing myself with a frown in the vanity mirror over the sink. *I am more than what I wear. What I wear does not decide my value or what men can do to me. I am stronger than my trauma.*

I patted my hair dry and fluffed it so it wasn't flat to my head. The thing blondes never want to admit even to themselves—we look like drowned rats with wet, translucent hair plastered to our heads, and pool parties are our nightmares.

I wrapped the towel tightly around myself so everything was covered and stepped out of the bathroom, determined to not be cowed by my vulnerability.

CHAPTER 11

JEB

The bloodlust was getting worse. I was able to ignore it in short spurts, but, heavens, it was getting bad. Carrying her up the stairs was fine, even though it brought her even closer to me and the scent of blood was so intense in my nostrils that I could taste it. But she kept talking in her tired, sleepy voice, and her questions helped to distract me. As long as we were making idle chit-chat, I was okay.

But then I parted from her for just a few minutes to raid my neighbor's medical supplies. Once away, and no longer talking, the sensations upped their ferocity. I should have stolen a sip from my neighbor while I was over there. Hell, I could hear his pulse through the two doorways between us. I should have, but I was too focused.

Reciting Hannah's list in my head, I collected as many supplies as I could find. Even the thing she'd called liquid stitches. I read the label out of pure curiosity. Man, modern science and medicine is just baffling. I hadn't had to really notice those kinds of advancements in a long time.

The last thing I found was something she'd called a painkiller—though the bottle said pain and fever reducer. Surely that was good enough. The bottle said ADVIL in big letters. If she was worried about a fever, she was worried about an infection, and this would have to help.

I returned to my apartment and carefully laid everything out on the counter. I once again could smell her clearly, and my teeth were practically pulsing in my mouth. I gripped the counter tightly as a wave of hunger swept over me, and I barely held in a groan.

Then she came out of the bathroom, and I could smell her all the better. She'd washed all of the blood off her arms and face. Now all I could smell on her was *new* blood, and it was...intense. Her speech wasn't distracting enough, as it had been earlier, and I found it hard to concentrate on her words over the sound of her heartbeat.

As she cleaned and bandaged her wounds, I retreated to the living room and tried to get a grip on myself.

Thankfully, the vile smell of hydrogen peroxide mixing with human blood was horrific. I could now smell that more than I could smell the fresh life-giving blood. *Thank god,* I thought, taking a reedy, hissing deep breath—though the air intake was unnecessary. My shoulders relaxed as the scent of the peroxide mixture and the fresh blood faded.

She came to the living room, freshly bandaged, but she kept her distance. Good. For both of us. Her arm was tightly bound starting from below her thumb up to her elbow. It looked professionally done, like she'd done it before. I commented on it, and that's when I realized she was a nursing student. Now I understood why she was so adamant about needing medical attention and stitches. She didn't just think she needed it, she *knew*.

When she went into the bathroom for a shower, it was another reprieve, but the pain in my veins and teeth was still growing worse. I got up and paced. I needed to stay focused and think, but it was getting hard. My pacing took me into the kitchen, where the medical supplies were still laid out, and I put them away, sticking them in random drawers that were completely empty.

Blood remained on the counter from where she was bandaging herself. I looked around for something to wipe it up with, but there was nothing. I don't cook because I don't eat, and I don't have any need for paper towels. Instead, I took my shirt off and stuck it under the faucet. I wrung it out and wiped the counter down, using the hydrogen peroxide to help disinfect the counter—like that mattered. I rarely even came into the kitchen.

After I retrieved a new shirt, I sat down on the couch and turned on the TV, just for a distraction. When the TV connected, it was playing a commercial where cartoon bears were hugging a package that said *Charmin*. I frowned at the commercial and sighed.

I left the apartment and snuck back into my neighbor's, making a mental note to pay for a decent chunk of his groceries this week to make up for everything I'd borrowed. I thought once again about taking a tiny taste of my neighbor's blood, just to tide me over. It'd have been easy; he was asleep on his couch. But it seemed odious somehow: you don't shit where you eat.

Instead, I returned to my apartment with a roll of toilet paper and another of paper towels—and a massive case of the cravings.

When I returned to the TV, a scene from *V for Vendetta* was playing that was a little too close to my current situation. Natalie Portman stormed off after finding out she had to stay hidden in the underground bunker for a year, yelling, "You should have just left me alone!"

With a groan, I shut the TV off and sat down heavily on the couch.

I didn't like this at all. She couldn't stay here. I couldn't babysit. I had things to figure out and things to do once I figured them out. And yet I had an obligation to her. I'd royally derailed her life because she couldn't go home—not yet at least. And yet she had school, people who would worry about her, she had...just life. Life to live, life to experience. And I'd ruined that.

I'd gotten her to agree to postpone going home at least until tomorrow morning. But it was going to be longer than that, and she wasn't going to like it. But staying here? I couldn't handle that.

First thing in the morning, I planned to take her to see someone who could heal her and could get her some kind of protection. And if I was super charming and accommodating, maybe they could take her in until things blew over. I could only hope.

I was in full craving mode by the time I heard the water shut off. I couldn't remember the last time I'd felt this crazed—this dry. My chest hurt, and my muscles were cramping. I needed oxygen, and without it, everything would deteriorate. I would go mad before withering, but first, I was going to get *very* unpleasant. I could already feel that coming: the irritation and the aggression.

I was still sitting on the couch, trying to coax myself into remaining in control a little longer, when Hannah came out of the bathroom in only a towel.

Fuck, she really was pretty. When I first saw her, she was covered in blood, and I hadn't paid any attention to her appearance since then. But here she was, scrubbed clean, her hair damp and falling over one shoulder, and very, very exposed. She'd been exposing a lot of skin all evening, but I hadn't noticed. Now I did, and—she was pretty.

"I don't suppose you have a robe or anything?" she asked as she stepped out of the bathroom.

"A *robe*?" I heard myself ask with a scoff. My chest was vibrating with laughter. "Who the hell wears a *robe* anymore?"

"Fine," she said, frowning. "Do you have anything I can wear?"

I smirked and looked her up and down again, appraisingly and languid. It was that or snap at her unfairly. Stupid craving.

"Why bother," I said, my voice slow and seductive. Her cheeks reddened. "I mean, you were crouching over me, giving my CPR, wearing a *very* short skirt. There's not much left to the imagination."

Her blush deepened, and she hugged the towel around her tighter. She shifted her weight and pressed her legs together in a kind of adorable self-conscious way. It was something so prim, and so human.

I was only selfishly relieving a bit of my tension. But when my eyes returned to her face, my humor evaporated. What I saw wasn't anger, like I expected, or even embarrassment. The only way I could describe the look in her eyes was *haunted*.

It made me think of my sister—not for the first time that day; I thought about her all the time, even after so many years. I'd seen a similar look in her eyes many times. And I'd seen variations of it over the years. The kind of veil shielding women's eyes as they remember something—something about another man's predatory gaze—or worse.

I am a dick, I thought as I realized this. She was remembering trauma, and the memory was caused by my callous teasing of her exposed form. My cravings quieted for the moment, overshadowed by seething self-loathing.

I hated my stupid damaged soul. Sometimes I was happy I couldn't feel more, but this was a moment when I wished I could feel worse. Trust me though—I felt as guilty as I possibly could.

"I'm sorry," I said, drawing fake emotion into my voice, making it sound as guilty as I should feel—as I wished I felt. "Yes, lending you clothes is the least I can do."

I stood and walked into my bedroom. She followed after a moment, and I pulled out a pair of sweatpants and the smallest T-shirt I had.

"You can wear these. They'll have to do for now," I told her as I handed them to her. *Until I can figure out what to do,* I thought but didn't say. *We might have to get you other clothes.*

She nodded. I wasn't forgiven yet, and that was fine. It was good she didn't forgive too quickly: I expected to be dreadfully unpleasant in the morning. It'd be a shame if she forgave me before I *really* offended her.

"I'm going to take a shower, too," I said, before we were standing there long enough for the silence to be uncomfortable. Because I was dead, I didn't sweat or anything. So I didn't need to bathe that often, but today I'd rolled around on a dirty street and was crusty with Hannah's dried blood. "There's TV. I have almost all the streaming options. Do whatever, just please don't leave. I promise it's safe here."

By the time I got out of the bathroom, Hannah was curled up in a tight ball on the couch, asleep. I stared down at her for a long moment, pondering the turn my life had taken in a matter of hours. I never had people in my apartment, and I wasn't prepared to have a human there. In a way, it was like housing an infant. Humans eat, drink, produce waste, have to worry about germs, and have to clean up their dishes. I lived such a minimalistic life; I didn't even own trash bags.

I needed to find a way to get her protection and return her to her normal life, or find someone else to take her in. I couldn't do this.

CHAPTER 12

HANNAH

I woke to a hand on my shoulder and a slightly less than gentle shake. A small groan escaped me as I opened my eyes. The stupid foil on the windows prevented me from gauging how early or late it was. But judging by how tired I was, it was still *very* early in the morning. A headache twinged between my eyes. I needed to hydrate. And I needed to inject caffeine and a healthy amount of painkillers into my system. Ugh, and food. I was starving.

"Hannah, come on," Jeb said in a soft but impatient voice.

With another groan, I uncurled my legs and sat up, partially.

"What time is it?" I rubbed my good hand over my neck.

"The sun is coming up soon," he replied.

"Great," I said, suppressing another groan. I sat up the rest of the way and put my feet on the floor. They were cold as ice, and he didn't have a rug over the hardwood floors of his apartment. I avoided wincing.

"We should get going. It's a reasonable enough hour to bother the person we're going to," Jeb said tonelessly. He sounded off.

Since when is almost-sunrise a reasonable time to bother anyone? I bitterly wanted to say, but I held my tongue. Instead, I nodded and looked over at him for the first time that morning. He was a few feet away from where I was seated on the couch, and he looked even worse than he had last night, before his shower. He was still model-beautiful—his hair simply could not misbehave, apparently—but he had dark shadows forming under his eyes and the whites of his eyes were bloodshot. He looked positively haggard but still unfairly gorgeous as hell.

"I guess you didn't sleep. Up all night thinking?"

"I don't need to sleep," he said simply and flatly. His face didn't change. "So yes, I was. Get your shoes."

I resisted more grumbling and retrieved my socks from the pile of clothes on the bathroom floor. I shuddered at putting on day-old socks, but at least I hadn't bled on them.

"I don't suppose there's time to stop for coffee?" I said as I finished with my socks. I meant it mostly as a joke, but I was partially serious. If he wanted me functioning and alert on three hours of sleep, I needed caffeine. "Or at least a Coke from a 7-Eleven?"

"There will most likely be coffee where we're going," he said.

I could hear the impatience creeping into his voice the longer we talked. And in turn, I was growing impatient with him. *He could chill out for half a minute, jeeze.* It was making me want to take even longer just to be petty.

I went to the kitchen and turned on the sink. I needed to drink water before I did anything else. I cupped my hand under the faucet and brought it to my lips. I'd checked the cupboards while he was showering, but he had no kitchenware, no glasses, and no food whatsoever. It made sense, I guess, but it was inconvenient.

After a few mouthfuls of water, I shut the faucet off. I turned, drying my hand on the leg of my borrowed sweatpants. Jeb was there, behind me, offering me a glass. Another thing stolen from his neighbor, no doubt.

"Thanks," I said shortly, taking it from him.

As my fingers closed on the glass, they unintentionally brushed his, and he withdrew his hand sharply. Luckily, I had a good enough hold on the glass so it didn't fall and break.

"Jeeze, what the hell?" I snapped, without meaning to. He'd withdrawn so quickly, as if I'd burned him or as if he was *that* repulsed by me. Frustratingly, he didn't say anything and just retreated back to the living room and sat on the edge of the seat of the armchair.

I filled the glass with more water and took my time drinking it. I eyed the Advil he'd set on the counter for me. It should be taken with food, but liver be damned, I needed it now. I downed the pills and another mouthful of water and set the glass by the sink.

"So where are we going?" I asked as I carefully put my feet into my sneakers. Tying them was going to be difficult.

"Boston" was all he said. *Is he being vague on purpose, or is he that short tempered in the mornings?* I was going to snap at him soon, I just knew it. It was too damn early for attitude.

Jeb seemed to notice me struggling with my shoes and softened infinitesimally. He knelt in front of me and tied them, with surprising gentleness. Then I realized it wasn't gentleness, exactly, but carefulness. I saw a tremor go through his hands.

"Thank you," I said as he sat back on his heels.

I glanced down at my bandages. I'd bled through them a little through the night. The gauze was stiff and undisturbed, though. Still, it probably wouldn't hurt to change out the bandage. I told Jeb this. Irritation flared on his face and his eyes narrowed, but not at me. He worked his tongue and jaw for a moment.

"Do you have to?" he asked gruffly.

Honestly, it was better that I kept the bandage on, now that the blood had finally clotted. Removing the gauze might sever the forming scab. So it was *technically* better if I left it on until we got where we were going. But his attitude was pissing me off and making me want to push back.

"Well, no, I suppose not. But since we're not going to a real doctor, I'm more than a little worried about infection. This person is probably just some rando that works out of a van, so I thought I would approach this with an overabundance of caution and keep this as clean and taken care of as possible. So, yeah, I think I have to."

He let out a growl of frustration but didn't retort. Point for me.

"For the record, they don't work out of a van," he grumbled, his eyes lowered. "She and her husband work out of a house. And they're nice people. If you're into that sort of thing."

"Yes, I'm into nice people," I said, unamused. "It would be a nice reprieve from present company."

Jeb set his jaw and looked away, rolling his eyes. Another point for me, but it just made me more angry.

"Seriously. What is your problem?" I said, done with the eye rolling and the attitude. He'd been playing hot and cold with me since we'd met on the street, but this was a whole other level of ice. Then there was his stupid lewd comment last night. I didn't deserve any of this from him. *I* was the one who was injured and in pain. He could have a little sympathy.

"My problem is that I need nourishment, and it's taking everything in me to not bite *you*," he said, suddenly forthright. "I was out last night to feed. And I never did that. So I am, as you would say, starving. And I'm only going to get more unpleasant."

I don't know what exactly I thought at that moment. There were several things, actually. There was bewilderment at forgetting that he wasn't human—even though I shouldn't have needed reminding. Then there was the *fear*, but the fear was only slight. He'd had the chance while I was sleeping, but he'd resisted and was still resisting now. Then, superseding that above all things, was a kind of dark amusement. Blame it on the lack of caffeine and the exhaustion.

"So, basically, you're saying you're just hangry?" I said, with an annoyed smirk.

He looked up at the ceiling and let out a sigh in his annoyance.

"Yes, and I'd really rather not go further down this trail of madness as I fight for control, so can we please get going?" he said with what sounded like his last bit of patience.

I rolled my eyes but decided it was time to cut him a break.

"Just let me pee, and then we can go," I said, getting up from the couch. I didn't wait for his permission or response, though.

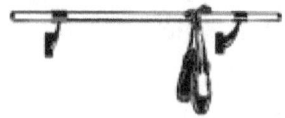

I'd never been to Boston, or many places on the northeastern coast, really. I lived and went to school in Portland, Oregon. Growing up, I'd traveled with my mom to see different ballet companies, but we primarily only did the West Coast. This was my first real time in the Northeast, and somehow it didn't occur to me before we left that it's damn cold in Boston in the early morning in October.

But I was done complaining aloud, even though my head was pounding, my chest ached from the seatbelt-bruise, my arm throbbed and itched something fierce, and now, on top of that, I was freezing in nothing but sweats and a T-shirt. The drive to snap at Jeb was strong, but as haggard as he looked, the last thing I wanted to do was invite that irritation down on me.

We were on the doorstep of a narrow, three-story house in a long row of narrow houses. The only thing that set this house apart from the others was the plastic skeleton wearing a Hawaiian shirt and a witch's hat on a porch chair by the door.

Jeb had been knocking for a few minutes, while I stood slightly off to his side, hugging myself, both for warmth and to hide just how pointy my nipples were in this cold. I wanted to pull my arms into the T-shirt like when I was a child, but I resisted, even though my teeth were starting to chatter.

"For Christ's sake, come *on*!" Jeb growled as he banged again on the front door.

The door opened partway, and the upper body of a beautiful blonde in her late twenties appeared in the opening. All I caught sight of at first was a small nose, blue eyes, and blonde hair in a messy bun on top of her head.

"Jesus, Jeb, what the hell?" She took one look at him and slammed the door—or she tried to.

Jeb was faster, and he wedged his foot in the opening before it could close all the way. He didn't even flinch as it crushed his foot.

"Libby, please," he begged, though his voice was still a growl.

"You're not coming in here like that," Libby said firmly. She was keeping her weight on the door—and on his foot. "What, did you just come up from underground? You look like hell."

"It's been a *bad* night," Jeb growled. He had his hand flat on the door, and I knew he could easily force his way in, but he was holding back. "Please, we need help."

"Go find blood the usual way. I don't know why the hell you thought to come here."

"It's not...for me." He put his hand on my back and nudged me so I took a step closer to him, into view.

The woman—Libby—seemed to see me for the first time. One eye narrowed as she took in my appearance. I could see the cogs turning in her head and getting stuck. She was probably wondering what the hell I was doing with this crazed, starved Lapsus and why I looked half-crazed myself. Apparently, my sleep-deprived eyes, messy, semi-limp hair, and the way I was hugging myself with my bandaged arm was enough to make Libby's anger soften. She let out a sigh of frustration.

"*Fine*. But *you* stay by the door. Any sudden moves, and my husband will drop you." She turned her narrowed eyes back to Jeb.

She opened the door wide for both of us, and Jeb hung back so I could enter first.

I took in the sight of Libby as I passed her and into her house. She was enviously full-figured with beautiful curves and a set of boobs I'd kill for. Her hair was platinum blonde, but with dark roots that looks intentional, yet effortless, and it was twisted into a messy top bun that my ballerina-trained hands could never manage. Her blue eyes were heavily lined with yesterday's eyeliner, and she wore gray sweatpants and a satin-lacey sleep tank under a floral kimono, which she pulled around her as she crossed her arms defensively. Her fierce eyes hadn't left Jeb.

The dark-skinned man standing at the far side of the room grabbed my attention. He was aiming a handgun at Jeb, who, as promised, stayed almost glued to the closed front door. He was a tall, rail-thin, attractive black man with a shaved head, brown eyes, and a lighter complexion that suggested he was mixed. He wore sweatpants and a tight white tank top.

He broke his steely gaze from Jeb and glanced at me, and he somehow communicated a gruff greeting with just his eyes and a brief nod.

I didn't ask for permission to move farther into the room. But it was warm and I was so grateful to be inside that I didn't care about rules of hospitality. I moved over to the first seat I found—a couch—and sat down on it, rubbing my bare arms.

The room was narrow yet spacious and had what I could only describe as a boho-witch aesthetic. The upholstered furniture was dark green velvet. The bookshelf across from me was mostly geodes, crystals, geometric knickknacks, and candlesticks. Various plants were peppered throughout the living room, and a large piece of fabric printed with the moon phases and cats hung on the wall behind the couch like a tapestry. The only thing that clashed with the aesthetic was the modern, run-of-the-mill, plastic playpen in the corner. The playpen was empty but for various toys.

Libby moved to an apothecary chest that I *loved* the look of. From one of the drawers, she withdrew a glass flask containing a thick red liquid. She tossed it to Jeb, who was still by the door, as instructed. He caught it and looked at it with disdain, but he cracked the wax seal without a word and downed the contents.

It was obvious it was blood, and unpleasant as it seemed, he drank it in two gagging swallows. His lips curled back in displeasure, and he shook his head, like a dog eating something horrible. But he put the vial back to his lips and drained as much of it as he could. After a moment of living with the taste on his tongue, he looked a little calmer. Like he was able to take a deep breath for the first time—though he didn't breathe.

"Thank you," he said, after he stood up straight again. His voice was a little hoarse.

"What was that?" I asked. I knew the obvious—blood—but didn't blood need to be fresh?

"A small portion of blood. Bewitched and sealed with magic so it stays as fresh as possible," Libby explained. She'd relaxed a little and felt comfortable enough to turn her back on Jeb. "Consider it a snack."

"Fresh as can be, but cold and...ugh," Jeb said with a shudder. "And hardly any kind of satisfying. Imagine being starving and someone handing you a fun-sized Snickers. It does barely anything nutritionally...but it takes some edge off."

"You still need to feed. Sooner rather than later," Libby said.

"Don't worry, I'm not staying," Jeb said tonelessly. "I'll go as soon as I know you can help her."

"What exactly does *she* need," Libby asked, turning to me. She took a seat on the coffee table, facing me. She glanced down at my bandages.

"She's injured and in danger. She needs healing and protection, food, and probably clothes after that." Jeb still obediently stayed by the door, though the man across the room had lowered the handgun to his side.

"That's a tall fucking order, Jeb, at 6:30 in the morning," Libby snapped, turning her torso so she could glare at Jeb.

"I will pay for it," Jeb said tensely, his eyes narrowing. "Just heal her wounds at the very least. I can find another witch for the rest of it if you're still so displeased with me."

"I'm not a healer, Jeb. It's not my usual forte," she argued.

"Please, Libby," he said, his gruff tone softening into a plea. "I didn't know who else to go to. This is important."

Her eyes narrowed further and a muscle in her clenched jaw twitched; she was obviously torn between her desire to help pitiful little me and her desire to kick Jeb's ass. I didn't blame her for the latter part. I stayed silent, however. I wouldn't beg, but it was interesting seeing Jeb do it for me.

"Fine. You'll explain when you get back, I expect," Libby said after a moment longer of hesitation. She wasn't requesting.

"I will," Jeb said. He nodded at Libby, then at the man with the handgun, who nodded curtly in return—his eyes still narrowed. Jeb turned and left through the front door.

After he was gone, Libby studied me with concern but also wariness. She took a deep breath before she spoke. "I'm Libby. This is my husband," she said, her voice much gentler than when she'd been addressing Jeb.

"I'm Colt," her husband said, holstering the handgun in the waistband of his sweatpants. "Are you a coffee drinker or tea?"

"Coffee, *please*," I said emphatically after I nodded to him in greeting.

He left the room in the direction of where I assumed the kitchen was.

"I'm Hannah," I said, realizing I hadn't introduced myself yet.

"Okay, Hannah, can I take a look at what we're dealing with?" she asked gently. I nodded, and she started to reach for the bandage, but she paused. "One sec."

She left the room and came back with a clear bowl filled with water and a cloth rag. She set it down beside her and removed the gauze. As I'd expected, the blood had clotted to the gauze itself, and it pulled on the scabs when she removed it. She wet the gauze with the damp rag. She'd slightly warmed the water, so it felt lovely on my cold arms, despite the pain.

"Did he do this to you?" she asked, but she sounded as if she couldn't believe it. "It's not his style at all."

"No, it was from a car window. There was an...an accident." I felt the grief again for Gerry from Uber, but it was fading.

Libby's eyebrow raised, but she didn't ask anything further. From her expression, I could guess she was thinking something along the lines of *Jeb has a lot of explaining to do.* I didn't blame her for her confusion. Everything about the past eight hours was weird, and I was only slightly less in the dark than she was.

She pulled the last of the gauze from my arm and hissed quietly at the sight of the gore. But she didn't look away.

"Do you know how to do stiches," I asked, staring down at the deep, horrible gashes. How did I not hit anything important? Or, if I had, how was I lucky enough to have not bled out?

"No," Libby said, but she was smiling like I'd said something funny. "But I can do better than stitches."

"What's that?" I asked warily.

"A poultice, to start with." She looked at me slyly and winked. "And a little bit of magic."

CHAPTER 13

I didn't waste any time finding my fix. I shifted away from Libby and Colt's house the second I was off the front porch. I chose a city in upstate New York at random—much like I'd chosen Portland, Oregon on a whim the night before—and much like I always choose my places to feed.

When I'd been waiting for the right time to wake Hannah, I'd misjudged the timing because I didn't account for time zones. We'd left my apartment thinking it was 5:30 a.m., but we'd arrived in Boston at 6:30.

Well, at least I gave Libby and Colt an extra hour of sleep, I thought as I realized my mistake. *They should be thankful.*

They wouldn't be, though. I had, as Libby said, placed a tall order early in the morning and while I was in the worst starving state I'd ever experienced. I had a lot of apologizing and explaining to do when I got back. If I went back.

The time misjudgment worked in my favor, however. When I left to feed at last, a lot more bodies were out in the open than would have been at 5:30 in the morning.

The first two were from relatively wealthy neighborhoods: one woman and one man. I took maybe a pint of blood from each; they'd feel a little off all day and maybe go home early and take a nap.

Two would have normally been enough to satiate me for the next day—two days tops. But I'd gone way further than I ever liked to, and I didn't want to experience that again any time soon, so I found one more person to feed on just for good measure. For this, I chose a nursing home in Louisiana.

Popular fiction implied that we feed only on the young and beautiful, the younger and livelier the better. But truly, there isn't really a *better*. There are varieties and flavors. The young are what you might call heady: full of life and energy. I tended to stay away from anyone with a "new parent" or "young one at home" vibe. They tasted flat and exhausted—and they didn't need me draining what little energy they had in their blood. The old, though, their taste was the heartiest. They tasted of experience and—though don't ask me how to describe this flavor—wisdom. There wasn't a lot of energy in it, though, and it tended to make me kind of sleepy if they're the only person I feed on. But since they were the third, it was like a dessert, and I could use all the wisdom I could get.

Full and satisfied at last, I could focus and actually *think* for the first time about what to do next. I'd said I'd go back. And I'd meant it as much as I could have at the time, but now I seriously considered whether I really had to—or even should.

Technically, my debt was paid to Hannah. I'd wanted to find her somewhere safe, and I'd done that. I felt no further obligation to the girl. In fact, I felt next to nothing toward her at all now that I was away from her and I knew she was being healed. That was to be expected, though: I don't feel much about anything or anyone on a good day.

Sure, a tiny voice in the back of my head was saying I should get her somewhere truly safe to lie low for the foreseeable future, until I figured things out or until things blew over. But there was nowhere really, truly safe, was there? And she was a spirited, *stubborn* twenty-two-year-old. She wasn't going to agree to lying low somewhere and ignoring her life and responsibilities for a fight she had no stake in. She was no one. She was a random. I owed her nothing.

Yes, she was random. But was she? Was she merely a coincidental bystander? I thought back to the moment before the car crash. Cassandra's gaze had grown distant and then she'd smiled and shoved me in front of the car Hannah was in.

Cassandra had seen the future in that moment, but what had she seen? Had she seen some significance in this chance meeting? Was she simply playing me? Did I dare risk ignoring the possibility that Hannah was significant, after all?

I'd chosen Portland, Oregon on a whim last night, with no rhyme or reason to it. If I'd chosen any other city in the US, what would I be doing now instead of having this internal debate? Where would I be instead if I hadn't discovered that there was this huge concerning plot? I'd be at home on my couch, watching something on one of the many streaming services, or even—if I could tolerate it—on cable. I'd be sitting there, completely content watching humanity from a distance but immersing myself in their culture so I knew how to exist within it, if I ever wanted to.

But instead, I had the weight of this discovery on my shoulders. What if I'd discovered Cassandra's plot when everyone else did? What would I even do then? How would I feel? Everything I saw last night—the chummy baddie-Lapsi, the cold-blooded murder of two seemingly neutral Lapsi, the conversation with the bad bitch herself, and the bad cops—all of it influenced how I was feeling right now. But if I hadn't seen those things and had simply heard mutterings about a community of Lapsi, would I have been concerned? Probably not. I would've found it curious, but I would have left it the hell alone.

I'd have chalked it up to some peace-love commune, and I'd have assumed it was organized by someone like the legendary Danielle. But this didn't scream peace-love commune. I didn't know what it screamed, but I knew it was something more *sinister*.

But what did I plan to do now that I did know something sinister was happening? I was no hero. I wasn't a doer. I didn't get involved or talk to anyone else or even associate. I didn't feel. But for some reason, I couldn't just sit and live with knowing that something weird was on the horizon. And I suddenly felt very, very alone.

After stewing and clearing my head for a while, I shifted back to the site of the accident. I wanted to reaffirm to myself that something was in fact *off* and I hadn't made a wild leap from bad cops to deeper conspiracy.

I returned to the same courtyard at the edge of downtown but remained in an alleyway. Completely opposite of last night, when there hadn't been a car in sight, there were plenty this morning. Sure enough, all signs of an accident last night were cleaned up, not so much as a piece of broken glass that I could see.

I wondered fleetingly about the driver. Had there been any official documentation or record of the accident? Had his body been disposed of or taken to a hospital morgue as a DOA? Would his family ever know, or would he forever be an unsolved mystery in their lives? I decided to keep this detail from Hannah as much as I could. I didn't know why I thought of it just then or why I felt like I should spare Hannah, someone I didn't care about or want to care about. But somehow I knew her heart might break to hear it.

Movement across the street caught my attention. At first, I thought it was just a pedestrian walking from a bus stop. But it wasn't.

A male Lapsus in a police uniform stood across the street. He was looking directly at me.

So I didn't get all of them, I thought as the newly digested blood churned in my stomach.

I didn't stick around for a confrontation. I shifted away from Portland as fast as I could.

CHAPTER 14

HANNAH

"Magic, really?" I said, trying but failing to hide my incredulity. I didn't know why I found it easy to accept the existence of a bloodsucker but couldn't wrap my head around the existence of magic.

"Yup, yup," Libby said over her shoulder. She'd gotten up from the coffee table and gone to the far side of the narrow living room. She returned with a blanket and a laptop. The blanket, she draped over my shoulders, being careful to not let any of it touch my right arm, which I kept propped on the coffee table.

She pulled an upholstered chair over and sat down, opening the laptop.

"It's weird that Jeb didn't mention I was a witch," Libby said, looking at the screen as it booted up. "Did he tell you I was a doctor?"

"He didn't tell me much of anything, really," I said with a shrug. I kept my eyes on my arm.

"Yeah, that doesn't surprise me at all," Libby grumbled. She looked at me over the laptop and rolled her eyes, then her gaze returned to the computer screen.

"So, what, you're going to ... magic-away these cuts? Like, magically heal them?" I said after a few seconds.

"That's the idea," she said without looking up. She was typing away on the keyboard. "Though, as I told Jeb, it isn't my specialty."

"I don't think he was listening, to be honest." I smirked.

"Ugh," she scoffed rolling her eyes again. "Yeah. I swear he was more pleasant when I first met him. Not, you know, much. But a little more pleasant."

I snorted and we both exchanged knowing grins.

"When did you meet him—or how?" I tried to sound casual, but I was intrigued. Mr. Privacy didn't seem to fit with this lovely witchy couple.

"I helped him out a few years back," Libby said with a slight wave of her hand. "With some wards on his home. Wards are my specialty, as it happens. So that was an easy gig."

"And why did he want the wards?" I couldn't help asking.

"I'm not sure really." She shrugged. "I think he might have killed another Lapsus and wanted to steer clear of his mate."

"I guess he makes a habit of killing other Lapsi." I didn't mean to say that aloud.

"Why do you say that?"

"Because he killed like ten last night," I said without thinking. I clamped my mouth shut, but it was too late. The words were out.

"What!? How or why!?" Libby lowered the laptop screen halfway and looked at me with bewildered blue eyes.

"I think you should wait for Jeb to explain it. He knows more of what happened," I said, grimacing. But then I couldn't stop the words. My stupid sleep-deprived brain was making a run for it. "I was just his bait." I didn't bother to mask the bitterness I felt at admitting that little detail.

"You were his bait?" she repeated incredulously. Her eyes fell to my arm where it rested on the coffee table. "That's how this happened?"

"No. This happened earlier. When my Uber driver hit Jeb with his car."

Libby put her head into her hands and shook it at the same time, baffled.

"Jesus, girl, I think you need to start at the beginning," she demanded.

Before I could say more, Colt walked back into the living room, carrying two mismatched mugs of steaming coffee.

"Coffee, but be warned. It is hella strong. Rocket-fuel strong," he warned me in a grave tone as he handed me the mug.

"Thank you, and that sounds wonderful, because I'm operating on at most three hours of sleep," I said, holding the mug close to my chest in my left hand, beyond grateful for the warmth and promise of caffeine.

"Okay, crazy girl. You sit there quietly and drink your coffee. I need a few minutes on The Server to figure out how to heal your ass." Libby turned her gaze back to the laptop screen, but her face remained bewildered.

"The what?" I asked.

"Booting up the ol' Dot-Cauldron?" Colt said as he passed behind Libby's chair. He handed her the second mug and kissed the top of her head.

"Still a more clever name, but unfortunately that's not what it is called," Libby said, gritting her teeth. This seemed to be a ritual exchange between them. I was still confused though.

"What...is that?" I asked warily.

"Witchy-pedia," Colt said with a grin, winking at me.

"*Silencio*, both of you, *please*!" Libby exclaimed, waving her free hand in the air. "I need ten minutes to research, and then we'll play, okay?"

Colt's grin widened, but he hushed and retreated from the room.

I sat in contented silence and sipped my coffee. It was mighty strong, as promised, and at last I felt the synapses of my exhausted brain firing at a more consistent, dependable rate. I started reorganizing my thoughts so that when I had to tell my side of the previous night, I could do it coherently.

Some time later, Libby placed the laptop on the coffee table and stood up. She went to the apothecary cabinet and opened some drawers. She walked back and forth between the coffee table and the cabinet, depositing and retrieving ingredients. I watched her, but not very intently—I wasn't interested in the exact ingredients she was grabbing. Mostly I watched her with a skeptical eye. Magic over medicine... I was ready to call bullshit, but I would do so nicely—I liked this woman, after all.

"Okay," Libby said. She rubbed her hands together. "I'm ready, but I want it on the record that I told both you and Jeb that this is out of my comfort zone. So you both are equally responsible if I fuck this up."

"You're instilling so much confidence," I said sarcastically. I took another sip of coffee and sat up straight on the couch, facing the coffee table. The blanket slipped from my shoulders, but it was preferrable to setting the coffee mug down. "If I lose my fingers, I'm going to be really upset."

"Shush. I promise you won't be any *more* maimed than you already are," Libby muttered, staring at her screen again. She portioned out ingredients—mostly dried herbs by the looks of it—into a large marble mortar. I sipped my rocket-fuel coffee and scowled skeptically over the rim of the mug.

She added something that smelled like castor oil to the mortar and started to grind and mix the ingredients with a matching marble pestle.

"Do you get a free one of those when you're initiated as a witch? Or do you just get a cauldron?" I asked, unable to help myself as I watched her work the pestle. The sound it made was soothing and comforting.

"What, this? No, this is from TJMaxx," Libby said. She didn't look up from her work, and her brow was furrowed in deep concentration.

I snorted softly into my mug. Next, Libby added a measure of something white and creamy. *Please don't be breastmilk*, I thought to myself, suppressing a shudder.

"Okay. That's that," Libby muttered to no one in particular, still focused. She set the pestle down and tapped her chin a few times.

She got up again and came back with a roll of something paper-like tucked under her arm and a weird looking antique bowl—about the size of a salad serving bowl. When she came back to the coffee table, she nudged items out of the way to make room for the large bowl. As she set it down, I saw the bowl was filled to the brim with coals. She opened a small compartment in the bowl and stuck a Bic lighter into it, lighting the coals from underneath. She put some of the ingredients away so there was open space on the coffee table again.

She spread out a roll of parchment paper on the table and cut off two portions. Onto these portions, she spread the herb mixture from the mortar in generous amounts.

"Okay. Arms out," she said, holding a hand out as if wanting an offering.

"What? Both?" I asked, wary. My left had scratches and minor cuts on it. "It's only my right that is concerning—"

"I can heal the cuts on your left just as easily," Libby said, snapping her fingers.

"All you've been saying is that this isn't easy for you," I argued, pulling my arms into my chest to shield them from what promised to be a horrifying experience.

"Give me your arms already. Trust me," Libby said. Her gruff impatience was only playful, it seemed, because her tone had softened on the *trust me*.

I sighed and, swallowing my pride, held out both arms over the coffee table. Libby gently nudged them onto the herb mixture parchment. She wrapped each of my hands and forearms in the parchment in a kind of cast and secured them with twine. She took out a stick of charcoal and, looking between the parchment and the laptop screen, drew symbols on the parchment.

"Okay. Now put your arms over the brazier."

"What?" I demanded. "No. I draw the line at putting my hands over what is essentially a stove."

"It's to seal the runes into the paper. This is the *magic* part of it," Libby said, trying to assure me. But I was beyond assurances.

"By cooking my arms? Bullshit."

"You're not going to be hurt. This is barely even hot. You want to call bullshit, fine. Do it, and then laugh at me if it doesn't work," she said. "Ugh, I'm not used to skeptics. Usually by the time someone comes to my door, they're believers."

"Yeah, your bedside manner is atrocious, too," I quipped bitterly.

"Please do this? It will work, I promise," Libby said, softening. "If it doesn't work, you can punch me in the face."

I sighed heavily in apprehensive defeat, then took a deep breath and placed my wrapped forearms over the hot coals of the brazier. I glared at her bitterly as I did so.

All I felt was a surprisingly comforting warmth as the parchment heated. The skin around my various cuts tingled, but not enough to be unpleasant. I was focusing so much on the pain I *didn't* feel, that I didn't realize at first that Libby was mumbling an enchantment of some kind. I raised an eyebrow and mused about how crazy my life had become in under eight hours.

Despite the caffeine I'd recently consumed, the warmth in my arms had become so comforting that I could practically fall asleep. My head was drooping forward when I felt a gentle squeeze on my fingers.

"You can take your arms off the coals now, hun," Libby was saying quietly.

I lifted my head, which was swimming, and refocused on the pretty woman in front of me. Oh. Right. Magic bullshit healing was happening. I lifted my arms off the brazier and held them out to Libby. She cut off the twine and removed the parchment from my hands and forearms. As she wiped the slightly caked herb mixture off my arms, I expected pain, but none came. When the mixture was mostly removed, we both stared at my hands and right wrist.

The superficial cuts on my hands were healed completely. The deepest of the cuts, those I'd adamantly demanded needed stiches, were merely lively pink scars. I clenched and unclenched my hands into fists and rotated my wrists. I was baffled into silence, but I wasn't quite ready to eat my words yet.

"If I had more skill in the healing arts, and if it weren't my first time at this spell, they would be completely healed," Libby said. "As it is, unfortunately I think the scars will be permanent."

"So I don't get to punch you in the face," I said as I continued to stare at my healed wounds. "Am I allowed a small slap for the scars?"

"I suppose that's fair," Libby said with a soft chuckle. She looked as relieved as I felt at the success of the spell.

I'll be damned. My stunned silence had returned.

Libby gathered up her supplies and walked them over to her supply cabinet.

"You can wash the rest of the poultice off your arms in the bathroom if you want. It's just past the kitchen, that way." She gestured in the general direction of a hallway at the other end of the living room.

I stood up but paused as I passed her.

"Thank you," I said, trying to intone the words with as much feeling as I could.

"It ain't nothing," Libby said with a shrug. But her grin betrayed the giddiness she felt at her success.

I returned to the living room after scrubbing down my arms with bar soap from the bathroom. I was just reaching out to take some things from Libby's heavily laden arms when a shrill shriek sounded behind me suddenly, making me turn.

Around the corner, into the living room, a tiny toddler clad only in a diaper came running, straight at me. She was a beautiful baby with tan skin, a perfect cherub face, and a puff of brassy blonde hair sticking in all directions. Her chubby little legs were more confident than they were powerful. The biggest semi-toothed grin split her bow-shaped mouth as she locked playful eyes on me.

She stopped and caught herself on my shins. She barely steadied herself before she was reaching up happily; though she spoke in babbling nonsense, she clearly was demanding that I pick her up.

I obliged the toddler without hesitation and took her into my arms. My heart was bursting with baby-love like I hadn't felt in years. I used to babysit back in my early teens—despite my mother's ceaseless protests. Since then,

I hadn't been around that many babies. Oh, how I missed their silly babble and giggles!

"And who is this beautiful one?" I asked, cheerfully bouncing the still-giggling girl.

"This is Sophie," Colt said. He'd followed closely behind the baby, carrying the shirt he'd no doubt been trying to put on her before she sprinted off. Still holding Sophie, I moved to Colt so he could fit the shirt over her afroed head.

"And Sophie knows no strangers," Libby said, slightly reproachful of the child, as Colt worked her arms into the sleeves. "I swear, she loves everyone she sees. She will go off with just anyone one of these days..."

"I was the same way, I'm told," Colt said, moving behind Libby and kissing her shoulder lovingly. "It'll go away, if she's like me."

Now clothed, baby Sophie erupted in more saliva-filled giggles and clapped as if it was the most interesting sound in the world. My heart was melting.

There was a knock on the door. Colt went to it and peeked through, then opened it to let Jeb back inside. It was weird to see him again, and I'd half expected him to just leave me here with these strangers and not return. I wasn't entirely sure if I was glad to see him back or not.

He stepped inside, and I saw the difference immediately. He looked much less dour and instead looked the perfect, unfairly beautiful picture of health. He didn't exactly look chipper, but he looked far friendlier than when he left.

He paused when his eyes fell on me, with the baby in my arms. Mild surprise showed in his eyes.

"Okay, I know I was out of it, but I know I wasn't gone *that* long," he said, raising an eyebrow.

Nothing in his deadpan tone suggested he was joking until he lifted one side of his mouth in the most half-assed smirk I'd ever seen. I rolled my eyes and turned back to baby Sophie and gave her a kiss on her chubby cheek.

But as suddenly as she fell in love with me, I was as uninteresting as chewed gum to Sophie. She leaned out of my arms and aggressively reached for Jeb to hold her next. Jeb looked even more startled as the child reached for him. He took a step instinctively away from her, and Sophie didn't like that. Her babble turned into grunting, and I could see her face reddening.

"Take her, Jeb, or she'll start to scream," I warned him, holding the struggling child out to him.

Showing the most emotion I'd seen him express, he warily took the child as if accepting a grenade. His touch seemed to soften immediately, though. Instinct took over, and he held Sophie as anyone would hold a toddler.

Sophie had left my long hair completely alone. But for some reason, she was fascinated by Jeb's brown hair. She reached up and grabbed a handful in her chubby hand. Jeb looked horrified and took Sophie's hand in his so she didn't pull too hard.

"Please don't, gremlin," he pleaded with her. "If you pull it out, it won't grow back."

He didn't mean for it to be funny. In fact, he was dead serious. But for some reason, I found myself laughing the first genuine laugh in a long time.

CHAPTER 15

JEB

"Jesus..." was all Libby could utter after I finished explaining everything.

We were sitting around their kitchen table—though Colt was going back and forth between the table and the stove. He'd determined that such a gathering and such an outpouring of heavy information required a heartier breakfast than the usual "Eggo waffles," whatever those were. I'd never understood waffles.

I'd spun out the yarn as best I could, from seeing the two Lapsi leave the brewhouse to killing the Lapsi cops, trying not to leave anything out. Hannah sat silently perpendicular to me. She'd let me take the reins on the story, since she claimed she was just a bystander through it all. She listened to the details she hadn't heard yet and sipped a second—or third?—mug of bitter-smelling coffee. When I got to the part about killing the Lapsi, I skirted around the detail that Hannah had been bait. Her eyes narrowed over the rim of her mug as I did so.

I still hadn't wavered in my conviction that I'd handled our escape as best as I could. I'd wanted her safe, and I'd gotten her to safety. I'd come back here, when I didn't have to, and I still didn't know why I had, which had to count for something. But at her glare, something shifted into place that nearly gave me pause.

Yes, I found it even harder than my tattered soul usually allowed to have regrets about our escape. But suddenly I regretted the *cost*. I'd needed authenticity, not acting, and we'd succeeded in that, but it cost me her trust. I hadn't cared about that at the time, but now? Had I come back to earn it? Or to prove I could be trusted to not desert her? *Interesting*.

"I'm still not getting the thing about it being strange seeing Lapsi together or the novelty of a gathering," Hannah said in the silence that followed Libby's exasperated response. "That isn't a thing?"

"Not usually, no," I answered. "At least, it used to be extremely uncommon. It's probably becoming more common in recent years, ever since the *chosen one* 'saved' us." I didn't bother keeping the bitterness and mocking out of my voice.

"What chosen one?" Hannah asked, like I dreaded she would.

"A few years ago, Cain was killed by a young naïve Lapsus named Danielle," I explained, rolling my eyes.

"Careful there," Libby warned, though her tone was somewhat mocking. "We do not take the *chosen one's* name in vain in this house. She happens to be my bestie. And this one here's best friend when she gets older, too!" She leaned over to the baby, seated in a high chair making a mess with scrambled eggs and syrup. She kissed the baby on her messy cheek, and the baby released a happy shriek. My stomach turned over at the sound. "A family tradition."

"And she's my aunt," Colt spoke up, putting a plate of bacon and another plate of eggs down on the table and taking a seat.

"Besides," Libby said, sitting up straight again. "She didn't kill Cain."

This was news to me.

"But I thought he was dead," I argued.

"Oh, he probably *is* dead. Undoubtedly." She was grinning, enjoying my confusion. "She spared him and made him mortal. No doubt the little pretentious prick was killed in an alley in the next town he went to."

"This Danielle sounds like a badass," Hannah said, sounding impressed. "Maybe we could use her help in this."

"No. Not interested in her help," I said firmly. *And where are you getting this "we" from? There is no we.*

"Why are you carrying such an attitude toward her? She won a victory for you Lapsi, didn't she?" Libby said. To her credit, she sounded legitimately curious, not defensive.

"I'm sure she thought so. But I lost a friend in that fight," I snapped, before I had a chance to hold that detail back. *Crap.*

"Adam?" Colt asked quietly. He set his mug down.

I held my tongue but nodded.

Adam. Or Adeimanthos—a fellow Lapsus with an atrocious full first name like myself. Arrogant, cocky, swaggering, pansexual Adam had been the closest friend I'd had in my four hundred years. He was attracted to anyone and everyone and wasn't afraid to make it known. He came onto me often, as well, and it worked a couple of times in his—and my—favor. Though that was all before I'd lost my

AMELIA ROSE

soul. Adam was the reason I still had part of my soul and wasn't *completely* an emotionless husk. I owed him everything for that.

He was also the reason I knew to never cut my hair, no matter how tired I might get of the lack of change. We're dead, and though we heal from wounds, certain things don't regenerate...like limbs or hair and fingernails. Adam had shaved his head back in ancient Roman times and forever had a buzzed head. Poor, beautiful bastard.

"I'm sorry," Colt said, genuinely sympathetic.

Sympathy. That was something I always failed to scoop up out of the remains of my soul. I envied people who could feel sympathy or empathy. I missed it.

"I'm sure she saw it as a victory, but I lost a friend, and her breaking part of our curse is the reason that bad Lapsi seem to be multiplying at an insidious rate."

"*What* part of *what* curse?" Hannah asked. The poor girl was trying so hard to keep up.

"Cain's curse. Immortality might seem great, but they were inherently forced to never belong anywhere—even with other Lapsi," Colt explained calmly to Hannah. Colt also sympathized with Hannah's game of catch-up. If I understood correctly, he was relatively newly educated in our lore. "And Danielle was able to break that part of the curse because, well, I guess you could say she was destined to?"

I suppressed a groan but rolled my head back and looked at the ceiling. Not this chosen-one theory I'd been mocking. They didn't really think I believed in the crap, did they? *Hannah, please don't ask. Just let it go, I'm begging you.*

"What?" Hannah asked. Of course she did.

"There was some astronomical timey whimey stuff she tries to downplay," Libby explained airily. "She was pulled into an astral plane, outside of time and space. And gave her blood to the witch that cursed Cain. When her blood again mixed with Cain's a few years ago, he became mortal, and their anti-community clause was broken."

"A witch made Lapsi?" Hannah asked, barely containing her exasperation.

"Yup!" Libby said cheerfully, stabbing a fork into her pile of scrambled eggs. "Witches did it millennia ago, wrote it into legend, which became the Bible. Yada, yada, yada. Witches actually used to hunt Lapsi, once upon a time. Until a few hundred years ago. But some Lapsi still harbor some hurt feelings."

"I feel like I'm at a high-stakes review session for a history final, but I haven't been there all semester," she said in a groan, throwing her head against the chairback. A chuckle escaped my lungs, surprising me.

"I'd love to say it gets easier, but it doesn't, really," Colt said, patting her hand sympathetically and holding the plate of bacon out to her. "Just eat bacon and try to absorb as much as you can."

Hannah took two pieces and bit into one, chewing grumpily.

"So technically, Danielle wasn't a descendant of Cain, and she'd never killed before. Thus she's been erected as the messiah, Jesus-figure of my race," I finished bitterly. I hoped to end this subject soon. Talk of god-figures, saviors, and religion made my guts boil. "But we're getting too far from the real issue."

"This Cassandra figure," Colt said, after swallowing a mouthful of eggs. "You think she is *the* Cassandra? Of legend?"

"Of actual Troy?" Hannah asked, raising her eyebrows. "Wooden horse and all that?"

"There was a Troy, though the epic poem greatly exaggerated the history," I said. I'd heard the real history of Troy and the great war through various grapevines over the years. Though this was my first time running into someone who'd *been* there. As far as I'd learned, the war did take eight years and there *was* a wooden horse, but it wasn't as big as the epic claims. Walls didn't need taken down to get it into the city. And only two or three Greeks were inside, along with a dead horse. They brought the dead horse out and hid it within the source of Troy's well water, poisoning it. Troy wasn't brought down in a final, upsetting siege with help from the gods; instead, it was slow, pestilent, and ugly. I didn't feel like explaining all of that right then, though.

"And Cassandra's deal was that she was psychic and prophetic but cursed to never be believed, right?" Colt said.

"In *verse*, yes," I said. "But, judging by...*all* of history, I'd wager she wasn't believed merely because she was a woman in that time period."

Libby and Hannah both nodded in a knowing, united way.

"But, I think the psychic part of her legend is true. She said she saw her success, but she didn't see me there," I said, remembering again the last thing she'd said to me. I looked at Hannah, who was nibbling her second piece of bacon. "And I think she saw you coming."

"Me?" she said, her head rearing back in surprise. "What about me?"

"I don't think she saw much," I admitted. I had no idea what Cassandra saw, but her eyes had glazed, she'd smiled, and she'd pushed me in front of the car Hannah was in. "I think she knew you'd hit me. And that it would keep me occupied at least for a while."

Her eyebrows came together as—I assumed—she was trying to figure out what part she really had to play in all of this. I hoped her part was over, as I'm sure she did, too.

"Keep you occupied so she can continue to build her cult," Libby guessed.

"Cult? No. I know cults—I was born into one," I protested. At Hannah's quizzical look, I turned to her and merely said, "Puritans." Then I turned again to the rest. "No, this feels more like some New World Order, Illuminati organizing. That handful of Lapsi was only the tip of the iceberg."

"What...what do you mean?" Hannah asked, though her face already looked worried.

I could tell the cogs were turning in her head and she was already guessing what had been rolling around in my head. At first it sounded crazy, but the more I thought about it, the more it seemed to fall in place. I steeled myself before saying the words aloud. Because saying them might make them true.

"It doesn't sound like she wants to build a city. She wants to *take* a city. And it sounds like she's closer than she wants us to think."

CHAPTER 16

HANNAH

S *he wants to take a city. My city,* I thought in horror. Not that I had that much hometown pride or anything. I had no stake in the city, and I had no stake in this. But my dad lived there, and I had a meager little lonely life there. I shuddered.

Libby instinctively put a hand on her daughter, as her way of showing her fear. Baby Sophie, blissfully unaware in her childish glory, let out another shrill happy baby noise. It didn't decrease the tension in the air from Jeb's statement, but the innocence of it jolted me out of my horrified silence.

"That's why you didn't want me to go to a hospital," I said, understanding dawning. "Because if a police station was overrun..."

"Then maybe other infrastructures are as well," Jeb said, finishing my thought for me. "And if I'm an enemy of Cassandra, so are you. You're not safe anywhere as long as she's still...plotting."

"So what do we do?" I asked, mystified by the impossibility of everything in front of us. *And when did it become we?* a little voice in my head piped up.

"I don't know," Jeb said, shaking his head. "I honestly don't know if there's anything I can do. I've just been taking this one step at a time. And now I'm at a loss."

I'd hindered and delayed him so much in the past several hours. He waited with me for an ambulance, to make sure I was safe, when he didn't have to—when he obviously had better things to do. He stayed to keep me alive when the cops turned out to be Lapsi. Then, while starving, he stayed in his apartment with me so he could get me somewhere safe in the morning. I'd been in his way through all of this, and I'd delayed him from finding out more about this Cassandra and her plan. I'd been a distraction.

Guilt brewed in my gut, but it paused when I thought more about Jeb's actions throughout the night. He might not have been doing it intentionally, but maybe he'd been embracing the distraction to avoid getting involved in something even bigger. I thought about his leave-me-alone lifestyle and that he still lived among humans, despite wanting distance. Then I considered his urgency to get me somewhere safe, his persistence through the obstacles that arose, and his insistence that I'd be killed if I left his side.

Then I remembered him with baby Sophie, earlier this morning. He'd been horrified at first to be handed the toddler, but I saw the instinctive gentleness that took over as he held Sophie in his arms. He was more in tune with humanity than he admitted.

He's lonely, I mused. *He doesn't realize it, but he's lonely.*

He'd been roped into this conspiracy and saddled with me, a random. He wouldn't admit it, but he was scared, and rather than drop me at a hospital on the other side of the planet, he'd reached out to two near-strangers because they were the only friendly faces he could think of.

Oh, Jeb, this might end up being the best thing for you, I thought with a perplexing mix of amusement, guilt, and bitterness. *And the worst thing for a lot of people.*

Sophie started to fuss as our contemplative silence stretched out. Colt grabbed a washcloth and wiped the stickiness from her fingers and face. He picked her up and carried her into the living room.

"Look." Jeb leaned forward in his chair toward Libby, elbows on the table. "I'm deep in this, because of last night. She's probably not safe anywhere, but she might be safer with you than me, given that you're the best in the business when it comes to wards and that you're clear across the country from Portland. Can she stay with you for a few days until I...until this blows over?"

He'd automatically started saying he *would* come back but had to alter it. Which was the grain of truth? He'd already come back once when we both knew he had no intention of doing so. Yet he'd come back. Had it only been to enlist their help or to pay his debt for them healing me? Or had he felt an obligation or a weird loyalty?

Honestly, the hot and cold act of his made it hard to guess his intention, and at this point, I didn't want to guess. Sure, signs pointed to him being a big, lonely softy at heart, but the jury was still out because of some of his actions over the past twelve hours.

Drawing myself out of my thoughts, my eyes slid to Libby, who hadn't answered yet. She'd withdrawn in her seat and was looking at the highchair next to her, even though Sophie wasn't there anymore.

I understood her hesitation immediately. This thing was deep and dangerous, and our presence was dangerous, the longer I was here. Libby probably wouldn't have cared two years ago, but she was a mother now.

"No," I answered for her. "We can't ask you to do that for me. I'm not risking you, or Sophie."

"Or me!" Colt called from the living room.

Jeb's mouth clenched into a tight line, but he didn't argue. He put his head into his hands and slumped forward.

"Okay," he said flatly into his hands, defeated. "But we do need protection. *More* protection."

"That much I can do," Libby said. She sent me a look that was both grateful and apologetic.

"All right. Then we'll go back home. Maybe lie low for a bit. Or brainstorm some more," Jeb said.

"I'll put an ear to the ground. Call in some favors, and see if anyone can sniff around Portland." Libby's eyes were distant. "In the meantime, I'll make Hannah charms to keep on her all the time and bundles to burn that will mask her scent. And reinforce the wards on your place."

"What about this Danielle person?" I asked. Jeb lifted his head high enough from his hands to stick me with some side-eye. "Can't she help? She'd at least be one person on our side."

"I can try, but she's not the easiest person to get ahold of these days. She's aloof ... especially with Sophie at this age." Libby winced. "I'll try, but no promises. I have a few others in mind I can call."

"And I think we're going to need food. And clothes," Jeb said, finally lifting his head from his hands and sitting up.

"I can take them," Colt said, appearing in the kitchen doorway, his hands in his pockets. "Target okay?"

"I thought I shouldn't go anywhere," I said, though clothes that fit sounded great: underwear at the very least.

"I have enough protection on me that I doubt anyone will fuck with us in a store. Besides, if there's a Lapsi underground movement going on in Oregon, I don't think they are going to be working—or shopping—at a Target clear across the country," Colt said, his stoic face at odds with the words he was saying—it just sounded so bizarre.

"I'll work on the protection charms and wards while you're gone," Libby said, getting up from the table. She walked around it toward her husband but stopped short. She took my hand and looked at me seriously. "Do you have anyone who's going to be worried about you?"

I could've laughed. That thought had crossed my mind a few times over the course of the night, but things had been so nonstop that I hadn't really paused to think about it. I wasn't going home for a while. And I definitely wasn't going to make my midterms on Monday.

"See, now you're asking the right questions," I said with a small laugh.

"You sound like a serial killer, babe," Colt said. His voice was quiet and probably meant only for Libby's ears.

"Do you, Hannah? Family? Friends?"

I didn't have to think about it for long. Honestly, there weren't many people in my life. I didn't bother worrying about what my mom would think about me disappearing.

We hadn't spoken in a few years. I didn't have any close friends, and none that were local. Really, there was only my dad. I didn't live at home, so it might be a day or two before he noticed. But then again, my roommate would notice and might call him, just to see if I was okay. By Monday, they'd be concerned.

"Just my dad, really," I admitted. Libby looked surprised that there were so few people that would miss my presence. But she said nothing. "And my roommate, maybe. I don't have her number though. I lost my phone."

"Do you know your dad's number?" she asked me. I nodded. "Do you want to call him? Let him know you're okay?"

"I don't know what I would even say," I said, shaking my head and shrugging at the same time.

"Tell him anything you want," she said. "I can give you a potion that will make you *very* convincing for a few minutes. You can tell him not to worry, and he'll listen to you."

The fact that a potion could do such a thing both surprised and intrigued me. What also surprised me was her sincere concern and kindness—though it shouldn't have. This woman had such a kind soul.

She took me to the living room and, after a moment of searching, handed me a small container. This one wasn't a glass vial, however; it was, humorously, a small Tupperware one.

"I ran out of the fancy glass vials," she explained with a what-can-you-do shrug. She handed me a phone and shooed everyone out of the room. Apparently, anyone within earshot after I downed the potion was going to find me very compelling. That made me nervous.

The potion was only about a mouthful of murky, tan liquid that looked like cider. I downed it in one go, and bitterness spread over my tongue. *I guess coercion shouldn't taste good*, I thought as I tried not to grimace. I let it settle in my stomach for a moment and dialed the familiar number.

"Hello?"

I almost started crying just from the relief of hearing his familiar, normal voice.

"Dad? It's me," I said before I had the chance to swallow the emotion in my voice.

"Hannah? Is everything okay?" he said, his voice instantly flaring in concern.

Crap. I reminded myself that it was early in the morning there. He knew I wasn't a morning person, and I'd never in a million years call this early.

"I'm fine. I'm fine. I promise," I assured him, automatically trying to sooth his worry.

"Oh, okay," he said, almost cheerful. Just like that, his worry vanished.

I need to be very careful, I warned myself. I didn't want to mess around with being so compelling and believable.

I decided to tell him that I'd met someone suddenly and was going away for a week or two with him. At first he asked about school—he believed me and accepted it, but he was still too much of a *dad* to not be concerned about my future. Again, I had to think carefully. If I said school was out for a week, he'd believe me. But when my roommate called, the jig might give itself up. I needed a lie that would make sense to my roommate too. I told him that I'd been feeling overwhelmed lately. That old trauma was resurfacing and upsetting me. I needed a little bit of time to figure myself out again. That was believable, and not *entirely* a lie. Old trauma *had* resurfaced and upset me last night, that was for sure.

He believed me without question and without any worry. I needed to get off the phone soon, before the potion or my resolve wore off, but I didn't want to go yet. I was scared suddenly and desperately wanted my dad.

"Dad," I said after our silence stretched for a moment. "I have to go now, but...Dad, I love you. Okay? I love you so much."

"I know, sweetie, I know." His voice was cheerful and worry free because of the manipulation of my compelling voice. I hated myself. "Be safe, okay? I love you too."

I didn't say anything else because I was about to cry. I hung up the phone and sat in the armchair for several minutes, collecting myself. When the bitterness had faded from my tongue, I got up and returned the phone to Libby. My tongue might not have been bitter anymore, but there was still a bad taste in my mouth that wasn't related to magic.

Colt drove us to the nearest Target, and it was so completely surreal to walk into such a mundane and consistent environment, a huge open space, full of merchandise and red shelves, after the night and day I'd been having.

We drove, rather than shifted—as Jeb called it—because Colt's wards made it impossible for him to be shifted, and he'd agreed to take Sophie with us so Libby could get to work. Jeb didn't go in with us at first. He wanted to feel out the space and make a few cautious rounds to make sure there weren't any threats around. Colt, pushing baby Sophie in a shopping cart, and I started collecting essentials from the shelves.

For clothes, I wasn't particular. I grabbed a pair of jeans and a few leggings, a couple sports bras, socks, underwear, some comfortable shirts and tank tops from the table displays, and a zip-up hoodie for warmth.

Jeb had zero food in his house, but he did have a coffee maker, a microwave, and a fridge, which apparently came with his apartment. I figured I could live on frozen dinners and coffee, so I grabbed these items as well as toilet paper. For good measure, I stuck a ceramic mug in the cart along with a set of silverware.

Jeb rejoined us in the personal hygiene aisles, where I was grabbing toothpaste and deodorant. We headed to the checkout area, but I paused at the start of one aisle.

"One sec, guys, I'll be right back." I left Jeb with the cart and darted down the aisle to my left. My period wasn't due any time soon, but I figured it was better to be prepared regardless.

Jeb and Colt hung back, giving me privacy to select the correct tampons. Actually, Colt seemed like the type who knew his wife's preferred brand and type and didn't have any qualms buying them for her. Jeb, I think, didn't even register what aisle it was.

"Pardon me," said a woman to my right that I hadn't noticed as I checked out the shelves. I didn't know how I hadn't noticed her though; she was a knockout. She was only a little taller than me, with beautiful, loosely curled red hair. She wore a simple, but pretty, deep blue dress that reminded me of Greece or eastern Europe. Her jean jacket toned down the elegance of her ensemble. She was smiling politely at me with perfect rosebud lips. "Could I trouble you to grab me one of those?"

She leaned into me and pointed a graceful hand at a box on the top shelf.

My heart fluttered at her sudden proximity. I once again noted all her beautiful details before I realized I was doing it.

'Um, yes, of course," I said, stuttering. I grabbed one of the boxes she'd indicated and handed it to her.

"Thank you, love," she said in a silky voice that gave me goosebumps. She took the box from me, brushing my knuckles with hers. "I know I could have grabbed them myself, but I wanted a reason to say hello." Her eyes unfocused and looked dreamy for a second. When they refocused on me, her coy smile turned into a beautiful, pleased grin. With her other hand, she gently brushed the backs of her fingers across my reddening cheek. "You really are quite the beauty, you know."

My stomach did a backflip. It'd been a while since a woman had boldly flirted with me, let alone in such an open public space. If I wasn't facing down an unknown threat against my hometown and operating on three hours of sleep,

I'd have come up with something *very* smooth to say back. But unfortunately, I stood there dumbfounded instead.

The woman's grin turned almost sly as her gaze moved past me, over my shoulder. When she looked at me again, she fluttered her eyelashes softly, and then she disappeared. The box she'd been holding fell to the ground with a thud, startling me out of my stupor.

"Hannah," Jeb said, suddenly beside me. I couldn't tell if his face was angry or concerned. "What did she say to you?"

"Uh, nothing. She just complimented me." I put a hand to my burning cheek, as if I could hide how flustered she'd made me. His concern seemed misplaced, though, like he'd known her. "Why? Who was that?"

"That was Cassandra," he said, looking all around him. He was rattled.

CHAPTER 17

JEB

Hannah crashed shortly after we finally shifted back to the vicinity of my apartment. The caffeine wore off, and she quickly devolved into something like a zombie from movies. I let her take the bedroom to nap, and while she slept, I put away the things I'd paid for in places I assumed they should go. However, organizing wasn't my strong suit, apparently, as I'd never had to do so before.

When everything was put away, I sat on the couch to think everything through. Six hours had passed since I'd had a moment to myself, and I still had no better ideas or better information.

Cassandra had gotten *so close*, yet I hadn't sensed her at all. And she'd shown up right next to Hannah, despite all of our precautions. It was as if she knew exactly where we'd be at that moment. It *scared* me, which was something I hadn't felt in years. She seemed to always be a step ahead, and she was toying with me.

This was such a mess, and it was so beyond me. It wasn't unheard of for there to be bad Lapsi out there. When there's power, there will always be someone who uses it maliciously. It's happened any number of times in the past: the Blood Countess, Jack the Ripper, the Zodiac Killer, to name just a few, were all Lapsi. But they were solitary and either grew bored and disappeared or met their end in some way or other. They preferred to shock rather than mystify, and they enjoyed the attention, so they killed in ways that didn't point to vampirism.

The Blood Countess was before my time, but I'd heard rumors that she was still alive and that her real name was Rosalyn. I was Lapsi by the time Jack the Ripper was active, but I wasn't yet exploring outside the United States, so I never had the pleasure of crossing paths with him—or her. I *did* meet the Zodiac Killer once, in San Francisco. He was an unsettling sort to put it mildly, and I steered clear of him after the one meeting. I don't know how *he* met his end, but three years later a human copycat tried to resurrect the reign of terror—before Adam killed him.

Adam. Soul or no soul, I missed my friend. Just like I missed my sisters even after four hundred years. Adam and I first met in the 1800s—the era of the ridiculously curly sideburns, may they burn in hell. We kept tabs on each other over the years and came together several times. It never lasted, however, because of that stupid nerve-itch that pushed Lapsi apart from everyone. We were occasionally lovers, but mostly he was the best friend I'd ever had.

Fleetingly, I mused over what Hannah would have made of Adam—if she'd have liked him or loathed him. Adam surely would make a pass—several passes—at Hannah if they'd met. She was his type. Then again, *everyone* was Adam's type. He pursued everyone equally, sincerely, and with good humor.

I hated that he was dead, and the smug bastard was happy somewhere knowing I was raging about it, even after years. He'd sacrificed himself for a handful of humans. He didn't have a bleeding heart for humans, humanity, and their precious existences. He'd done it spur of the moment, like the stupid bastard did everything.

Not for the first time that day, I sent a quiet, muted, wish into the ether that Adam were here. He wouldn't know what to do, necessarily, but he would at least have suggestions of plans of attack. He was a cocky, gunslinger-type, and a blowhard, but he'd be somewhere to start.

He would have toyed with Cassandra twofold, just to prove he could. Whereas I'd just stood there, assessing the risks and the odds, he'd have attacked.

But he wasn't here, and I felt like a fly in Cassandra's perilous web. Everything about Cassandra rankled me, and she knew it. She knew everything, it seemed.

Hannah said Cassandra didn't say anything to her, but somehow in the one look she gave me over Hannah's shoulder, she's said volumes. Her face was sly and mischievous, and almost threatening: silently telling me that she would kill Hannah if I interfered further. As if she thought I cared.

Did I care? I cared that she was toying with me. I cared that she was toying with society and infiltrating it in such an insidious way. I cared that a lot of people were probably going to die. I cared that the world was changing so damn fast after being the same for so long. I cared that I was scared.

But did I care about *Hannah*? Was a weird bond forming because of her dependency on me and my weird, new sense of honor? Yeah, sure. That was bound to happen after twelve hours of complete insanity. Was it more than that? No, probably not.

I didn't know anything about her life, her interests, or her goals in life—beyond survival. In the brief amount of time I'd known her, I'd gleaned that she was kind, spirited, and stubborn as hell—but also incredibly adaptable. She'd accepted the existence of Lapsi without blinking. Her entire universe had changed in that instant, and she'd just accepted it.

Yes, she was interesting. I admired her strength and intelligence, and I wanted to know where it all came from. I wanted to know how she was apparently so alone that only her dad would notice she was gone. Many things about her were perplexing and fascinating.

It would be interesting to know her, I found myself thinking, which surprised me.

Perhaps it was just the novelty of her presence. I avoided people so much that being forced together with this girl made her interesting. Maybe it was just the boredom of my soulless existence that made her interesting.

Or maybe she was a new toy to unwrap and tinker with. I hated how that made me sound, but it was partly the flat truth. Lacking empathy and feeling made me more than a little bit of a psychopath. Yeah, I hated it, but a part of me found her intriguing just because I wanted to dissect her mind for fun. And it was probably better if that was all it was: forming a friendship or a bond with this human was futile and stupid with a war about to start.

I could already guess what she felt about me, or how she saw me: interesting but cold. In twelve hours, what had I shown her about myself? That I'm an unfeeling dick and I'm mighty unpleasant when "hangry." That I use strangers as resources and want to be left the hell alone. Yet I was simultaneously adamant about keeping her safe, which was at odds with everything else in my personality.

I wouldn't blame her if that was all she saw in me, because none of it was false.

I turned the TV on and browsed for something to put on purely as a distraction for my brain. I selected a Disney Marvel show that I usually liked, but it wasn't sticking. My mind was too occupied with other things. As the show played, I continued combing through various subjects in my brain: Cassandra and my basic grasp of what she was planning, just how topsy-turvy my life had become in such a short span of time, and how oddly interwoven and tangled my life was with Hannah's now.

Hannah. Hannah. Hannah...

CHAPTER 18

JEB

It's easy for a Lapsus to lose track of time. When you have eternity, time becomes somewhat meaningless. A year is nothing, and an hour seems like minutes. I didn't realize that a couple hours had passed since I'd sat down until the bedroom door opened.

I didn't move from my spot as she stepped into the room, and for a brief moment, I was convinced she'd come up behind me and put her arms around me. The daydream was so visceral, I could almost feel where her arms would go and what her hair would feel like brushing my cheek. *What the hell?*

I wasn't sure if I was relieved or disappointed when she *didn't* do this, but my muscles didn't relax until she'd climbed over the back of the couch and settled into the cushion, two feet from me.

"Oh, I've seen this," she said as she took in what was happening on the TV screen. "Have you?"

"Yeah, once or twice before," I said with a shrug. "I'm honestly not paying attention to it."

She was dressed simply in leggings, a gray tank top, and a zipper sweatshirt. She raked her long blonde hair over one shoulder.

"Too busy thinking about how evil Lapsi are going to take over an entire metropolitan city and how the evil leading lady is a *smoking* hot redhead?" She leaned back, stretching against the arm of the couch.

"You could say that, I guess," I said with a half smile. "Beautiful, deadly, and a bit insane."

"But aren't they always?" she mused. She ran a hand through her hair and looked dreamily past me.

"Were you into her?" I asked, purely out of curiosity.

"Very," she said, grinning. Then she grimaced playfully at me. "It is absolutely unfair how attractive all of you are."

"Part of the gig," I said with an amused huff. "Our beauty both attracts prey and inspires animosity with our neighbors..."

"And were you into her too, when you had your run-in with *Cassandra of Troy*?"

"I suppose, yeah." I shrugged. "But then I saw her murder someone and steal the soul of another. It kind of killed the vibe."

She chuckled softly. She dropped her hands into her lap and drew her legs up onto the couch, crossing them like a pretzel. After a few seconds of collective contemplative silence, she looked my way, cringing.

"So what do we do now?"

"Lie low for a bit, I guess." I shrugged one shoulder lethargically. "See if Libby turns over any rocks. I don't know what else we can really do."

"Sounds relaxing enough. It was almost fall break anyway," she said, imitating my shrug. She grabbed the streaming remote from the coffee table with surprising grace and returned the TV to the home screen. "Wow. You really do have *all* the streaming."

"My neighbor can afford it," I said with a smirk.

"One can easily watch the world from a distance with all of this," she teased.

"Yeah, the lonely life suits me this century," I said with a shrug. Her smile wavered at my casual reference to centuries. "Besides, I can learn all I can about humanity from right here."

"Oh, yeah? And what have you learned so far?" she asked. "That humans are garbage?"

"I wouldn't say *that*," I protested lightly. "But you put too much drama into baking competitions."

"That's because baking is chemistry and an art form, all in one. It's intense."

"I guess I just don't understand baking because I've never had to do it," I admitted. "Never even tried cake in my life."

"What? How?" she said, genuinely surprised.

"I was but a poor goat farmer in a Puritan village," I reminded her. In truth, I knew *of* baking, but I'd never had to do it. My younger sister prepared our meals, while I tended our farm all day. "Not a lot of cake to be had in Puritan times."

She leaned her elbow into the back of the couch and her head against her hand.

"What is it like?" she asked quietly, her expression quizzical. "To have so long, when others don't?"

"It's kind of boring, actually," I admitted, finding no reason to lie about it. "You find things to amuse you, but they get old after fifty years or so."

"Had many midlife crises, have you?"

"There is no such thing as 'midlife' for me. But in terms of mid-centuries..." I shrugged, waving one hand lazily in the air. "I don't know. Identities get old and people start to notice you don't age. You get bored. You move on. Try different things. Technological advances happen, and you have to try them out."

"Like...?"

I understood her curiosity. She couldn't fathom centuries of time, and I couldn't fathom millennia on this planet, but there are Lapsi out there who have been alive for *several*. It was weird, though; I couldn't remember the last time I got to talk about my life.

"I've dabbled in a lot of things over the years. I've helped build monuments. I learned to fly when flying was still brand new. I flew gliders over Nazi Germany, for the hell of it. Germany wasn't allowed to have motorized aircraft, so they had these cool gliders. I was a sideshow act for Barnum for about fifty years. Adam was an Olympic medalist for javelin in 1896...and sometime in the sixties, I think?"

Her eyebrows lifted in surprise, but she bobbed her head a little, signaling me to keep going.

"I tried the college thing back in the seventies. That sucked, a lot."

"What, why?" she asked.

"Imagine being the only one who just *cannot* get high or drunk. It's a drag," I explained with an eyeroll. "Let's see, what else? I crossed the nation on one of the first trains. Experimented with TNT in the gold mines. Did some cave diving."

"Cave diving?" she repeated, interested. I felt my eye involuntarily twitch.

"Yeah, and skydiving. Halo-diving. Lots of diving," I continued, not wanting to dwell on the cave diving. It wasn't a pleasant memory.

"But nothing stuck?"

"No, plenty of it stuck. It wasn't a matter of not enjoying things. It just...things get old." I held my hands up in ambivalence.

"I'd love to have so much time to do things I love," she said wistfully. Her eyebrows had drawn together slightly.

"Yeah?" I asked. The longing in her eyes intrigued me. "What would you do with eternity?"

She hardly missed a beat in answering.

"Dance," she said simply, almost sadly.

"Dance?" I repeated in mild surprise. I didn't know what I'd expected, but it hadn't been such a quick answer full of conviction. "Really?"

She nodded. One corner of her mouth lifted, but still sadly.

"What kind?"

"All kinds," she said, again answering with simplicity and certainty. "There would be no limit. No need to focus on just one kind."

"I thought you were studying to be a nurse."

She nodded solemnly. "That wasn't what I was always going to be," she explained, relaxing into the couch, as if preparing to tell a long, sad tale. "Practically from the moment I could stand, I was dancing. My mom was a ballerina, and she didn't want biological kids." I guess my eyebrow raised slightly, because she backtracked. "Weight and body image are priorities for dancers, and Mom didn't want to ruin hers by getting pregnant. But Dad wanted kids, so they compromised by adopting *me*. A little clone that she could turn into a dancer."

She rolled her eyes and shook her head to communicate exactly what she thought of her mad scientist ballerina mother.

"But regardless of her selfish, helicopter motives, I absolutely loved it." Her wistful smile returned. "I still do."

"So why...?" I didn't know how to ask.

"I never had a real formal school experience until later in life," she continued, with a shrug. "I was homeschooled so I could devote as much time as possible to ballet. In my teens, I was in this dance academy that grooms you to be good enough for the major dance companies." At my slightly uncomprehending expression, she quickly explained, "It was a *big* deal: just trust me. I never fell out of love with ballet, but..."

She paused. I didn't want to interrupt her thoughts. She took a deep breath before continuing.

"Professional dancers have an amazing, glamorous, beautiful...but very *short* career," she said sadly. "If I got a job in a company at seventeen or eighteen, I'd have maybe ten years of a good, solid career. After that you're considered too old, too fragile, and undesirable. I...I didn't want to feel worthless at twenty-eight." She paused again. "So I left at sixteen, before I was too locked into it. That way I didn't have to face that heartbreaking time of my life. It hurt, and it really sucked, but I wanted to do something with my life that had more...permanence."

Now her fascination with an endless life made perfect sense. She hated eventuality and looming failure, and with immortality, she wouldn't have to face that kind of finality. It was endearing, and so human. I'd never looked at immortality that way before—but, of course, I hadn't chosen this life; it'd been forced on me.

"My mom didn't take it well." Her eyes darkened, and her jaw tensed against the painful memory. "She couldn't accept it, and she couldn't forgive me. She...said a lot of hurtful things. But Dad was on my side through it all, and they divorced because they couldn't agree. I moved away with Dad and went to high school for the first time. But then, that same year, the Covid pandemic hit and schools shut down."

"Oh yeah, that was a rough time for my kind, too," I said, remembering. "Food was hard to find because no one was leaving their homes."

She looked surprised at first. Then her mouth turned up into a smile to acknowledge my joke, but her eyes still looked sad.

"Virtual learning was just like homeschool. So, yeah. No real-life school experience for me, but it turns out I liked school—learning at least. I wanted to help people, so I chose nursing. Which I know is crazy, because of the whole Covid pandemic and the nursing shortage and massive burnout in the aftermath. But I don't know...I would always be needed. I would be helping. It's..."

"Permanent," I finished for her.

Deep in the tattered remains of my soul, something shifted. At first, I thought it was just muted awe of her drive and adaptability, and a fierce protectiveness of her—and it *was* that, but it was more. It rattled around in the hollow cavity where my soul had been, simultaneously grounding me and making me feel lighter than I had in centuries. Someone with a soul might call it the first palpitations of love, but *I* couldn't call it that: I wasn't capable of that.

But I did know one thing for certain: if anything ever happened to her and her beautiful spirit, whatever remained of my soul would *ignite*, and people would perish.

"I still dance though. I take classes and practice all the time. It's just more something I love to do, rather than something that is a life goal," she explained after a moment, looking almost proud. "I'm in a few professionally made videos on YouTube. An old acquaintance introduced me to the choreographer. It's funny. The girls were always super competitive because of the limited promised spots in ballet companies. But once I left, or once they found their spots in companies, they became so much nicer. Anyway... do you want to see one of the videos?"

"Sure," I said honestly. Looking at her now, I could see the ingrained grace and fluidity in her movements and her physique. She was slim, and while I wouldn't say she was the stick-skinny dancer type, I suspected she had been once.

She took up the remote again and switched over to the YouTube app. It didn't take her long to find the video she wanted and pull it up.

The video started, showing her and a male dancer in the center of a studio loft, with large windows filtering plenty of natural light. They begin with an upbeat song I didn't recognize, with lots of lifts and chemistry; though on her part, she seems *shy*. She straightens her skirt over her legs when his lift pushes it up or pulls it free when it gets trapped between them. Quickly, their rhythm falters and becomes disjointed. She starts moving away from him more, only to be pulled back into another lift, and their body language suggests impatience.

Subtly, her movements become sloppier and almost sleepy until finally she slips from his grip and slowly slides to the floor. He lowers himself gracefully on top of her and puts a hand to her mouth. She raises an arm, but his other hand presses it to the floor.

Oh shit. I'd been so caught up in the grace of the duet that I hadn't noticed the tone change until it hit me like a wall of bricks.

She rolls onto her stomach and lunges away, to be pulled back by him and forced into an embrace. It's still graceful and subtle and doesn't linger long enough to be triggering, but the message is there all the same. Then Hannah's alone in the frame, and the song's changed to something quieter and slower.

Still on the floor, she curls, then uncurls, rolls to her back and lifts her shoulder blades off the floor, then contracts and lowers again. She shoulder-rolls backward into a crouch as the song's tempo picks up a notch. Slowly, the song builds, and as it does, Hannah raises herself off the floor in levels: from a crouch, to her knees, then finally to her feet. Many of the moves in this part include spins followed by powerful, sweeping kicks, followed by jumps. Then another sweeping kick into a cartwheel-kick.

She was beautifully talented, and I could almost feel the raw emotion of the dance piece. This third act of the dance was about healing and finding her strength. It was so well done that the fluttering weight stirred again within my damaged soul.

"This part of the dance actually uses a lot of Capoeira moves," she blurted animatedly, while the Hannah on the screen did a powerful full-bodied sweeping kick.

I glanced over at her, and she was looking anywhere but at me. Like she realized how vulnerable she'd just made herself by having this be the first video she showed me.

"It's an interesting kind of martial art from Brazil." She plowed on, speaking quickly, as if to keep me from asking about it. "Enslaved people created the fighting style to be mistaken for a dance. I took several classes in it a few years back, as a kind of therapy. The choreographer liked my idea of incorporating it here."

"Does it work?" I asked. I knew she expected me to ask about the subject matter of the video, not the fighting style. Admittedly, I was curious, but I wasn't going to pry into her trauma until I felt I'd earned enough trust for that.

"Oh, no, it doesn't," she said with a chuckle. "I mean I don't think so. It's more of an art-art than a martial art. But learning self-defense in the form of dance made me feel better...it helped." She shrugged, looking away from me. "But I've never used it practically: just in choreographed routines and performances. I doubt it works."

"Do you want to try it?" I asked.

"Try what?"

"Try and see if it's applicable in combat. You want to try it on me?" I smirked. I was genuinely curious, and we could use the distraction. She might need to fight or defend herself, and I wanted to know if she could use this in any way.

"Jeb, it's just a dance style, basically," she protested, eyeing me warily while I climbed over the back of the couch.

"Strong kicks can go a long way," I said with a shrug. I was half-lying: strong kicks could go a long way against a mortal. I pushed the couch—with her on it—and the coffee table toward the TV, clearing the floor so the space was open. Then I held my hand out to her, to help her over the backrest. "Come on. Try me. I won't hit back, I promise."

She still looked wary, but she begrudgingly took my hand.

"Besides, I'm sure you want to hit me after everything last night. I did use you as bait, after all. I'll let you do your worst, without defending myself."

"No, you shouldn't hold back," Hannah argued. She hopped over the back of the couch and stood facing me, releasing my hand. "If we want to test it for real, it has to seem at least somewhat real."

"You don't want me to do that," I assured her, shaking my head. "But I'll semi-block and move, okay? Come on."

She debated internally with herself for another moment, but ultimately, her eyes focused and her body relaxed into a beginning fighting stance. She stepped around me, then she quickly crouched low and delivered a quick spinning kick to my shin. It was surprisingly strong and would have easily unbalanced a human, but it wasn't enough to knock a Lapsus down. I knelt anyway, to see how she'd attack next had she successfully knocked me over.

"Good," I said as encouragement. "Keep going."

She stepped back and put her hands to the floor. She lifted up into a headstand, spinning on her hands and kicking out both her legs, like a tornado of limbs. She didn't connect any of these kicks to me; she was just showing off. I moved in and grabbed her waist, lifting her, upside down, off the ground.

I tried to move one arm below her legs to support her better, but she twisted in my arms. Her body went simultaneously limp as her upper body twisted in my arms. Cursing through clenched teeth, I went to one knee so it didn't hurt her if I dropped her.

She slid out of my grip and righted herself before I could recover, then stepped onto my knee and pivoted smoothly. She brought her leg up and around and her foot connected *hard* with the side of my head. Temporarily stunned, I fell sideways and backward, and she jumped gracefully off my knee before I crashed to the ground.

"Jesus," I huffed in surprise when my back hit the floor. It was hard to keep the pride out of my voice: she was lithe and strong and reacted quickly. She might not survive against a Lapsus, but she could give them a frustratingly hard time.

I got up and again attempted to grab her, but she twisted and managed to slide out of my grip, laughing.

"Don't laugh," I said, though I felt my own chest vibrating with it. "I am a *real* attacker."

She did another cartwheel and attempted to kick me in the chest again. This time, I caught her foot, just to show she could be stopped. I pushed her foot away, disrupting her balance. She rolled to the floor, and again she spun into a crouch and kicked my legs. Again, it didn't unbalance me, but I exaggerated a fall to the floor.

"Okay, okay, that's good for now, I think," I said, holding my hands up in surrender. She hopped onto her feet and spun on one foot, using her other leg to kick herself into a series of effortless pirouettes. Her back arched back as she did so, and her arms extended gracefully above her. She looked serene: like she was finally releasing some tension and letting herself loose. It was beautiful.

I felt myself relaxing too, in a way I hadn't in a long, long time. Emboldened, I stood quickly and caught her hand just as she stopped spinning. With a gentle yank, I pulled her, spinning into me. She wasn't prepared, so she collided with my chest instead of catching herself.

"Oof," she said, her cheek hitting my shoulder.

I shifted her hand in mine and placed my other hand below her shoulder blades. My mind worked quickly to remember the proper steps, which I hadn't used in years. I moved us one step forward, then a step back, then to the side. She fell in with me and picked up on the rhythm with no problem.

"My word, Jebadiah, can you dance?" she said quietly.

"Don't use my full name, you'll break my concentration," I said, gritting my teeth. I lifted her arm and she spun with no difficulty. We took a few more steps, then I shifted my weight to support her and dipped her low and slow. As I pulled her back up, she laughed, and I found myself almost smiling.

"You don't seem like the kind of person to do ballroom dance," she said as we stopped.

"Please," I scoffed, spinning her out again and then back in. "You don't make it through the eighteen and nineteen hundreds without knowing how to dance in a room full of people."

"Oh yeah? Well, what else do you know?" she challenged.

I shifted gears and guided her into faster steps, this time swing dancing. She kept up well and was good enough that I felt confident in lifting her correctly. I kept it simple, but lifts in swing weren't small and trivial. We stumbled a bit, but were both laughing by the time her feet were back on the floor.

We paused so she could catch her breath, but we didn't step away from each other. She closed the distance between us and put her face into my chest, still chucking a little. My arms circled her automatically, relishing the simple, friendly embrace and the momentary relief from the stress around us.

I felt lighter than I had in more than fifty years. It wouldn't last, but I savored the simplicity of it while I could.

Fifteen minutes later we'd moved the furniture back to their original spots and were seated on the couch again. I left her plenty of room, and she used it to stretch sideways across the cushions. Her feet rested in my lap, and while I hadn't expected such casual intimacy from a girl I'd put through hell, I found I didn't mind it.

"So how old were you?" she asked casually. She was idly running her hands through her hair. "When you were changed?"

"Twenty-four," I said with a shrug. I felt that we'd somehow bonded enough in the past hour that it was okay for me to ask her something personal: something she'd probably expected me to ask earlier. "How old were you?"

"When I was changed?" she said, lifting an eyebrow.

Yes, but not into a Lapsi. "The subject of that dance video. How old?"

Her idle smile wavered into a frown. Her hand dropped from her hair into her lap.

"Eighteen. Just after high school," she said, her voice as deadpan as mine usually was.

"Was it someone you knew?" I was on dangerous ground. It wasn't my place to ask, and I didn't want to press it. It was her story to tell, but only if she wanted to.

She shook her head. "I don't even know his name."

CHAPTER 19

HANNAH

I shouldn't have been surprised that he'd ask. And I suppose I kind of wanted him to ask; otherwise, why would I show him the video of my dance? It wasn't the only one I'd done with that director, after all. It was just the only one I'd really contributed to creatively. It was another step I'd taken in confronting what happened to me, and, like learning Capoeira, it had helped.

I could have denied it and lied to him, but I felt like we were beyond that now. We'd had a moment earlier: a genuine, stress-relieving, friendly moment. I wanted to tell him, but not all of it. *I am the one in control here,* I told myself, like my therapist would say. I told who I wanted, when I wanted, and how I wanted. I wore short skirts to dates to feel in control and because I would *like* to trust men again. And bad things happen no matter what you wear, so who cares?

So I sat up straight, curled my legs under me, and told him the details I was comfortable sharing.

It was your typical, horrifyingly common story of a girl at a party where she knows no one. She was slipped something in her drink, made docile and semi-conscious, then raped.

I was visiting an old dance friend at her college. She hadn't landed a job in a ballet company, so she'd gone on to college instead. In the fall of her freshman year, she'd invited me out for a visit to reconnect. I missed having friends, and I missed the closeness of my little troop of dancers, so I flew from Portland to her college in Boulder, Colorado.

My friend was pledging for a sorority, which was close with a neighboring fraternity. She wanted to go to the fraternity's Saturday night party, and of course I'd agreed. I'd never experienced one, and it sounded like the typical college experience everyone should have.

It started out okay. It was noisy and kind of gross and dirty, because it was a house run by boys. But everyone was lively and laughing. There was beer pong, flip cup, and video games. I played some beer pong, but I had only one drink that night. I was in an unfamiliar place, so I wanted to retain control of everything, and I definitely didn't want to use the toilet in that filthy house, either to pee or to vomit.

The night got fuzzy after that one drink.

I remembered bits and pieces. I remembered the predatory gazes of several of the fraternity boys. They were older students—upperclassmen. The ones my age were treated practically like slaves to the older boys.

I didn't remember where my friend went or when we got separated. I remembered doing a shot of whiskey with her and a group of her rush-mates, but instead of swallowing the shot in one go, I spat it into the cup of whiskey-Coke I used as a chaser. It made the drink stronger the rest of the time I drank it, but at least I didn't down it all at once.

I remembered feeling dizzy, weirdly fluid, and unfocused. I remembered wandering for a bit and searching for somewhere quieter to sit, so I could get ahold of my swimming head. I didn't know if I'd found this quieter place myself or if I had been *led* there.

I woke relatively alert before it happened, most likely because I didn't take the shot. I heard him tell me I was beautiful, and I felt his lips on mine. I felt his hand moving up my leg, up my skirt. I snapped fully alert then and pushed his hand away. When I did this, something sparked in his eyes just before they darkened into those of a predator—like the cops' eyes had last night—and he lunged for me.

I think he wanted me to fight and scream—that had been the spark in his eyes. I'd snapped alert, and he'd smelled a fight. His hand went to my mouth, muffling me as he pushed me down onto the bed, but his grip over my mouth was halfhearted—like he wanted to hear me scream and bite at him. I didn't though. I completely froze: limp and paralyzed with panic, even when he pinned one leg to the bed, and...

Robbing him of the fight he wanted and retreating into my head while he did what he did was the world's tiniest victory. Of course, I didn't realize it at the time or for years after because, really, I was the one who lost everything.

But after years of playing the memory over in my head, I'd been able to convince myself that I'd won in a *tiny* way. He'd acted disgusted through the whole thing and was far rougher than he needed to be, as if punishing me for underperforming. He was brutal, but I'd robbed him of a little bit of his savage satisfaction.

Fuck him.

I didn't go into all this detail when I told Jeb. I only told him that I was at a party out of town where I knew no one, and I was abandoned, drugged, and assaulted while passed out. I didn't tell him that I was awake and aware, but frozen. I sugarcoated it for him because my calm would break if I glimpsed anything like pity in his face, and then I'd cry.

What I *did* admit was that I couldn't remember how I got back to my friend's place and that I haven't really spoken to her since it happened. I knew it wasn't fair. It wasn't her fault, and for all I knew, she'd been assaulted too—she'd taken a shot from the same bottle of whiskey, hadn't she?

I didn't even tell her what happened, but she guessed. She felt responsible and apologized so many times, but I never replied. In my traumatized mind, she represented that night, and I wanted to bury that night. And four years later, it felt too late to reach out.

But that was the extent of what I told Jeb. I didn't owe him the gritty details of that night or of the long road of digging myself out of the experience.

And it had been a long, stupid, fucking road.

On the plane ride home, I'd broken down in the bathroom and couldn't pick myself up off the floor. A stewardess had to break me out of the tiny bathroom, and she was the first person to truly comfort me.

I saved my clothing from that night: everything but my panties, which I'm convinced the rapist kept. I sealed my clothes in a plastic bag, for evidence. Then, months later, I had a breakdown and destroyed them using my dad's paper shredder. Which was stupid because then I had to explain to my dad about his broken paper shredder, unloading all my trauma onto him in one tearful, blubbering explosion.

Eventually I told my mother, in a moment of weakness. We only talked on holidays, with an obligatory telephone call that always quickly turned into her guilting me and berating me for quitting ballet. I told her about my assault, thinking if she pitied me, she might finally give me a break. But it was worse than I could have fathomed. Rather than pitying me or comforting me like a mother should, she essentially told me that I never would have been at that party if I'd stuck with ballet. That was the last time we spoke.

For a year after it, I spiraled. The strangest things at the strangest times brought everything back up. The memory robbed me of sleep before important exams and popped into my head at the worst times, sending me into panic attacks. Even when I could sleep, I'd jolt awake in a panic, convinced I'd felt him on top of me again or heard his ragged breath in my ears. A year after the event, I caught a whiff of his same awful, potent cologne in a store and vomited on the spot.

It was why I was twenty-two and still only in my second year of nursing school. It'd wrecked my focus, my sleep patterns, my ability to retain information. I'd had several false starts at school, thinking I was better: convincing myself I was better. But finally, I found my therapist—and she was a godsend—and I threw myself back into dance more than I had since quitting the academy.

Somehow, I crawled out of the hole my assault threw me into, and I carved out a semblance of *normal*. All, of course, before Gerry the gentleman hit Jeb with his car and threw everything into a different kind of chaos.

We sat in silence for several moments after I finished telling Jeb all I wanted to tell him. I wasn't expecting him to hold me or reach out to me—nor did I want him to. Instead I welcomed the silence, even though it was a heavy, pensive one.

"Were you..." He hesitated, as if hoping for better words.

I'd already guessed what he wanted to ask. *Had I been a virgin?*

"No," I said, shaking my head. I felt the smallest smile start on my lips. "Hadn't been a virgin for quite a while."

His head tilted—the telling sign that he was surprised. I smiled at his discomfort as he struggled to ask another question.

"Dancers." I shrugged and gave him a sly, but coy grin. "My academy kind of slept around..."

My first time had been with Paolo, an eighteen-year-old professional dancer on tour with his company. They used our studio as their rehearsal space while they were in town. I was fourteen—yes, I know the age difference raises red flags *now*, but it was consensual, and it meant nothing. After Paolo, it was every straight boy at our academy—and once or twice with a female dancer.

We were young, hormonal, high strung, and poorly chaperoned. Life at the ballet academy was grueling and stressful, and sex was a stress reliever. I loved it because it was the only aspect of our lives where I didn't feel like I was *competing* with the other girls. Girl dancers were my rivals: for roles, for attention from our instructors, and for jobs in the future. But we didn't compete for the boys: we shared. It made us all closer, as dancers and as companions through the hell that is ballet academy.

I missed sex, and I loathed what happened to me. Being assaulted had taken something I enjoyed and made it something ugly.

"I haven't had sex since," I admitted. I only realized a second later that I had spoken aloud. "I haven't been ready, but...after four years, I really miss it. You know?"

Jeb smiled, and I half expected him to make a smart comment about being willing, whenever I wanted it. But he didn't. He just smiled sadly and looked away, thinking about something. His smile faded after a moment.

"I had two younger sisters," he said. My brow furrowed in confusion: it was a random segue. "When I was alive, I mean—*way* back in the early 1600s. When I was maybe seventeen, my oldest sister was fifteen and she was raped by a man in the village and forced to marry him."

I was too surprised to respond, but my heart ached for his sister. It was bad enough going through it in the twenty-first century, but I couldn't fathom going through it in the seventeenth century and being forced to marry the attacker and bear his kids.

"I couldn't protect her, both before or afterward. Because what could you do back then? If she stayed unmarried, she'd have been ostracized. We would have starved because no one would associate with us. Her marrying him 'saved her soul' and saved us." He said it bitterly—or as bitter as his typically toneless voice could be. "I could never look her in the eye without feeling like

I should've done something, or without feeling somehow responsible. If I'd been older, and man of the house, I'd have fought for her..."

"I'm sorry," I said. It was a simple statement, but it was all I could think to say. "And I am so sorry for her."

"Years later, when I was twenty-four, a man came by my farm," he continued after a moment. "My father died a year earlier, so it was my farm now. My youngest sister at seventeen was still living at home. The man approached me, and he offered to pay me for her..."

I gasped softly, before I could stop it. I covered my mouth in my horror.

"She was pretty and young and, you know...virginal," he said with a grimace. "He was Lapsi, and he was only offering to pay me as a disgusting formality. He offered a lot, but I refused him, and he took everything."

My stomach churned because I could see where this tale was going.

"He changed me to be a spiteful dick," he said, looking away. "And he...took my sister. But he didn't change her."

"Oh my god," I uttered automatically. Both of my hands were over my mouth now. "I'm so sorry, Jeb."

"No, *I'm* sorry," he said, with more feeling than was usually in his voice—and it still wasn't much. "I really am. For you. For my sisters. For all women. Not much has changed in four hundred years, and it fucking sucks."

I lowered my hands from my mouth and gave him a small smirk in agreement. *Too true, friend.*

"And I'm sorry that I sound so disingenuous," he continued, running a frustrated hand through his hair.

He looked like he was debating whether he really wanted to say what he was about to say. I waited. Whatever it was, it was his decision to share it, like it'd been mine earlier.

"About fifty years ago, I was cave diving with a friend—a Lapsus named Adam," he said. I remembered the name from earlier. "Have you...have you ever seen the movie *The Descent*?"

I nodded.

"Well, I think the writer of that movie was writing from some *experience*. If you go deep enough, to caves that are never touched by humanity...there are holes."

"Holes?"

"Doorways. Into Hell, for lack of a better word. They're rare. And they're small. Not much can squeeze through, but some do. I...came across one such being while exploring. They don't have a sophisticated name. They're just known as Soul Eaters."

Oh. Things were starting to make sense.

"They suck out your soul and consume it. It's what Cassandra used on that one Lapsus that night, though I don't know how she's controlling it. It wasn't the same Soul Eater I encountered. That one is dead, thanks to Adam, who managed to kill it shortly after it took my soul. But...there wasn't much left of my soul after Adam killed it."

So, in a way, you're like me. And like your sisters, I thought but stayed silent.

"Within your soul is your capacity for feeling: your emotions...your empathy," he explained. "I can *remember* feelings, but I don't feel much of anything anymore. I know how I should feel or react to situations, so I react as I *should*.

I pretend. So, I'm sorry, but I'm not. I sympathize, but I don't..."

"So that explains why you're a dick sometimes," I said, teasing him gently.

His smile was fake and humorless. "I'm not trying to one-up my sisters' or your experiences," he said, his voice surprisingly soft. "I just...I can relate."

"I know." I took his hand in one of mine and gave it a friendly, reassuring squeeze. "And thank you. You've made it easier to understand you."

He nodded but didn't say anything more. He kept looking forward at the coffee table, his eyes unfocused. After a moment, he gave my hand a friendly squeeze in return.

CHAPTER 20

HANNAH

We spent the better part of the next week lying low in Jeb's apartment. It reminded me of early days of the Covid pandemic, when the gears of society screeched to a halt and my state enacted a shelter-in-place protocol. Only this time I was in lockdown with a friend, rather than just my dad, but I had no social media.

I did a lot of baking back then. I'd just quit dancing and no longer had to worry about counting every calorie to stay dancer-skinny. In those early post-academy days, I discovered that I loved chocolate and became obsessed with making things with chocolate chips. My dad might have gained more weight during that time than me.

But for this lockdown, my diet consisted entirely of semi-healthy frozen meals, peanut butter and jelly sandwiches, coffee, and water. It wasn't as bad as it sounds, and a lot can be said about the simple joys of a PB&J—though poor Jeb couldn't wrap his head around it.

He left once every evening so he could get his fix of blood, but he was never gone long. I assumed feeding had been his sole social interactions for years: like a glass of wine at the end of the day. I felt bad robbing him of that, since with me here, he felt the need to just grab and go, but it was desperate times.

We hung out in silence a lot, watching movies and TV shows. I logged into my school account and worked on coursework—purely for the purpose of occupying my mind and making sure I wasn't too far behind if I ever returned to normal life.

And we danced.

I needed to move and get exercise to keep me from scratching the walls, so for a good portion of each day, we pushed the couch and coffee table out of the way so I could dance. I warmed up with basic barre, using the back of the couch as my support, then I practiced a dance I already knew before working out some new ones. There was something centering and freeing about dance, about watching your arm lift gracefully into the air or about shoulder-rolling on the ground into a different fluid move.

It didn't take long for Jeb to realize that my warm up dance was the one from the second half of the video I'd shown him—minus a lot of the kicks and Capoeira. Over the two years since choreographing it, the dance had become a kind of mantra for me. I loved how it perfectly followed the progression of the song: the transitions from floor to standing matched the song's uptick from a slow, sad tempo to powerful and kickass. The dance was a ritual to remind me that I didn't and couldn't stay down.

Jeb joined me for part of my exercise every day. At first it was just to do partner dancing with me. We did classical ballroom, salsa, and even tango, but we enjoyed swing dance the most: it was faster, more buoyant, and involved bigger, bolder movements. And the lifts! I've always loved lifts in all forms of dance. The level of trust in the partners, the feeling of flying and of being supported by another. And in swing, the lifts were *exhilarating* and, even more than ballet, involved a lot of trust. Swing wasn't sexy like a tango, but it was damn fun.

Later in the week, Jeb joined me in different kinds of dance, not the typical face-to-face partner dancing. He let me direct him and choreograph pieces with him in it. He didn't do any classical ballet moves, but he was okay with turns and leaps and, of course, *lifts*. It passed the time, but it also bonded us in a way that we couldn't do when just watching TV or sitting around, waiting.

Mid-week, we made another quick trip to Boston at Libby's request. She'd been working diligently researching and feeling around about what could be going on in Portland. She still didn't have much to report other than small whispers—and nothing outside what we already knew. But she'd been working on better wards and protection charms, and she had a few that she wanted to try out and to hand off.

"You look like you've lost weight," Libby said as I lifted a squealing baby Sophie out of her playpen. Sophie gave me a hug and then snuggled her head into the crook of my neck. Her puff of hair pressed into my jawline.

God, this kid, I thought, my heart melting at how precious and loving Sophie was.

"Just been exercising a lot. Trying to stay active while cooped up inside," I explained. I would have shrugged, but Sophie's head on my shoulder prevented that.

"So, you said you have some 'new toys'?" Jeb said stoically.

"I absolutely do!" Grinning, she practically skipped over to her apothecary cabinet.

Since we hadn't woken her up at the crack of dawn, she wasn't in pajamas this time. She wore some cute ultra-high waisted jeans, with double-breasted buttons on the wide waistband. She had a loose cotton shirt tucked into it and a long tan cardigan. Her blonde hair was tied into a bouncy ponytail. Nothing about this girl screamed "witch" other than how she decorated her house.

Sophie moved her head from my shoulder and poked at my face. I kissed her noisily on the cheek, sending her into a fit of giggles, then dipped her slowly upside down and brought her back up. She shrieked in happiness.

Libby returned with a medium-sized box and took a seat in the armchair that angled toward the sofa. She gestured for us to have a seat. I put Sophie back into her playpen—she happily returned to the light-up toy she'd been playing with before I arrived—and walked over to the couch. I took a seat, but Jeb shook his head and stayed standing off to the side, his hands in his jeans pockets.

"The first one is for you, Hannah." She pulled something small from the box and handed it to me.

It was a ring with a wide silver band and a large, flat, cushion-cut moonstone set in prongs. The band was a little on the big side, but I could probably wear it on my thumb.

"This was a thought-child of mine, and mine alone," Libby said as I inspected the ring. "It's purely experimental and one of a kind. I've had the idea for a while but never had a reason to test it out. It changes the aura of its wearer. It makes you appear Lapsi to other Lapsi."

"What? How?" I said, though I knew I'd never be able to understand the how.

"Highly complicated. Just trust me," Libby said, waving her hand. "But it masks your scent and the sound of your heartbeat completely and makes you seem *very* Lapsi. You'll be able to blend in if you need to go into covert situations." She winked. "So, if you end up going to Portland, you have this added layer of protection. As long as you stay away from anyone who actually knows you're human. Like our bad bitch."

"Sounds cool," I said, turning the ring over between my fingers, still admiring it. I loved moonstone, and I wondered if Libby chose it for its beauty or its qualities.

"Sounds expensive," Jeb quipped from where he stood several feet away but he was kidding. I'd asked a day or so ago how he afforded things like rent and groceries, and he'd explained that he had a legacy account in stocks that he set up over a century ago, and he transferred it every few decades, as if passing it to the next generation of Endecotts.

"I do it for the science, thank you," Libby said, putting a hand to her chest as if offended. She winked at Jeb and turned her attention back to me. "Try it on, let's see if it works."

I shrugged, glad I at least wasn't putting my arms over a fire this time. I slipped the ring onto my thumb and slid it into place. I didn't know what I was expecting, but when I looked at Jeb, he seemed different somehow. Nothing had changed in his appearance, except maybe a reflective quality to his eyes that I hadn't noticed before, but something about him was just *off* from the rest of us in the room.

He stood frozen, eyeing me warily.

"That is bizarre..." he said as he stared. "I can't separate the human from the Lapsi sense of you."

He looked sad and apologetic, like he was trying to tell me he'd never wanted this for me, even if it was fake and temporary. He didn't want the Lapsi life to be my life, while I didn't exactly see a downside.

"I'd say it works," Jeb said with a huff, giving Libby the proper admiration she was due. "Incredible job."

"Excellent!" Libby said, clapping in her excitement. Sophie mimicked her mother from her seat in the playpen. "Wear that any time you go out, *please*. And stay safe."

I nodded but slipped the ring off and put it into my sweatshirt pocket. I wasn't going anywhere just yet, and I didn't like unnerving Jeb like that.

Libby held the box out for Jeb to take. He looked both surprised and impressed when he opened the lid and peered inside. He pulled an object out of it and turned it over in his hands.

It was about the size of a golf ball and silver in color. It had a ring on the top, attached to a pin. It was small and shiny silver, and undeniably a *grenade*.

"Those weren't an easy task. No one's used silver fulminate since the hunting ages," Libby explained. "I had to call in several favors and scrounge around to get that much silver *and* silver fulminate. There's six in there."

"Not easy, yet you had enough supplies and time to make *six* of these in four days? I'd hate to see you tackle something *really* 'impossible.' What would you need for that, a week?" Jeb teased in his toneless voice. He put the grenade back into the box and hugged it to his chest. "*Thank you.*"

My heart hurt to leave Sophie again, but I said a long goodbye to her that she didn't understand. While I kissed her several times, Jeb handed Libby a stack of bills for payment for all her services. She frowned at the stack and handed most of it back, shaking her head.

"I don't need generosity. Just your promise that you'll be careful," she told him firmly.

Jeb agreed and took the portioned money back. But as we were leaving, he tucked the bills into a jacket hanging on a hook by the front door.

We returned to his apartment and stayed cooped up again. Three days later, we were called to Portland.

CHAPTER 21

JEB

I didn't think we'd be back in Portland so soon. If I'd had my way, we'd never be going back at all, but I was the one who knew what was going on, had opposed it, and lived to tell the tale. I couldn't say that about the Lapsi cut down in that alley. And I'd had Libby looking into everything: it would be a superior dick move to then do nothing with her hard-researched information.

Even so, I wasn't a doer or a hero. I still didn't know what I, a soulless Lapsi driven mostly by curiosity, would be able to do to stop or damage Cassandra's plan. My honest aim in returning to Portland was to find out what was going on, get out, and find someone who could stop it. If that person was Danielle, the supposed Messiah, then so be it. As long as it wasn't me, and as long as Hannah wasn't involved.

Hannah.

It was absurd how, in just a week, Hannah had changed me in ways I never thought needed changed. I was always a loner, even when I was alive. As a goat farmer in a small, boring village, I saw the nastiness of life and was powerless to do anything about it. My church and its God dictated who was righteous and who was damnable, and it cost my sister any semblance of freedom. Because of this, I had never planned on marrying, and once my youngest sister was out of the house, I'd planned on going full hermit.

No matter the *how*, being turned Lapsi freed me. I left my village before anyone even found my sister's body. From there, I wandered and explored, always running from my grief, and I generally stuck to myself. I didn't even really know about the anti-community part of the Lapsi curse for a long time. After two centuries, I mingled a little more with humanity, and it became almost recreational: going out, having a good, seductive time, then feeding and disappearing again. The early 1900s were my favorite; with the Roaring Twenties, the speakeasies, and the dancing. It was around then that I started to appreciate humanity again: their resilience, their lust for life, their spirits.

But then the Great Depression hit. I killed during that time more than I ever did in the past or since. I did it out of mercy: ending poor souls' misery when they were truly out of hope. It was a small service when their government and economy failed them. Then, finally, what pulled the economy out of rock bottom? War. A horrifying, despicable war on top of a mass genocide, run by a tiny, insane man. A human.

I went to Nazi Germany to check out their scientific advancements: I wanted to fly a glider. But what I saw there broke my heart and ruined my outlook on humanity for a long time afterward. Then I lost my soul, and I didn't feel much of anything anymore.

It was no problem for me to watch humanity from a distance, through their media and their art. My faith in them was shaken, and I had no interest in repairing that faith.

But Hannah changed that. I hadn't wanted her there with me: I *really* hadn't. But in her, I'd found a friend for the first time since Adam. At first, I'd thought getting to know Hannah would be amusing, just because it was something new. But now I was almost grateful we'd been thrown together.

She was intelligent and stubborn, so kind and empathetic. She wanted to be a nurse, despite the demands and thanklessness surrounding that profession, purely because she wanted to help people. She'd been nearly destroyed by trauma but had pulled herself out of it, and still she wanted to help. If more people were like her, humanity might be worth saving.

With her here, I was alive again. She made me want to be better and to care about what Cassandra was planning—more than mild curiosity—and do something about it, even if it was just recon.

Libby called us after a full week of us being cooped up in my apartment together. She said she'd been talking with a Lapsus who was in touch with another Lapsus who could get us into some more informative meetings. That way we could find out more of what Cassandra was planning.

We were going to be back that same night, so we didn't bring anything with us aside from the various charms Libby had made for Hannah, my weapons, and my precious silver fulminate grenades.

We shifted to a park in the northern area of downtown Portland known as the Pearl District. There, in a dense batch of bushes, I hid the bundle of grenades in a nondescript bag. They were warded so humans would stay away, and I didn't expect any Lapsi to be poking bushes in a park. I couldn't conceal them all on my person, so I kept just one with me. I didn't anticipate needing it, but erring on the side of caution had saved our asses in the police precinct, so I would continue to do so.

Before we left the park, I had her put the ring on. As soon as it was situated on her thumb, her aura became undeniably Lapsi. I frowned and had to remind myself it was just an illusion, but I hated it. I didn't want the Lapsi life to be hers. I wanted her to *live*. Sure, she'd be happy with immortality and being able to dance without worrying about her body aging, but she had goals and dreams and a family—a father at least. I'd seen her with baby Sophie in her arms and how good she was with her. I wanted her to be able to be a mother if that was what she wanted.

"If we want this to be believable, you've gotta stop looking at me with those big sad eyes every time I put this ring on," she said, breaking through my pensive thoughts.

"Right," I said, giving her a half smile, which was all I could muster. Libby hadn't told the Lapsi we were meeting that Hannah was human, so we had to sell it. I had to get out of my head about how Hannah's façade was doing things to me.

We shifted to the meeting place: the basement of a tap house that wasn't in operation yet. It was a cold cellar full of beer kegs and posters meant for the walls upstairs. There was a table with chairs, and a couch for some reason.

When we arrived, one Lapsi was already there. I'd never met him, but I recognized him as one of the members of that

Lapsi rock band from years ago. I didn't know which one he was—two of the bandmates had looked nearly identical.

He was seated at the table, but he stood when we entered. He was tall and thin as a rail, with a face of sharp angles outlining his piercing blue eyes. His hair was dark and choppy, and it stuck out at all angles.

"Hi, guys, I'm Riley," he said, holding out a hand. He hadn't moved away from the table, only stood up, with the chair still behind his legs.

"Jeb. And this is Hannah," I said, motioning to Hannah beside me and taking the hand he offered. "You're from that band, right?"

"Yeah, that's me." He shook my hand but ran his other hand through his hair, tugging at it awkwardly. When he released my hand, he shoved both hands into his pockets. "And they tell me that you knew Adam?"

I stiffened at the mention of his name. *Why the hell is that important?*

"Yeah, he was a friend," I said, trying not to sound defensive.

"I–I'm sorry," he said, dropping his gaze from mine. He seemed surprisingly sympathetic for a first meeting. "I didn't know him long, but...he...he was a good man."

Ah, now I see it. He'd been in Adam's thrall. It made sense; Riley seemed like Adam's type. Even though everyone was Adam's type, he was particularly alluring to the quiet, sad ones. Riley gave off serious sad-puppy vibes, one that'd been kicked too many times. *Damn Adam and his arrogant charm.*

"No need to say anything else, man," I said, grinning. Even soulless, I couldn't keep the amusement out of my voice. "I get it. Thank you for the condolences."

"Awe, am I walking in on a tender moment?" a voice from behind me said.

I recognized the voice—though it'd been years—and my shoulders tensed. It was a power move to shift into a room directly behind someone. It was *my* power move.

I turned toward the newcomer. He looked the same as the last time I'd seen him: frozen at age eighteen. He was shorter and stockier than me, with his shoulders wider than his narrow waist. He had shoulder-length dark brown hair, framing his painfully beautiful, youthful face with its aquiline nose and gray-green eyes. He looked at me like he was sizing me up, similar to what I was doing.

"Mason," I said, taking his hand in a brisk, firm, no-nonsense grasp. Classic machismo stuff, but I had my reasons.

"Jeb," Mason said, returning the macho grasp with a smirk. "You look different from the last time we met. A little harrowed. Like you've been to hell."

You don't know the half of it, I thought bitterly. *Losing your soul alters you.*

"Yeah, this guy quite enjoyed the social sphere when I met him," Mason teased. He was looking at Hannah, who I'd arranged myself in front of.

"This one?" Hannah said automatically in disbelief. I wished she wouldn't.

"Yes, quite the jitterbug. He liked the *sock hops*," Mason said, still teasing me, but his tone was more mocking than teasing.

"Yeah, and if I remember correctly, I had to pull you off a girl that was maybe fifteen. Your hand was all the way up her dress." I kept my voice low and level so he knew I wasn't teasing.

Mason's smile faltered, and he visibly bristled. "Yeah, well, being stuck this youthful limits my choices of dance partner at times, doesn't it? And just because she was young didn't mean I was *forcing* her." His voice had dropped an octave—not quite a growl, but not friendly. Then a shadow of guilt passed over his features. "But you're not wrong to judge. You caught me during one of my...unsavory stints. I'm working on it."

"Really?" I mocked. "A leopard can change his spots?"

"Yeah, yeah, I know. I don't expect you to believe me." He started proud but looked away at the end. He strolled past me and Hannah and took the seat closest to Riley, giving him a playful punch to his shoulder. "But Riley can vouch for me. Not that I care about defending myself to you."

I narrowed my eyes in suspicion and watched Riley for any flicker of disdain in his face or even annoyance at being asked to vouch for the dick. His smile morphed into more of a wince of discomfort—whether from the attention or from the playful love-tap that might have been more of a real punch. But that was the only change in his demeanor, so somehow the sad puppy trusted the asshole. It didn't lower my opinion of Mason, though. He'd given off big asshole vibes the last time we met, and he still did, but they were surprisingly *less*.

"Shall we?" Mason said, waving to the empty seats.

Still glaring at him, I circled to the seat opposite his. Hannah followed behind me, and I put a hand on the corner of the table, subtly indicating where she should sit: not directly next to me, but not too far away.

"And since it seems Jeb, here, isn't going to introduce us," Mason said, leaning his elbows on the table and giving Hannah an extremely charming smile—but not flirtatious thankfully. Or I'd have to murder him. "Hi, I'm Mason."

"I–I'm Hannah," she said, fumbling her words at first. But she caught herself, like she realized that, though she appeared Lapsi to them, she had to *act* it too.

"And how did you get together with this lug?" Mason asked, angling his head in my direction. "You seem newly made. Did he change you?"

I ground my teeth in irritation. We hadn't discussed a backstory for her because we hadn't expected that kind of question. I leaned forward to interject, but Hannah surprised me and beat me to it.

"Not together, and no, he didn't," she said firmly, leaning against the back of her chair. "We both had a run-in with Cassandra a week ago, uncovering this little endeavor of hers, and we want to know more."

"A run-in with Cassandra?" He let out a low whistle and bit his lip. "I've been here a year, and I haven't even had that pleasure. We've even met before, and she likes me, yet I haven't seen her." He propped his head on his hand and looked at both of us with manic interest. "Tell me, what was that 'run-in' like?"

"Let's just say it ended with a car crash and a dead Uber—"

"As well as one Lapsus murdered, another's soul devoured, and a room full of dead Lapsi cops." I leaned forward, pulling Mason's attention away from Hannah, again. If he was a creep, I was prepared to squash him. I moved my gaze between him and Riley impatiently. "All right, so we're here. What are we doing here?"

"Well, Libby reached out yesterday, asking me if I knew anything about Portland, not knowing I was already here, investigating," Riley explained, sitting up straight, as if thankful for the handoff. "It's just been a few weeks for me, though. Mason's been here longer. We haven't been able to track down Danielle for her help, so…"

I looked away from him and rolled my eyes, involuntarily. I caught Mason's eye across the table and realized he'd done the same eyeroll. *Huh, another Danielle-skeptic.* My opinion of him raised a fraction.

"Yeah, fortunate for you guys, I'm the next best thing to Danielle," Mason said with a grin. He spread his hands on the table, palms up. "Like I said, I came on the scene about a year ago. Apparently, word hasn't traveled yet about my turning over a new leaf, so I still have clout with the baddies. I'm not helping, or on their side, but they don't know that."

"So, what are they doing?" It seemed he wanted me to be impressed that he was a spy, but I wasn't. I just wanted the info he had.

"Well, it's what you've previously assumed. She wants to take this city for herself. For Lapsi," Riley confirmed.

"Why here? Why Portland?" Hannah asked.

"Cassandra was at the fall of Troy, and she wants her city back—but a *modern* Troy. Portland is a sister city to Istanbul: back-in-the-day-*Troy*. Similar climate, similar terrain, blah blah blah, it's her perfect New Troy." Mason paused to shoot us all a mocking sneer. "Cassandra is sentimental *to a fault*, and she's taking full advantage of the change to our curse. She isn't interested in building a city from the ground up. She wants to take an already established city, keep its infrastructure, economy, and everything intact, just with Lapsi involvement and control."

"But how...how do you do that with such a heavily populated, educated, and often *armed* civilization?" Hannah asked.

"Infiltration, mostly. And other things." He didn't elaborate on either detail. "She doesn't plan on taking the whole city all at once—it's over a hundred forty-five square miles. Troy itself was only maybe two square miles, and far less densely populated. She's focusing on a small section of this city, with intentions of expanding."

"And how does she plan to contain everyone? If something like this goes down, people will just leave—they aren't walled in," Hannah argued.

"She has a solution for that," Mason said.

"And what is that?" I asked, impatient with his vague answers.

"It's, uh, it's better if I show you," he said with an apologetic grimace. "I can't explain it."

That sounded like a trap if I ever heard one, but he held up his hands in defense.

"I know, I know but trust me," he said calmly. "I could try to explain it, but you won't believe me. Not unless you see it. I can take you there."

Yes, the classic you "have to see it to believe it" trap. But I was backed against a wall. I needed to know what was going on. I needed to know what Cassandra was planning so I could figure out how far to run away or how to disrupt it.

I didn't trust this guy or his "I swear I am atoning" vibe, but he was offering to take me deep behind the enemy lines so I could see the fine details of her plan. I could handle myself with the weapons I had on my person, but I doubted I could do it while also protecting Hannah. I didn't want to part with her, because she was safer with me, but I didn't want to take her into the heart of it all—especially if it was a trap.

I thought about Riley, too. Mason and I could handle ourselves and keep up an act among the worst of the Lapsi. I doubted if Riley could be covert, like Mason, but he could protect Hannah, even if he thought she was a Lapsi. Thankfully, Riley spoke up with an answer to my conundrum.

"I was going to see if I could talk to some other Lapsi," Riley said. "Get some on our side, to at least get them to be on high alert."

"Where are you going to be doing this?" I asked.

"I figured I would start at the typical haunts," Riley said with a shrug. He meant bars and parties, probably: Lapsi preferred social gatherings to private, intimate spaces.

"Okay, I think we split up, then," I said, after debating in my head for another moment. Much as I didn't want to separate from Hannah, it made the most sense. "I'll go with Mason to get more insight." I looked to Hannah. "Hannah, you go with Riley and try to rally some alliances."

She looked like she wanted to argue, but she closed her mouth and nodded. I could tell she was scared to leave my side. I felt the same, but I wasn't going to admit it.

Riley will keep you safe, but please still be careful, I sent telepathically to her. She masked most of her surprise at hearing my voice in her head. I didn't do it that often. She couldn't reply, but she nodded, almost imperceptibly. *I'll be careful too. I'll come back,* I promised her.

CHAPTER 22

HANNAH

I wished I'd gone with Jeb.

Not because I was a glutton for danger and wanted to go into the heart of Cassandra's scheme, and not because I'd forgotten how to exist away from Jeb. No, it was because Riley's idea of "typical haunts" was *parties*. Bars, I could've handled, but college ragers? I'd never wanted to see the inside of another party as long as I lived.

Ordinarily, I'd have been a supporter of the "face your fears" mindset, but that only works for fears that either are irrational or that could never happen to you again. But going into a raging, uncontrolled college party wasn't facing a fear in a safe way, because what happened to me could *very* easily happen again.

But I couldn't tell any of this to Riley for many reasons. One, he was a complete stranger, and although he had big German shepherd energy, I couldn't tell him why the thought of being inside the walls of a college party had me shaking with real, cold fear. And the other reason was that he thought I was a Lapsus. Lapsi are powerful, immortal and strong, and wouldn't be afraid of being at a *party*.

I told myself that this time was different and I wasn't there for a party. This was purely reconnaissance, and I needed to keep up the façade of being a Lapsus. And Lapsi only drink blood, so there was no way anyone could slip me drugs. Nothing was going to happen to me.

There were three large colleges in a small square radius. Put that many young and stressed bodies in such a small area, parties will abound. The first party gave me the most anxiety as we entered it. The crush of bodies and the smell of booze brought back so many memories.

I let Riley do most of the talking at each of the parties, once we found a few Lapsi. I didn't trust myself to speak without my voice shaking. Mostly, we just talked to other Lapsi to see if they knew anything going on, and if they didn't know, we informed them so they could be on alert. It was simple enough, but I was having trouble focusing on their conversations. My nerves were wound so tight they might snap at the wrong word.

When we were walking up the lawn to the fourth and largest party, those tightly wound nerves nearly exploded. It was a big house, located near the Portland State University campus, just outside the football-shaped area of downtown, caused by the 405 and the 5 freeways that circled downtown and divided it from the rest of the city. I'd never been to this area, but from my fellow nursing students, I understood that this was mainly fraternity and sorority houses. The thudding bass that hit me at the edge of the lawn, the trash and exorbitant amount of empty beer cans littering the grass were dead giveaways that this was a fraternity house. My worst nightmare.

But the smell was what hit me first, halting me on the steps and making me nearly lose my dinner. Stale beer, musky BO, and that same damn overpowering cologne that brought all my trauma crashing viscerally back to the forefront of my mind. *Do all pledges all over this damn country get a bottle of that cologne upon initiation?*

Riley stopped and turned to me with a questioning frown when he noticed I wasn't following him anymore. To hide the panic that must've been painted on my face, I dropped quickly into a crouch, pretending that my shoe needed fixing. While I fiddled with the laces of my sneaker, loosening the knot, then retying it, I forced a deep breath into my lungs as quietly as I could, trying to push the trauma memories back to their hiding places by breathing through the horrible aura of scents and focusing on the less triggering notes within it.

Campfire. I could smell campfire as well. There were no awful memories connected to campfires, so I seized on that. It sort of worked. I was still a millimeter away from full panic, but I could hold it together. Probably.

Keep it together, girl. Keep it together, I told myself when I finished retying my shoe and made myself stand up straight. *This thing is bigger than your trauma. Stop being selfish.* I stepped back to Riley's side, and we continued into the pulsing house of nightmares.

Riley was much better at spotting Lapsi than I was; I was still getting used to the sixth sense the ring gave me. He found one immediately when we walked in, and he made a beeline for him. I was a useless recon partner, but Riley had it well enough in hand, so once again I stood back and let him talk. I was recovering from an almost-panic attack, but the effort of repairing the damage to my nerves was exhausting. I hoped we'd be done soon, but I didn't know how long Riley intended to do this. I considered sneaking away to the kitchen for a can of soda. Caffeine sounded like a good idea, but even if I could drink it without Riley or the other Lapsi noticing, was it worth the risk of drinking anything in this house?

I glanced around, trying to ascertain where the kitchen was and whether they had anything *sealed* to drink. Across the crowded living room, a girl was stumbling up a flight of stairs, supported by a tall, strong man my age. Instantly, alarms went off in my head, and all thoughts of caffeine evaporated, as did my fear.

I started across the room, not even bothering to tell Riley I was leaving—which, admittedly was dumb, but I was thinking about only one thing at that moment. On the way to the stairs, I grabbed the hand of another girl my age.

"Help," I said, without really looking at who I was grabbing. She complained a little but followed me when she caught a look at my face, or maybe it was the aura my ring was giving off.

We stomped up the stairs and made it to the top in time to see a door close. I didn't even think about whether the door was locked: I just slammed my foot flat against it—right above the doorknob. The crummy lock broke immediately, and the door swung inward.

I took in details only one at a time as I burst into the room. Messy room. A desk. Hardwood floors. Bed. Girl on bed. Man with one knee hovering above the bed, his pants already undone. Thankfully, his dick wasn't out yet.

"Hey!" I heard myself yell—eloquent, I know—as I burst farther into the room. I advanced on him and he was so surprised at our sudden appearance, that he backed up by two steps.

I put myself between him and the bed. Why—I don't know. It was dumb. I did all of this very *dumb*—but valiantly, I might add.

The girl I'd dragged up the stairs saw everything too, though she probably perceived it with more detail than I did in my singular trauma-fueled mindset. She pulled the other girl, who could barely stand, off the bed, supporting her, and they moved out of the room while the man recovered from his surprise at being interrupted.

Get out of there, a voice was screaming in my head. I was alone in the room with an attempted rapist, and any second he'd realize how painfully blue his balls were about to be. But I was still registering single details.

Man.

Tall.

Door. Door. Door!

I lurched around the bed, angling for the door as fast as I could, but not fast enough. The man grabbed my upper arm—and some of my hair—jerking me backward. I spun out of his grip but fell backward against the bed, onto my elbows.

"Fucking slut!" the man shouted. Spittle splashed against my face from his snarl. I hadn't realized he was hovering above me, so close.

"Fucking rapist!" I screamed back, bucking against him.

I pushed off the bed, but he was still between me and the exit. I put my weight into his chest to shove him off balance, but he was so tall and so strong. He put a hand to my throat and pushed me back down onto the bed and pressed his hip against my leg so I couldn't move it.

"This will show you, you stubborn bitch," he hissed, spraying my chin with more of his spittle.

His other hand tugged roughly at the waist of my jeans. The button pulled loose. *No, no, no, no, no...*

I felt the familiar paralysis spreading through me. The disbelief. The shock. The powerlessness.

No, not again. This will not happen again. A firm voice spoke in my head. Firmer than I felt right then. My brain was finally waking up, and with it came *anger*. I wasn't going to let this happen again. I wasn't going to be a victim. Again. I was stronger than this.

And more than that, I had more *important* things to do. I was up against actual *vampires* and a potential hostile takeover of an entire goddamned city. I was not going to cower under this *mortal* man. This pathetic human man that got a stiffy by degrading women.

"Fucking pig," I spat at him when I realized the hand was on my throat, not over my mouth this time.

He froze for a second, no doubt bewildered to see the anger replace the fear in my eyes. I brought my knee up as hard as I could. I missed the mark, but my knee connected with his tender inner thigh. He grunted and snarled, but he released me and backed up.

"Bitch!" he yelled. He was hunched over, with a hand to his leg.

"Asshole!" I countered, with a hand to my neck.

Get out, get out, get out, my inner voice was screaming. But he was still between me and the door, and before I could move for the door again, he righted himself. His arm and shoulder jerked, as if to strike me.

Instinct took over. Rather than blocking, I went low and dropped into a spinning crouch, kicking out with a powerful leg. I'd tried this kick on Jeb, and it barely shook him, but this was just a man. I broke his footing, and he stumbled backward. In trying to recover, his feet slipped on a piece of clothing on the floor, and he toppled, *hard*, backward against a desk.

The crack seemed to echo as he fell to the ground like a rock.

At last, I caught my breath, but it faltered again when I felt the deafening silence in the room pressing in around me. I stared at the man, still lying where he'd fallen. He wasn't moving—or breathing.

I went to my knees and crawled toward him, but it was difficult with my hands shaking so violently.

Please move. Please move.

He wouldn't. Ever again. I didn't have to get close enough to feel for a pulse. I could see the angle of his neck. He was dead. I'd killed him. I'd killed a man. A human man.

I was a killer. I was a killer. I was a killer. I put my hands to my mouth, as if I were saying the words aloud.

"Well done, love," a familiar voice said behind me. I was in too much shock to turn toward it, but my shoulders shuddered to hear her approaching me from behind. "Hey, hey now. Don't worry. No one will know. No one needs to know."

She stepped from behind me to stand near the body. She was in a knee-length white dress, with gold embroidery at the empire waist. Her long red curls fell over her shoulder as she tilted her head to the side and looked down at the body.

Then Cassandra turned toward me.

"I mean, honestly, his life was forfeit the moment he took that girl up here and closed the door." She knelt in front of me, and she froze, taking in my face. She looked surprised to see me, but then her smile widened into a pleased grin. "It's *you*."

CHAPTER 23

JEB

M ason brought us to a large open space east of the Willamette River and northeast of the city. When transporting a human, or objects, it's done through touch. With another Lapsus, you could also do it through touch or you follow behind them by latching onto their signature, but you can only do it if they *let* you. Otherwise, they can disappear without a trace and you can't follow.

"Where are we?" I asked as I looked around. I knew where we were in relation to the river and downtown because of an innate inner compass, but I didn't know where exactly he'd taken me.

The whole area was packed soil, with cargo trailers scattered about and *lots* of train tracks.

"Union Pacific Railroad Company train depot," Mason said, pushing hair out of his eyes. Wind was blowing roughly off the river, and my own hair was whipping aggressively across my eyes. "Come on."

"Is this a meeting place that you're showing me?" I assumed he was taking me to some planning meeting or a recruitment rally so I could hear the plans. Or rather that's what I assumed *Mason* wanted me to assume. Really, I thought I was shifting directly into a trap. I expected to be surrounded by at least a dozen Lapsi, and maybe Cassandra herself, all out for blood. This big open space wasn't what I was expecting.

"Sort of," he said, keeping up with his aggravating vagueness.

I gave the silver grenade in my pocket a loving caress for reassurance. The silver was unnerving to my skin—not quite a burn, not quite rash-inducing. We're sensitive to silver, and silver only. If it pierces us, we don't heal from it like we heal from everything else. If it pierces deep enough, or pierces the heart, we're dead. Forever. Skin contact is just a mild irritation, though.

He walked toward a hangar-like metal structure nearby and opened a door in its siding. He went in first, which perplexed me. If it were a trap, he'd make me go in first. Was he trying to build trust or throw me off guard? Regardless, I followed.

Inside was a warehouse full of crates, ladders, and tools. He led me to an interior door, which led to a stairwell.

"Is this the entrance to whatever perimeter she's setting up? Does it run under the tracks?" I asked, after we stepped through the doorway. I stayed on the platform landing of the stairs and leaned against the railing, looking down. The stairs went down two or three flights, then a hallway went off in two directions.

"Yes, it's an entrance. Technically, the perimeter runs under the 405 and the 5, but this is my usual route," Mason explained. He leaned against the railing too, but with his back against it. "Look," he started, in a hushed tone. "I know you don't trust me. And you don't have to."

"So you're not going to try and convince me to?" I said, skeptical.

"No, I'm not going to try and convince you," he said with a soft, quiet chuckle beneath his voice. "I'm going to tell you to lean into that distrust. Because people down there...none of us trust each other. It's kind of the whole point. But we're all down there to accomplish a task, because we want what it promises."

"What does it promise?" That unsettled feeling was surfacing again, as it always did whenever I tried to fathom what Cassandra was planning.

Mason gave me a sidelong look, his mouth turned up into a grin. But the smile didn't reach his eyes. "Control. Power. Debauchery without consequence." His tone was meant to sound enticing, but his eyes didn't agree.

"What happened to you, man? Why the sudden change in you?" I asked. This was the man who had inspired Oscar Wilde's debaucherous character, Dorian Gray.

Mason frowned and shook his head. *Not here*, he said telepathically. He moved back to the door to the outside and held it open for me.

I followed him back outside into the bitingly cold autumn wind blowing off the river. Mason stepped away from the building and turned into the wind, so his long hair would stop blowing in his face.

"Look, if you must know, it was a girl. Yeah, cliché as fuck, right?" Mason said, slightly defensive. "But yeah. A girl and her kid brother woke me up. She helped me realize that I needed to *be* better to deserve better."

"And where is this girl now?" I pressed, not believing him. If he'd met his soulmate, he probably would have changed her. So why wasn't she here too?

"My past caught up with me, and she was thrown into the middle of it," he admitted, frowning. "I was forced to change her because they nearly killed her." He looked off into the distance for a second, thinking about the past. This must have been fairly recent for it to still bring such emotion to his face. "I'm still a mess, though, and she deserves better than that. So she's off, living through immortality, and I am working to better myself. It doesn't matter how long it takes when you're immortal. All things can be forgiven after a couple hundred years."

Strangely optimistic for a Lapsus. Optimism for our kind felt so novel, but maybe it was just me that was the perpetual pessimist. His admission, and the hope in his eyes did nothing to lower my guard though.

"So...shall we?" He turned back to the building. This time, he held the door open for me to walk in first.

Keeping me guessing with his motives, I thought, frowning.

Down we went. Two flights below was a tunnel that reminded me of a subway station, minus the platform and tracks. The hallway went both ways from the stairs and didn't seem to turn for a while. Mason led us to the right. We walked for a couple hundred feet and passed only a few Lapsi in the hallway. I had to lean into my inner sociopath just a bit to blend in. It was a delicate balance to figure out: I had to appear just enough of an asshole to not be fucked with, but not enough of an asshole to make people want to fight me.

Not that I expected my face to be on Most Wanted posters lining the hallway, but I would have thought that killing twelve Lapsi in a police precinct would somehow activate people's Spidey senses. However, for the most part, everyone kept their guarded eyes forward. Now what Mason'd said made sense.

A couple hundred feet down the hall, Mason turned into a large auditorium space lined in tile. It reminded me of a lecture hall—if lectures were held in a subway. There were maybe two hundred Lapsi in attendance. We stood at the back, and I wondered about being seen eavesdropping, but if Mason wasn't concerned, neither was I.

On the lower level of the hall was a large table with a map rolled out onto it. The map showed a detailed shot of downtown Portland, specifically the football-shaped area within the 405 and the 5 interchanges. Outside the freeway lines were several large red X's. *What the hell could those mean?* But I had a feeling I already knew.

I'd expected to see Cassandra addressing her troops, but she wasn't in sight. Instead, a handful of people were standing there, as if at a blackboard.

These people took turns giving presentations on containment, tramping down on rebellion and panic as soon as possible. Then there were presentations about seemingly trivial things, but things that hadn't occurred to me. Things like how they'd keep power operational, cell service and internet functioning, and plumbing uninterrupted.

One person gave a report about how many doctors had been changed and were ready at the hospitals and clinics to accept wounded. No one seemed to pay attention while this person spoke, because in the face of a Lapsi uprising, what Lapsus really cares about wounded blood banks?

Finally, the last Lapsus in the lineup stepped forward. He walked to the middle of the floor, right in front of the table, so that he had everyone's attention.

"Lapsi brethren!" he said in a loud clear voice. I nearly snorted aloud at his greeting, but I stopped myself. "Tonight begins a new era! Plans have been in place for so long, and tonight they roll forward. For too long Lapsi have been forced to be outliers and outcasts, hiding in the shadows and taking only what wouldn't be noticed. But after tonight, we will forever be a force to be reckoned with! Finally, we will have a seat at the table, and we will have a place to call home. But above all? Finally, we will have the power and control that we are due!"

As he finished, several in the audience cheered and whooped, but many remained stoic, watchful. I chose to follow their example as I digested all I'd just heard. This man's boastful speech sounded like a page out of Cassandra's book all right. She'd spouted verbiage to me that suggested we'd been second-class citizens and not the powerful, predatory creatures that we were. It just wasn't true, and I didn't understand how anyone could believe that.

Tonight? I asked Mason telepathically. I needed to get out of there and find Hannah. *Now.* We needed to get out of the city and back to my apartment before anything went down tonight. But if this was really a trap I'd willingly walked into, was there any point?

Mason glanced sideways at me, and I tried to glean anything from his expression—whether cunning or distress—but he gave me nothing.

They've moved it up, apparently, he told me. In his telepathic words, I could *feel* the wince he was hiding from his face. *I thought we had another week or two. Come on, I still have the big thing to show you.*

He jerked his head back toward the hallway, and I followed him out, hoping our departure wasn't noticed by the Lapsi in attendance.

A little farther down the hallway, it doglegged to both sides. The new hallway was about five times as wide. Mason walked across it and opened a door to the left. He jerked his head in an "after you" gesture.

This is what you have to see to believe. Because, frankly, I don't know how to explain it, he told me. I resisted the urge to stroke the grenade in my pocket again for strength. When I stepped toward the door, he lifted an arm and pointed at the hallway ceiling above our heads. "Right now, we're directly under the freeway that circles downtown."

"And the significance of that?" I asked, pausing at the door and eyeing him.

"You'll see."

The wards were stronger here than I'd ever felt. I'd been able to smell the wards all over this facility the second we entered the hangar aboveground, but here they were worse. Far worse. Either this was a heavily laid trap—in which case I was kind of flattered that they took so much precaution to contain *me*—or this was protecting something *big*.

Steeling myself for an ambush, making my peace with imminent death, and hoping at least I wouldn't die in any embarrassing fashion, I walked through the door that Mason was holding open for me.

Inside was a medium-sized room with a dirt floor. The room was completely bare except for a cylindrical pillar in its center. It was as wide as a tree trunk and made of clear crystal or glass. At first, it appeared to be a lightly glowing pillar of selenite crystal, but when I stepped closer, I realized it was a glass tube *full* of a swirling, silver, ghost-like mist. Toward the ceiling, a thinner tube, like a pipe, exited the pillar on either side and went off through the walls.

My stomach twisted when I made myself approach it. This was beyond unsettling. This was *horrifying*. I could feel the tattered remains of my soul shuddering in a way I'd never felt it do before. I fell slowly to my knees, and my hand reached out to touch the glass of the pillar. The pillar of...

"Souls," I said aloud, though barely over a whisper.

"Those pipes run the entire perimeter of their intended initial territory," Mason explained quietly. He was inside the room now, somewhere behind me. "*This* is their method of containment."

How in the... I'd never heard of this kind of magic before. This was horrendous. This was *monstrous*.

"I need to find Hannah," I said, not realizing I was speaking aloud. "I need to get to her before things start happening."

"Okay," Mason said nonchalantly behind me.

Wait, what does he mean "okay"? I turned around and stood up, facing him.

He was standing by the wall where several sigils that made up the strong wards in this room were painted and holding a rod-like device that started whirring. I eyed it suspiciously, half expecting it to be a Bond-like gadget that would entrap me somehow. But then I noticed the wards painted on the walls were fading—no, not fading but flickering a little, like they were temporarily disrupted but fighting it.

"What are you doing?"

"Go get what's-her-name," he said gruffly. He was gritting his teeth and looking at the device warily. He glanced at the wards around him, frowning. "Shit, it needs to be higher, but they'll notice. Go as soon as you see these fade, okay? You'll only have a second, and I gotta clear the area before anyone can get here to investigate. Shit, this thing is scaring me."

"But..." *I thought this was a trap,* I finished silently.

Mason rolled his eyes and hissed—whether at me or the whirring device in his hand that seemed to be hurting him.

"I said you didn't have to trust me," he said. "Not that I wasn't trustworthy. Now go! Get out and fight, or get out and run. But *go.*"

Still, I hesitated. He was letting me get away when I thought he was trapping me. In a split second, I decided to trust him. I might need him again.

"In a park north of downtown, I hid a package with weapons in it. In case I don't make it, you find it and protect yourself."

"And you tell Libby her device needs work!" he snarled through whatever jarring pain the device was giving him.

FALLEN SOULS

The wards faded, and I didn't wait to see if it held. I shifted the hell out of there.

CHAPTER 24

HANNAH

Dead. Dead. Dead. Dead. Dead.

I didn't even know his name, but he was dead. Another person around me, dead. Yes, he was a rapist, and he'd been about to assault me, but that didn't mean he had to die. Dead. I was a killer.

"I knew I'd see you again," Cassandra said dreamily as she knelt in front of me. She put herself between me and the body, blocking my view of him. It didn't matter: it was burned into my retinas. Cassandra looked perplexed as she studied my face, and she narrowed her eyes like I was a puzzle. She reached toward my face. "But he...I didn't think he would have it in him to do it."

She means Jeb. The small part of me that wasn't in shock for the second time in a week reminded me. *She thinks Jeb made me Lapsi.*

She still looked at me with narrowed eyes, like if she looked hard enough, she'd see through the illusion. Faintly, I could see something dawning on her.

"I killed him," I heard myself say aloud. Vaguely, I was aware that the still-perceptive part of my mind was trying to distract her from finding out I was still human.

"He was going to rape you," she reminded me gently. "You defended yourself, and you did so *valiantly*. It took me so long to realize I could defend myself."

"Defend myself was the aim, yes," I argued tonelessly. "But killing him? He didn't—"

She cut me off. "He didn't what? Deserve that? Would it have been better if he'd lived? What, did you expect reformation from him? Can you honestly imagine him making love to someone without shuddering? Men like him can't repent. Once they violate one woman, they violate us all."

I thought of *my* rapist and where he might be today. Was he still hurting women? Or was he married and making sweet, affectionate love to his wife, while imagining my gagged face? I shuddered at the image.

How would I feel if I heard that he'd been killed somewhere, by accident or otherwise? Relieved. Honestly and truly relieved. Did I prefer the thought of him dead to the thought of him still out there somewhere, enjoying life? Yeah. Yeah I did. So why was this different?

It was different because *I* was the one who killed him. How was I better than him now? I'd been assaulted, but this man had been *killed*.

"See, you understand," she said, her head tilting in her curiosity. She'd seen my hands clench and my eyes go distant. "But not about this one. This wasn't the first attempt, was it?"

"Not my first rodeo, no," I confirmed, shaking my head sadly. "It's how I knew what he was going to do to that other girl."

Her eyes softened, and the corners of her mouth turned downward. But there was a sparkle in her eyes, like I'd become even more interesting to her.

"Come on, love." She gently took my arm and stood up, helping me to my feet. She led me to the bed and made me take a seat on the creep's comforter. She put her hands to either side of my face and placed her forehead to mine.

"It's astounding," she said, as her fingers slid through my hair. "Thousands of years separate us. And yet we're connected by the same trauma. Thousands of years and nothing has changed for us."

Someone near the doorway cleared their throat, and Cassandra pulled away from me with an irritated hiss so quiet it was meant only for my ears.

"We've finished collecting all the other Lapsi in the house, ma'am," a deep-voiced Lapsus said. He stood just inside the doorway, his hand resting on the broken doorknob.

Riley, I thought fleetingly. Riley'd been captured, and I was sitting here with the would-be queen herself. Yet I was focused solely on one shitty human?

Snap out of it, my inner voice screamed at me. Listening through the shock was easier said than done, though.

"Wonderful," Cassandra said sweetly, though I sensed annoyance. "On your way out, kindly remove this." She pointed to the body on the floor. "It's upsetting her."

His eyes narrowed, but he complied. He lifted the body and hefted it over his shoulder as if it were nothing but a pillow. He glanced at me and paused.

"And what about this one?" he asked.

"Don't worry about her. She's with me," Cassandra said. "It was her first kill. You know how it is."

"Sure," he agreed, but his frown and narrowed eyes said he didn't understand at all. He'd probably killed before he was even a Lapsus. He turned from us and disappeared.

Leave, the voice was saying. My thoughts were starting to normalize again, slowly, now that I didn't have the body to stare at. *But what's the point? I'm caught, either way.* Despite Cassandra's weird tenderness toward me, I hadn't forgotten how deadly she was.

"That's better, isn't it?" Cassandra said, turning back to me with a smile. Her eyes were still boring into mine, simultaneously intrigued and studious, like she was trying to find the crack in the illusion.

"I was first raped at fifteen. By a *priest*," she explained, walking back to stand in front of where I sat. "Though religion was different back then: less...righteous and stuffy, but still. Rape is still rape. I saw our city's destruction coming, but no one believed me. I was silenced and ignored because I was a woman. Then, as my city was falling, I was taken as a prize for the enemy's king and forced into his harem. I was made to pleasure him and his men, whether I wanted to or not."

"Wait...did you ever not-not want to?" I asked, confused by her choice of words.

Her lips turned up into a smirk, and she bit her bottom lip seductively.

"Yes, actually. When they wanted to just watch two women..."

She put her hand gently to the side of my face and slowly brought her lips to mine.

My surprise melted under the heat of her lips, and the sensations of being kissed overwhelmed me instantly, making my lips tingle and my face redden. It had been *so long* since I'd been kissed by anyone, and as scared and startled as I was, it was thrilling. My eyes fluttered closed, and I brushed over her bare arms as lightly as I could with my fingertips.

Her tongue brushed my lips as her kiss deepened. My lips parted, and a small moan escaped my mouth and flowed into hers. Her hands found the zipper of my hoodie, and she slowly undid it. As she slipped it off my shoulders down my arms, she put her mouth to the sensitive part of my throat where it met my shoulder. I released a sound between a sigh and a groan.

She cupped my small breasts in her hands, and her mouth found mine again. I pulled eagerly on her dress by her hips, and as she stumbled closer to me, I placed two hands firmly on her backside, squeezing.

I felt her body vibrating with laughter at my boldness. She gripped my breasts a little rougher, and I let my hands travel lower, to the hem of her short dress, then upward again, under her dress. It was her turn to moan in surprise and pleasure.

Was I still trying to distract her from looking too closely at my fake-Lapsi aura? I'd like to say I could be that manipulative, but, no: it was the furthest thing from my mind. It'd just been so long since I'd even thought about enjoying something like this that when she kissed me, I lost myself in the intimacy I'd been missing.

I only got far enough up her legs to tell she wasn't wearing anything under her dress. Then her hands were sliding down my arms to find my hands and hold onto them. She pulled her mouth away and instead pressed her forehead against mine.

"My, you sure know what you're doing," she said huskily, as if out of breath.

Her hand stroked my right hand, and when it brushed the ring on my thumb, she paused. Her eyes opened and she looked into mine, slyly. She gently tugged at the ring and pulled it off, then moved back to look at me.

Fuck. I shrank back, barely stopping my arms from wrapping around myself. It was just a ring, but I suddenly felt naked under her gaze, which was terrifying yet thrilling. I dug my hands into the comforter and kept my shoulders squared.

"There you are," she whispered, smiling in satisfaction. She could tell now that I hadn't been changed and that I was still just human. "I like you better this way."

"Weak?" I said quietly. *This is when she kills me.*

She shook her head and put a hand gently to my face again. "Innocent," she replied instead. "Fragile."

Right. My ears and skin were still buzzing with arousal, but I told them to cool it: the moment had passed. She enjoyed my innocence and fragility. She enjoyed toying with the weak, like me, and she was toying with the world.

Suddenly, my thoughts cleared, and the questions I should have been asking surfaced.

"Why did you capture all of the Lapsi at this party?"

"So they don't interfere with everything that's about to start," she said simply. She'd pulled back enough to stand up straight and took her hand from my face.

"But you didn't kill them?"

"No, of course I didn't." She shrugged. "I'll need them later."

"Need them for what?" I couldn't help asking. She was being casually forthcoming, but I didn't expect her to continue being so.

"I'll need their help in reestablishing order," she responded, surprising me. "And in cleaning up the Lapsi that just want chaos and death."

"Why involve *those* Lapsi in the first place? The ones that want chaos and death?" I prodded further. *Why the hell hasn't she stopped me from asking questions yet?*

She fixed me with a look that made me feel like a student who'd missed a question in a history review game.

"Every capturing of a city requires *infantry*," she explained patiently. "Ruthless but expendable. Promise them power, and they will do anything you ask."

"How many people are going to die in all this?" I put my hands under my legs so I didn't clench them in anger.

Her eye twitched. At last, I was nearing the end of her patience. I knew I shouldn't be trying to test it, but if was going to die, I wanted to go down curious rather than afraid. Just call me Cat.

"Many, probably," she responded. "But there will be peace when the dust settles."

"You're so calm about causing so much human death to get what you want." I could hear irritation sneaking into my voice, which was possibly a mistake, but oh well.

"What should I care about *humans*?" she snapped. "Humans, with their wars? Humans killing each other over skin color, land, *women*! Seizing women in their wars or just off the fucking street. Raping them. Selling them. Forcing them to bear children. Locking them in empty rooms because they had the *gall* to touch themselves. The human race is a mess. Good fucking riddance to them all.

"I was raised in war. I was taken away from my people and raped countless times. My home was destroyed by the people who took me away. I was changed into a killer and kept by a killer. Even though we both couldn't stand being near each other, he wouldn't let me go. His presence was torture to me, and mine to him. He was *that* cruel; he would torture himself if it meant I hurt too. Until I killed him. But then I truly had no one. For years and years. I was changed into something strong and beautiful and deadly, but still, I was denied a place to belong. But now, at last, I can have a home, and no one will stop me from taking it!"

I've cracked her armor, I thought with a bit of satisfaction. But it didn't matter at all. What good was this tiny victory when I was a mouse and she was a lion?

Then another question rose to the forefront of my mind.

"If you're not killing the Lapsi that oppose you, why did you kill the two in the alley last week?" My eyebrows drew together in confusion, remembering the murder and soul-theft Jeb had witnessed.

"Oh, them," she said airily. Her smile returned, but it was a sly, mischievous one. "I did that because I knew Jeb was watching. I cannot abide spying."

"So you killed Lapsi to manipulate him. And you're toying with him, still, because..."

"Because I find him interesting. Like I find *you* interesting," she said, smiling. She put a hand to my face again. I resisted pulling away, though I wanted to.

She found me interesting. Me. But why? She'd said she knew she'd see me again, and she'd been almost elated to see me here tonight. Had she seen me before meeting me at that Target?

"Why did you push Jeb in front of the car I was in? Did you know I was in it?"

"You specifically? No, child," she said patronizingly. "I saw the accident, yes. But you weren't the significant part of it. I used it as a distraction for Jeb. Something to keep him busy for a little bit, while I left. I expected it to distract him for maybe thirty minutes. Imagine my surprise to find him still occupied with you twelve hours later—and having killed a troop of my Lapsi to keep you safe. *You*, this accident of timing: a wrong-place-wrong-time anomaly. You were a coincidence, yet you've captivated my soulless plaything. Therefore, you're interesting."

I was silent, absorbing. It was comforting and a relief to find out I wasn't an important piece in this game. I'd been afraid she would tell me that this had to do with my birthmother; that I was some long-long-long descendant of someone important. I wouldn't have been able to cope with that, but I was happy to be an accident: happy to be unimportant.

"So, you have your plaything's plaything," I said calmly. "Are you planning on ransoming it? Or killing it?"

"I am asking it to join me," she said seriously, in a sultry tone.

What the fuck, I almost asked aloud, but I held it in. She couldn't be serious.

"You can entertain me, and keep me tethered to humanity, if you so desire it," she said. Was she mocking me? "What do you say?"

I say it's time to get out of here. I was done playing the game. I'd found out I wasn't an important piece, and now she wanted me to *be* an important piece. No thanks.

"No, ma'am, I respectfully decline," I said, surprised at how even my voice came out. I stood up from the bed, startling her enough that she took a step back.

"No?" she said quietly.

"No," I repeated. "I think I should go now."

As I walked to the door, I knew that every move I made now was inviting death, but I didn't care. I'd rather die walking away from something like this than live in it.

"But you can't—"

"Do you intend to *force* me?" I demanded evenly, stopping and looking her directly in the eye. She knew what I meant by force, and I knew she wouldn't do anything that resembled removing my consent. Okay, I didn't know it, but I believed strongly in it, and I *hoped*.

"No," she said quietly, resigned. Her eyes narrowed, but she didn't move to stop me.

I turned my back on her and walked out of the room—thinking all the while how foolish it was to turn my back on a lion.

The party downstairs had thinned, but it didn't seem like anyone even knew anything amiss had happened in the past several minutes: be it rounding up a handful of Lapsi, an almost-rape, or their classmate *dying*. I made it out the front door and onto the porch, but I had no idea where to go next. I didn't know this area of the city, my escort had been abducted, and Cassandra had said something was happening *soon*. *Where the hell is Jeb?*

I walked off the porch and onto the lawn, thinking as quickly as I could about my next move.

Halfway to the sidewalk, the house behind me exploded.

The force threw me forward several feet and I landed, gracelessly sprawled on the grass. The back of my shirt was destroyed, and I felt hot air blustering against burns on my back and arms, but none of this manifested the pain it should have. *Shock. I'm in shock. Again.*

I moved up onto my hands and knees, retching and coughing from the acrid smoke behind me. I took a moment to steady myself and got to my feet.

I'd been thrown to the edge of the lawn, which hovered over the sidewalk, held back by a decorative retaining wall. It was a four-foot drop, but there were stairs just to my left.

"Hey, girlie," a voice behind me said.

I turned just as the Lapsus behind me lunged. With a shriek, I jumped back automatically, and fell over the retaining wall, landing flat on my back on the sidewalk. Shock kept me from feeling the pain of the hard cement grinding against the burns on my back, but the fall knocked the air from my lungs. While I struggled to get my reflexes back in line and take a breath, my attacker jumped down to the sidewalk and knelt over me. I saw the flash of a knife and lifted my hand to defend myself.

Somehow, I managed to deflect the knife into the guy's upper thigh. I could never reproduce that fluid, spectacular move if I had a million years. He let out a string of curses, and the back of his hand struck me across the cheek so hard that I saw spots in front of my eyes.

I groaned and turned over as I tried to clear my vision. I was pulled back, however, and pinned.

"That was a good trick back there, little girl," he snarled. I recognized his voice now. It was the Lapsus who had taken the body away. "You like to play at being a Lapsus, hmm? Well, we'll see how you like this."

"She said not to kill her," a nearby voice warned. I couldn't see the owner of the voice. "We're supposed to keep her intact."

"She'll be *intact*. But we can still have a bit of fun," the first Lapsus snarled.

A hand covered my mouth, and a vile liquid poured over my lips. I sputtered and bucked, trying to get away, but they held me fast, forcing me to swallow several mouthfuls of whatever it was. It tasted metallic.

Then another form stood over me. I could only make out pointed ears, and large, sunken holes for eyes. The hand he lowered over my mouth had a dark, gaping hole in the center of its palm. I wasn't usually a screamer when afraid, but the instant his hand went over my mouth, a scream ripped from my throat straight into the void in his hand.

CHAPTER 25

I t took several tries to find her. Before parting ways, I'd taken a strand of her hair to use as a tether. It doesn't always work to track people, but it was better than nothing. I shifted to three spots she'd previously been that night with no luck.

I cursed Riley and his unplanned meanderings of the city, and I cursed myself for not thinking to ask for his destinations or his phone number. Then a series of low concussive tremors shook the night. The explosions were far off, but I could see them in the distance. They seemed to be just outside the freeway overpasses that marked the territory.

I let out a string of expletives and tried one more time to shift to where Hannah's scent was. I appeared near the aftermath of one of the explosions. My heart trembled in my throat, but I refused to panic. I couldn't panic. Panicking meant that I *cared*, and I was incapable of caring. Yet why did I feel like panicking?

"Hannah!" My voice echoed into the night. Why did it sound so scared? I should've been quiet, but it escaped my mouth before I could stop it.

Aside from the roar of the fires still blazing in the houses around me, the air was surprisingly quiet. No sirens. Just like that night a week ago, there were no signs of aid coming.

I stomped around the debris for a bit, trying to ignore the bile climbing up my throat and the panic thrumming in my chest. Then I retreated to the street to look at the wreckage from a distance, and I practically stumbled right over her.

She was lying on her back on the sidewalk, and I dropped to my knees by her side, putting my hands to her face. Her face was warm, thankfully; I'd been afraid to find it cold. I sat down heavily and pulled her head and shoulders onto my lap, inspecting her for injuries. She seemed surprisingly unharmed, despite the ash on her forehead. As I slipped a hand under her, I felt smooth, bare skin. Most of the back of her shirt was in tatters. She'd been close to the explosion but not in it. But how was she so unharmed?

Then I caught a scent on her. Lapsi. Her ring was gone, but she smelled and *felt* like a Lapsus, despite her warmth. I put a hand to her neck and let out a breath of relief when her pulse beat against my fingers. She was alive and not changed. But they'd given her Lapsi blood. *Why the hell would they do that?*

It wasn't enough to change her, but it would have healed any wounds—more than our saliva would. She'd have a cranky kind of hunger that she couldn't do anything about, she'd heal quickly, and she'd acquire some of our unnatural strength, but only temporarily.

My fists clenched in anger, but I forced them to relax and not shake. I didn't have time to be angry about this. I had to get Hannah far away from here, but first I had to retrieve my weapons.

I put my hand to the side of her face and sent a little bit of my power into her mind. I'd only done it twice to her, and I'd vowed never to do it again, but I needed her awake.

"Hannah," I said softly to her. I was surprised to hear a hoarseness to my voice. I blamed it on the smoke—despite not having inhaled any of it. "Hannah, wake up."

Her eyes opened and looked up at me. Her eyebrows twitched together in mild confusion, and she blinked a few times, then looked away from me, almost bored. She rolled out of my arms and sat up on her own, looking around at her surroundings.

"What happened, Hannah?" I asked, watching her carefully. She was in shock, surely, but she seemed *off*. It wasn't like I expected her to hug me or be relieved to see me—mostly I expected her to be scared and bewildered—but I'd expected *some* kind of emotion.

"Uh, a lot," she said vaguely, uninterested. She seemed to be ordering her thoughts, prioritizing what was most important. "Riley's gone."

"Gone? He's dead?" I said warily. I couldn't afford to lose an ally tonight.

She shook her head and looked away, back up at the blaze.

"No, she took him. He and the other Lapsi we were talking to. She's containing them."

"She? Cassandra? She was here?" I was alarmed now.

Hannah nodded and turned her head back toward me. "I told you. A lot happened." Then she looked down at her hands, looking perplexed again. She clenched and unclenched her hands, as if testing them. She looked up and around again. "Why do I feel weird? Why am I...hungry? Why isn't it still dark out?"

She was probably thrumming with energy that she couldn't explain, and though it was nearly midnight, it only appeared to be dusk to her. But it was my turn to prioritize *my* thoughts. I could ask questions and answer hers later, but first, we had to get my weapons and get out of there.

"We gotta go," I said calmly. I stood up and helped Hannah to her feet—not that she needed the help. Once we were both standing, I shifted us away.

We reappeared between two buildings on the edge of the park where I'd left the grenades.

People were everywhere. Of course there were; they'd all heard or seen the explosions in the distance. They'd poured out of the bars and out of their residences to see what was going on. People were going to panic, and when people panic, people become stupid. Violence happens, and looting happens. I didn't want to be on the street when *that* started.

In the park, around the brush where my bag was hidden, were crowds of people and Lapsi alike. The Lapsi were on full alert, like they were waiting for the right moment to pounce. Not good. Not good.

It was going to be nearly impossible—no, *completely* impossible—to retrieve my things without being attacked. Before I could decide my next move, another explosion rocked the ground, but this one felt like an earthquake. I backed us up against the building wall, with Hannah behind me. I glanced back at her to gauge her level of panic, but she was looking past me, *way* past me. With more wariness burning in my veins than I'd felt in eons, I turned and followed her gaze.

The freeway overpasses shuddered and toppled straight to the ground. As the tons of cement and iron fell, a massive dust cloud burst upward and kept climbing, but it wasn't just any demolition dust cloud. It shimmered like a silver net, creating a dome over all of us, laced with countless *souls* that Cassandra had collected.

This was her containment: her pilfered souls created a boundary, impenetrable by anything manmade. The city was about to discover what I already knew: we were trapped. I'd wanted to be gone before this happened, but I'd failed, and now we were trapped within that barrier. All I could think of right then were swear words.

"Something tells me we aren't going anywhere for a bit," Hannah said behind me.

Her words and her tone froze me in my panic. She wouldn't say something like that. She would be freaking out and demanding to know what we should do or demanding to get off the street. She wasn't acting or reacting like *my* Hannah would.

In hindsight, I already knew, but I'd been refusing to think it. Because if it was true, I knew I'd lose it. But now I had to ask.

"What happened to you?" I turned toward her. We were still in the cover between two buildings. Beyond us, I could hear screams. The Lapsi had pounced, and the humans were panicking.

She shrugged, her expression impassive, as if it wasn't important.

"I told you. A lot," she said again.

"You were attacked?" I stepped closer to her and put my hands on her shoulders. She nodded. "By what?"

She looked away, as if trying to remember, but she shrugged again.

"What did it look like? Tall and bald? Tattoos?" I could hear the emotion in my voice, emotion that was usually too deep for me to reach.

"It was dark…" She shrugged again.

"Did it have eyes?" I demanded impatiently. "Or did it have sunken black—"

"Holes. Yes. And a hole in its hand…"

Before my hands could involuntarily clench and crush her clavicles, I released her and backed away. I hadn't felt this emotion in over fifty years—even longer than that, really. I almost didn't recognize it, but my hands shook with it, and my teeth chattered as my jaw clenched. I felt it welling up in my throat, and I couldn't hold it back, nor did I want to.

I turned and thrust my fists against the brick wall. The bricks shuddered and cracked, and the bones in my hands shattered. I barely noticed as the scream of rage bellowed out of my throat.

CHAPTER 26

JEB

After a moment, I was able to reel the rage in enough to think straight. I tucked most of it into a neat little package within myself, to unleash it upon the next Lapsus I saw—or upon Cassandra. No doubt she was behind this. But I held a little of the rage just beneath the surface to fuel my motivation to keep going.

As promised, the internet was still active, so I used it to find a nearby Airbnb that wasn't booked. I didn't bother booking it: I just needed to know of a place that was for sure unoccupied. We needed off the streets while the chaos raged through the night.

I shifted the two of us into the empty residence, which was located at the top of a tall, upscale apartment building. Once there, I took off my jacket and outer shirt, and sank onto the minimalistic posh couch. I buried my head in my hands.

I'd failed. I didn't get us out of there in time, and I didn't do shit to stop this. I had nothing now but one grenade and a few knives against an unknown number of malicious Lapsi and a barrier of some magic I'd never even *heard of* that used souls. Many *many* souls.

They'd stolen Hannah's soul, and I was responsible. I'd dragged her through my shit rather than leave her alone. I tried reminding myself *again* that she would have been killed anyway, but it did no good. This was yet another person I'd been powerless to save from rape, assault, or death. I lived every day with the guilt of my sisters' experiences. And now Hannah—the person with the most vibrant, most interesting soul I've ever taken the time to know—had been reduced to a shell.

Somehow, I knew Cassandra had done this to spite me. But why? It wasn't like I'd damaged her grand plan, or even grazed it. What were twelve bad Lapsi to this malicious army? I was her chew toy for no reason, and Hannah'd gotten clobbered in the path of destruction.

"They're all tearing each other apart down there," Hannah said, breaking through my thoughts.

She was standing at the window, looking down at the city below. A good eight inches of her long blonde hair had been singed away in the explosion. It looked choppy and windblown yet still effortlessly styled. She'd kicked her shoes off, and the frayed open back of her tank top fluttered in the breeze from the ceiling fan.

We don't even have any extra clothes on us, I mused miserably.

"It's like they're rioting, but there's nothing to riot about."

"It's just fear. And chaos." I rested my elbows on my legs and put my hands together. They'd stopped shaking, but a small tremor still hummed in the tendons of my forearms.

"And opportunity-seizers looting and killing because there is no one to stop them."

"Chaos," she repeated tonelessly.

I wanted to go to her and embrace her from behind. I hadn't wanted to embrace her like that in all our time together, but I wanted to now, to see if she still had any warmth in her. I'd taken it all for granted, and now it was gone. But I didn't move from my spot on the couch.

"Why do I feel like this, Jeb?" she said, turning from the window. A zing lanced through me at hearing my name spoken in her cold, unfeeling tone. She was turning her hands over in front of her, flexing her fingers. "Like, I have so much energy ... I feel like I can lift a bus over my head."

"They gave you Lapsi blood," I explained as carefully as possible.

Her hands stopped moving, and she looked at me. A question was on her lips, but she didn't ask it.

"You haven't been changed," I assured her calmly. *Except for your soul.* "It'll wear off, but right now you're...I guess, *part* Lapsi." *And all the way soulless.* "You're stronger, and you'll heal quickly. But you'll probably be a bit jittery."

"Like I had, like, eight espressos," she said, nodding. "This feels good though. I feel...powerful."

"Yeah, imagine dancing while you're hyped like this." I felt a small smile on my lips as I imagined it.

She didn't smile though. Instead, she froze, and her eyes looked distant. Her eyes moved back and forth a little, as if she was thinking through something or trying to draw something out of herself. Then she shook her head and looked at me.

In her soulless eyes, I saw the closest thing that she could muster to sadness. Then, quickly, muted anger. *Oh. Crap.* I realized I'd been thoughtless.

Dancing brought her joy and happiness. It gave her a tether in a mean, chaotic world. But joy was contained in the *soul*, and now comfort, joy, happiness, enjoyment...those were all *gone*. She was trying to conjure up the feeling dancing used to give her, and it simply *wasn't there*.

"They also set a Soul Eater on you, as by now you probably realize. And it...took your soul," I explained slowly and delicately. "Cassandra is using harvested souls for her barrier. So it's possible yours wasn't consumed. It's a small comfort, but..." Her eyes showed me nothing but the same would-be sorrow as a moment earlier. "I'm sorry, Hannah," I said softly. I wanted to get up and go to her, but I didn't. It wouldn't help. "I am so sorry."

She shook her head as if to dismiss the subject and turned back to the window. Before she crossed her arms in front of her, I saw the tremor in her hands.

We were both silent for a while. We could hear the screams and panic down below, but it was distant. After a few moments, Hannah turned from the window and walked, determined, to the kitchen. Curious, I followed. I reached the kitchen as she was twirling a corkscrew into a bottle of wine she'd found.

"What are you doing?" I asked, deadpan, and took a seat at the counter. I was drained from my rageful outburst. I couldn't put any more feeling into my voice.

"We lost, Jeb," she said simply. She didn't need to leverage the cork from the bottle. She just pulled with one short tug and out popped the cork. Her lips twitched into a semi-pleased, semi-impressed smirk. She put the wine opener down, cork and all, on the counter. "We're stuck in this *New Troy*, run by a crazy bitch, and we have no plan. *But* we have this lovely space for the night. And we have wine." She held the bottle up in a kind of *cheers* gesture. "So I'm having a drink."

"That's not for us, though. This stuff isn't ours to use," I said, purely for the sake of arguing.

"Who's keeping track right now?" she said, shrugging. "There are people down there looting. They're either stealing what isn't nailed down or breaking and burning what they can't carry. Oh, no, I'm taking a bottle of wine? Sue me." She took a swig from the bottle.

I released a humorless snort in response. She wasn't wrong, but it felt weird that I was being the voice of moral reason. I pushed a wine glass on the counter toward her. She picked it up and looked at me with an unreadable expression. Then she smiled mockingly, lifted the glass, and dropped it. It shattered on the counter, spraying shards everywhere.

"Jesus," I said without meaning to.

I stood and brought over a trash can. I started brushing the shards off the counter into the can. Hannah picked up a large piece of the broken glass and looked at it. She squeezed it in her palm and stared as it cut into her flesh. She laid her hand flat, and the wounds healed within a moment. She looked at her hand curiously. Then she shrugged and tossed the shard into the can, picked up the bottle again, and held it up, near her mouth.

"You think I can even get drunk when I'm like this? All hyped on Lapsi blood?" she asked, looking at the lip of the wine bottle.

"I don't think you can." I honestly didn't know, but I doubted it.

"Is that a challenge?" she said, lifting an eyebrow.

I shook my head. "No, it's not a challenge. Do what you want," I said with a tired shrug. I didn't have it in me to banter with this soulless version of my friend. I leaned my back against the wall of the kitchen, a few feet from her, and shoved my hands into the pockets of my jeans.

She paused in bringing the bottle to her lips, her mocking smile faltering. She looked at me with an unreadable expression. Her eyebrows knitted together, and she lowered the bottle back to the counter.

"I don't *want* anything, Jeb," she said quietly. "And it's a first for me, not to have a single want, a single care or worry. I don't know what to do with myself."

She looked so lost suddenly, but still unfeeling. I reached out and put my hand over hers on the counter. A poor comfort—one soulless hand on another—but it was all I could manage.

"What all happened tonight?" I asked after a few seconds. Maybe changing the subject would make this less sad.

She shrugged nonchalantly. "I went with Riley to some parties—conquering several fears at once, mind you—" She paused. She was trying to conjure up this feeling of fear, I knew, but she only had the memory of it. Like an aftertaste or a wisp of perfume that stirs up a distant memory of a loved one. "At the last one, I saw a guy leading a drugged girl up the stairs..."

Oh no. I could see where this was going.

"I chased after him, into a room."

"Why did you leave Riley?" I blurted unintentionally. "You were safe with him."

"Oh, yes, *so safe.*" She scoffed. "Don't forget he was captured shortly after I left him. If I hadn't run off, I'd be with him, not here with you."

But you'd still have a soul, probably, I almost said but refrained because I didn't know that for certain. She would probably be dead, or they'd still have taken her soul to spite me.

"I confronted the guy. The girl got out of there, then he attacked me instead and started pulling at my clothes, but I defended myself. He tripped and broke his neck on his desk." She paused for only half a second at this admission and plowed forward. "Then Cassandra showed up. I made out with her for a bit. She asked me to join her, but I told her where to shove it, and on my way out of the house, I was attacked by another Lapsus. And I lost my fucking soul."

There were *several* details in that list of events that I desperately wanted to circle back to, but right at that moment, I found myself smiling, despite the somber mood. These were her soul's last moments, and they were being told to me with such banality. It was so close to humorous that I found myself *almost* laughing.

I closed the distance between us, shaking my head incredulously. I put a hand behind her head and pulled her into my chest. I rested my chin on the top of her head and stood there for a moment, savoring the feeling of her. She stood stiffly at first, but then her hands brushed my forearms, running softly and distractingly up my arms to my shoulders.

I pulled back and looked down at her. I opened my mouth to question her, but before I could, she reached up and pulled my face to hers. Our lips met and I was too startled to object—*if* I was going to object.

This wasn't a slow, sensual kiss, however; there was a *demand* to it. I put my hands to her hips as she pressed herself closer into me. Her fingers ran roughly through my hair, her nails grazing my scalp. It raised a growl in my throat that escaped my lips as a ragged hiss. Any protest I might have had left my body through that hiss. I returned her hungry kisses with a fervent hunger of my own, nipping at her bottom lip a little before exploring her mouth with my tongue.

She shoved suddenly against my chest, and my back hit the wall behind me with a soft thud. With the Lapsi blood coursing through her, for once we were equals in strength. I started to pull her against me again, but she resisted. Her hands went to the buckle of my belt, and staring hard and mischievously into my eyes, she undid the belt, and with a rough tug, it was gone.

Ordinarily, I would probably protest this. We were *friends*, and crossing this line with a friend required a little more discussion than the assumptions and challenges we were making. But I'd reached a point in my mental exhaustion that shut all of that down. I—and from her signals, I assumed Hannah agreed—just wanted to say *fuck it* and enjoy a moment or two of pure, passionate *release*.

She tossed my belt aside, and I let out another growl before pushing myself away from the wall and closing the distance between us again. With one hand, I cupped the back of her head and kept her lips pressed firmly to mine. With my other, I grabbed a handful of her ruined shirt and pulled. With one tug, the last few tatters at her back came loose, and I tossed the fabric away. Beneath it, she wore only a thin lacy bra, also nearly ruined at the back.

I traced a line of rough kisses from her ear down her neck. My fangs started to sharpen at the feel of her pulse against my lips, but I held them back. She shuddered against me, feeling the brief point of them before they retracted, but I knew it wasn't from fear or revulsion. I continued moving my lips down her neck to her shoulder, and I unhooked the back of her bra and slid the straps from her shoulders. As it fell to the cold tile floor without a sound, I cupped a small breast in each of my hands and returned my lips to hers, trying but failing to not kiss her too hungrily or grasp her warm flesh too eagerly.

Her hands found the front of my jeans again, and she managed to get the button loose before I dropped my hands to her hips and lifted her against me. I turned and pushed her back into the wall—gentler than she'd shoved me against it, but not by much. She responded as I expected, wrapping strong legs around my hips and linking her ankles behind me. She grabbed the hem of my shirt and lifted it over my head. She tossed it aside, and I pinned her wrists against the wall by her head.

I was losing myself in her kiss, her feel, her scent. I nipped again at the soft flesh of her neck and growled against her skin while she shuddered against me with pleasure. Her hands tangled in my hair again, pulling my head into her neck. I wrapped my hands around fistfuls of her hair and growled her name over and over as I breathed in the scent of her. She smelled of fire and smoke and Lapsi, but beneath all of that, it was *her*.

With my eyes closed, her scent conjured a series of images in my head. Her laughing at me as I warily held baby Sophie. Her legs across my lap as she stretched out on the couch. Her dancing and spinning in my arms as we danced together. I felt an unfamiliar pain in my chest as these images flitted across my mind, but I forcibly shut down my thoughts to avoid that pain. *Not now*, I told myself as I brought my lips roughly back to hers.

Putting my arms around her back to support her, I shifted us to the bedroom of the suite. We reappeared at the foot of the bed, and I let us fall onto it. She gasped softly in surprise as she fell against the bed. I hovered above her, holding myself up on one knee and an elbow. I kissed her from her mouth to her bellybutton, and her hands entwined again in my hair. I found her mouth and kissed her, while letting my fingertips brush lightly over the skin of her naked breasts and torso.

She undid the front of my jeans the rest of the way, and the sound that escaped when she coaxed my dick out into the open was a cross between a groan and a growl. *Oh god, how long has it even been? I need this...*I thought feverishly as she ran a thumb over the sensitive tip. I pulled myself away from her to stand at the foot of the bed. Grabbing the waist band of her jeans at her hips, I pulled them and her panties

FALLEN SOULS

off in one swift motion. I let my own jeans fall to the floor and pulled her toward me, to the edge of the bed.

I dropped to my knees and kissed my way up her inner thigh, pacing myself, when I desperately wanted to bury my face between her legs. I wouldn't admit it to her, but it had been over fifty years since I'd done anything sexual with another person. It was difficult to feel good about sex when it just felt *selfish* without *any* feeling behind it.

Her scent was driving me mad, and it grew stronger the farther up her leg I traveled. And beneath the scent of fire, spent adrenaline, and frat party, she smelled *heavenly*.

My lips paused just over her femoral artery, near the inside of her hip joint, and my senses were overwhelmed on all fronts. My hand gripped the curve of her ass, her pulse thrummed beneath my lips and in my ears, and her heady scent—so close—within reach—*fuck*.

I managed to drag myself away from the pull of her blood, though it still pulsed in my ears, and instead dove my head between her legs with a groan.

I was only at it for a moment when she let out a ragged breath and tangled her hand in my hair. Gently, but urgently, she pulled me away from her clit. Following her lead, I stood, and she scooted farther back on the bed.

I crawled over her, nudging her legs apart so I could angle myself between them. She pressed her knees to either side of my hips and reached between us, wrapping deft fingers around my cock. It was my turn to let out a ragged sigh while she stroked me. She clasped her legs around my waist and, her hand still on my dick, positioned the tip at her entrance, guiding me in. One thrust and I'd be buried inside her.

I paused and cupped the side of her face, angling it up to look in my eyes. I wanted to savor this for just a moment. The distraction of carnal release would evaporate as soon as we finished, and then we'd be back to the real world. But looking in her eyes and seeing the determined lust there, and nothing else, woke my brain up.

This should *mean* something for Hannah—and it would if she still had a soul. This was the first time she was having sex since her assault. Shouldn't this be a little more—not *special. Special* is such a human word—but, I guess, more *meaningful*?

She'd lost her soul today. She wasn't the same person she had been three hours earlier when we'd parted ways. She was still reeling, and she was semi-high on Lapsi blood. Could I really consider this consent? But we were both letting go tonight. This wasn't love, this was stress relief. But was it?

"Wa–wait—" I sputtered out, surprising myself, pulling my hand from her face. "Shouldn't we—Let's just think for a second."

"No waiting. No thinking. Just do it," she said huskily, shaking her head.

Her hands were on my dick again, fingers brushing over the most sensitive flesh of my body. Pleasure coursed through me again, and I moaned. *Fuck*.

"I–I can't," I heard myself say. My voice was husky and breathless, but I realized I meant the words. But my traitorous hand went to her bare hip and upper thigh, where it pressed against my side. *Fuck*, I thought silently even as I said, "Not like this. Hannah, let go."

I pressed my fists into the mattress by her shoulders, ready to push myself away, if only she'd release her legs from around me. She didn't at first, though, and instead tensed, as if to latch on tighter. Her hand was still on my dick, and if she moved a single muscle in that hand, my resolve would break. All she'd have to do then was flex her leg muscles and she'd pull me into her. I'd be a lost man, and I'd hate myself for it.

But I trusted her to respect the rules of consent. Soul or no soul, she'd never take from someone what was taken from her. I knew it from experience: moral principles—especially those lodged in experience—remained, even after the attached emotions vaporized. She just needed a minute to navigate her selfish, soulless drives.

I watched the subtle emotions on her face, knowing the cogs were turning and that moral compass was surfacing. Her eyes bore into mine, no doubt assessing that I was barely—and desperately—holding onto my resolve. Her mouth set into a hard line, and her nostrils flared in irritation, but after an agonizingly tense moment, her legs released me, and her hands and feet fell heavily to the mattress.

She released a frustrated sigh as I crawled off the bed. I tried not to look at her, still naked and gorgeous on the bed and staring at me stoically while I pulled my jeans back up and zipped them. I ran my hands roughly through my hair, then over my face.

"I hope this isn't the part where you tell me you're a 400-year-old virgin, and your Puritan upbringing says you can't fuck outside of marriage," she said sarcastically after a moment. She pulled herself to the foot of the bed and crossed her legs.

"Shut up" was all I managed to mumble through clenched teeth. Even though *I* was the one to pull away, my dick and its army of blood vessels hadn't yet caught up with the program, and it was as irritated about my decision as Hannah was. I couldn't fight both battles at once.

"Then what?" she demanded impatiently, not giving me the moment I was silently begging for. "Because that's all this is. That's all it can be, now, right? Sex without feelings."

"Is it? Is it really? Shouldn't it be a little more than that?" I blurted before I'd completely sorted through my thoughts. I didn't know what I was trying to say. "After everything, do you really want sex between us to be meaningless?"

"I thought *I* was supposed to be the one with these hang-ups," she said, rolling her eyes. I looked away from her to keep myself from glaring at her. "It's just basic sex. Don't bring feelings into this, because I have none. *You* have none."

"But it should *mean* something to you," I argued. I put my hands into the pockets of my jeans to keep them from fidgeting—or reaching for her. "It should mean something to you whether I care. Like it means something to *me* whether *you* care."

Her face changed subtly. One eye narrowed, and she tilted her head, perplexed. She stood up from the bed and walked toward me.

She was ambivalent at standing before me naked, and it was yet another reminder that she'd lost part of herself. Not that she'd been prudish, but she had that adorable human trait that makes them want to cover themselves or attach meaning to letting another see them so exposed. But here she was, uncovered and uncaring, and it startled me how much it hurt to see her like that. The rage bubbled to the surface again, but I tamped it back down and looked away from her as she approached.

"Do you love me?" she asked quietly. There wasn't anything in her voice: no hope, or wonder, or even real curiosity. It was just a basic question.

"I don't know," I said honestly. I made myself look her in the face. "I don't think I can. In the usual way..."

"Then I can't either, can I?"

"Yeah, but did you?" I found myself asking, but I had no idea why. "Before this, did *she* have any feelings toward me? Did she care?"

"Don't talk about 'her' like I am not 'her,'" she snapped, her frown deepening. "Don't talk like she's dead. She is me, and I'm alive, and I'm stronger for it. It could be a lot worse."

But sometimes it felt like it would be better to have died than live like a shell. *You don't realize it yet, but you will someday,* I thought but didn't say aloud. *Unless I can reverse this somehow.*

I'd meant it when I told Hannah her soul probably hadn't been consumed. It was possible it was being used in the soul-barrier grid. Or, more likely, Cassandra had it with her, as a trophy.

I took Hannah's face in my hands and looked her in the eyes.

"I promise I will find a way to reverse this," I told her.

"Whatever," she said, pushing my hands from her face. "I'm going to shower."

She turned her back to me and walked away. She seemed calm, but I saw the tension in her bare shoulder blades. I also realized as she walked away, that she'd never answered my question about caring about me.

CHAPTER 27

HANNAH

I'd known something was drastically different about me as soon as Jeb woke me up on the pavement. It wasn't just that I suddenly felt strong and unstoppable, but something else. I'd spent too much time in therapy, analyzing my thoughts and feelings, to not notice the sudden, complete *absence* of them. I was completely numb, and because of that, my thoughts came more clear, more rational, and more calculating. So having Jeb describe the monster to me, like he knew the type personally, confirmed what I already knew.

I wasn't afraid or sad or worried. I just *was*.

Jeb's reaction on the other hand was puzzling. He turned into a being of rage, and I would have found it startling—terrifying, even—if I still had a soul, but instead, I just watched, curious. He'd told me he couldn't feel, but apparently, emotion did still exist in us, just *very* deep down.

When he made me think about dance, I tried for a moment to conjure up the usual feelings I associated with dance: the release and creation, the happiness of doing something so beautiful and so *me*. But nothing came. I was hollow.

It's why I'd wanted sex so badly. Because in those moments I *could* feel. Even if it was just the physical feelings, it was pleasure and it was *something*, and it felt great, but Jeb pulling back and refusing brought the hollowness back.

Emotions aside, the shower *felt amazing*—and not just because I finished for myself what Jeb wouldn't. The hot water was enough to send me moaning with pleasure. I'd been covered in grime from the atmosphere of the parties I went to, the probably disease-ridden bed I'd been forced onto, and the ash, smoke, and debris from the explosion. It felt wonderful to get all of that off my skin.

As I scrubbed my hair and my scalp, I realized that I'd lost about eight inches of my hair. It now hung two or so inches past my shoulders when wet. Oh well. It was still long enough to be pulled back into a ponytail, even though I had no hair ties, no hairbrush, and no makeup. I hadn't had any of these things for over a week now.

I didn't bother covering myself with a towel when I left the bathroom. Who the hell cared? Jeb? He could eat a dick if he "cared" that I was naked. He was on the couch as I emerged, with the TV on. He glanced briefly my way, but he didn't react. *Good.*

I moved immediately into the bedroom and retrieved my underwear and jeans. I pulled them on and went to the kitchen to retrieve my damaged, but still functional bra. I didn't have a shirt, though. Jeb had retrieved his from the floor of the kitchen and put it on, so I didn't have the option to steal that.

I grabbed the bottle of wine from the counter and brought it with me into the suite's living room. I didn't really want to drink it, but I was embracing this new "why the fuck not?" mood. I sat on the couch, as far on the edge as I could so I didn't suggest a want for intimacy.

Jeb had the news on, oddly enough. We were technically in a dystopian hellscape at the moment, and you don't usually imagine that scenario with the news or cable or hot water, even.

"We have power," I said. It came out as a statement, but I really meant it as a question. *Huh. Inflection and facial expressions require actual effort when you don't have a soul. Interesting.*

"Yeah, Cassandra made sure that most facilities and conveniences stayed operational," Jeb explained. He had more practice being soulless than I, so he'd been able to read the question in my voice. "I imagine she did so to cut down on a lot of the panic and fear, and to keep us somewhat functional. But I think her main reason was—"

"To communicate with the outside world still," I finished for him. I was quickly realizing that, when you remove emotion from things, your brain gets to conclusions faster. Psychopaths really did have an advantage, apparently. "She wants this to be broadcasted and noticed."

"Exactly." He nodded, but his eyes were still on the screen. "I figured our new queen will be making an announcement to the outside world any minute."

"Oh, did I miss it?" I said, feigning intrigue. I think it worked, but it sounded flat. It was sarcasm anyway, though, so it didn't matter.

"No, I haven't seen anything yet." He turned the sound up on the TV.

On the screen were on-hand reports—mostly cell phone footage of Lapsi attacks, looting, and general panic, from the past two hours. Some—Jeb identified them for me—were filmed and explained by Lapsi. Most, however, were by humans. And then it would cut to anchormen and desk-reporters analyzing these videos for the public.

It was weird hearing people on the outside—people with no knowledge of magic—try to make sense of what was happening in Portland. They thought it was Antifa or foreign terrorists. It was almost laughable, but it wouldn't be long until they were enlightened.

In fact, it wasn't long at all. A moment later, the report cut to a video recording of Cassandra addressing the outside world.

Both Jeb and I straightened up involuntarily as Cassandra's face appeared on the screen. She looked beautiful and serene—like a queen at her coronation—wearing a red satin dress that still resembled a Grecian gown with gold embroidery on the empire waist. She looked like a true Classic queen—while I was squatting in an Airbnb in only a pair of jeans and a black bralette from Target.

Distantly, I realized she'd cut her long fiery red hair, and it now fell in waves just past her shoulders. *My length, now*, I noted absently. It was strange though, because Jeb had implied that after being changed, hair never grew back. Cassandra had gone millennia with her long, gorgeous locks, and she cut them off now?

"Hello human world," Cassandra said to the camera. Her smile was flirtatious and mocking. "By now, I believe I've caught your attention. If I haven't, then there's even less hope for humanity than I thought. If the loss of hundreds of human lives across such a small space of land doesn't capture the eye of the free world, probably nothing will.

"I have captured only a portion of this city, but rest assured. Expansion is our goal until we have the entire city to call our own. Who is we, though? Foreign, politically motivated terrorists? Aliens? No, hardly. We are Lapsi, the Fallen Favorites. Nothing but a small offshoot of the human species that you all unsophisticatedly call *vampires*. Until recently, we were unable to come together and form a community of our own. But we are no longer denied this, and we deserve a city. We deserve a civilization with rules and order, and a seat at the table of *humanity*. It is our world too after all, isn't it?

"I know this looks violent now, but it had to be done to seize control. My eventual, unyielding goal, above all else, is peace. So I implore you all to sit back and wait for us to establish this. We are self-sufficient. We have retained electricity, water systems, health systems, and law enforcement systems. Food transport and essential supplies will not be interrupted; we have seen to everything. Your people who are now contained within our boundaries of this New Troy will be—majorly—unharmed.

"That being said, I'm not naïve. I've been around too long to know how humanity will react to such perceived savagery. But I advise you, interference and infiltration is futile. We are protected by a dark, powerful kind of magic. And I also advise against your trigger-happy knee-jerk response of *bombing* this city, as I'm sure you are already considering doing. This will be unwise. We do not die easily, and all bombs will do is kill more defenseless humans. And there are far more of your precious humans in this city than there are of my kind."

This serene, but menacing note of finality was a good threat against potential violence, convincing the enemy that it would backfire. That the ends wouldn't justify the means. It was chilling, but would it be believed? I had no idea.

"Magnificent use of rhetoric," I said sarcastically as the report ended.

More reports followed that one, but it was more of the same madness we were living. Jeb switched off the TV and looked over at me, taking in my appearance for the first time since I'd showered. I imagined how I must look. Scrubbed clean, but wearing dirty, singed jeans. My hair was clean but recently shorn and very uneven—the pieces in the front were still eight inches longer than the rest.

Jeb stood and walked around the couch. From a chair by the door, he retrieved his jacket and button-down flannel and handed me the latter, with apology in his eyes. I wrapped it around me, not bothering to button it, and realized for the first time that Jeb had a distinct scent. The Lapsi blood really did heighten all my senses. *If only it could heighten my feelings, too*, I found myself thinking, to distract me from the scent invading my nostrils, *then he wouldn't look at me with sad-puppy eyes all the time.*

His eyebrows drew together, and he looked at his jacket. From one of his pockets, he pulled out his phone. He thumbed through it briefly, then handed it to me and sat back down on the couch.

"Texts from Libby," he explained. "Apparently texts can still come in."

The earliest text was from ten p.m., around the time we were meeting with Riley and Mason. That was only a few hours ago, but it felt like a lifetime. This first text was asking for an update. The next text was just after midnight, after the explosions that leveled several houses, and after the freeways fell.

The texts were in quick succession after that, each one more panicked than the next. She wanted Jeb to call her. She wanted to know that I was okay. She threatened to kill Jeb if anything happened to me—I wondered if losing my soul forfeited Jeb's life in Libby's eyes. It probably did.

The second to last text brought up baby Sophie. Sophie knew something was up, sensing her mother's panic, and her usual sunny disposition had turned stormy. Sophie was worried about me, according to Libby. In her small, baby brain, she somehow knew I was in trouble.

I tried to conjure up feelings about this. I remembered baby Sophie, and I remembered the immediate feeling of love toward her. It'd felt like my heart was melting, but in a good way. I remembered laughing as Sophie laughed her guttural, baby laugh of pure, untainted happiness. I could recall all of this, but they were just little whispers of memory that told me how I *should* be feeling. I was still just numb.

The last text was Libby resigning herself to the possibility that he—and consequentially me—was dead. But she still had hope. She hoped that maybe he just couldn't text back, and insisted she was ready to help if she could, if he would just text her back.

"Shouldn't we call her? She might have advice or insight," I said.

I was about to touch the phone icon to call her, but Jeb put his hand over mine and took the phone from me.

"I don't want to call outside the territory," he said, shaking his head. "In case it's being monitored, I don't want it revealed that I have outside help. It would put her and her family in danger."

I nodded and looked away. I got up from the couch and went to the window. The sleeves of Jeb's shirt were too long on me, and I worked at folding them over on themselves so they came to just above the bend of my elbow.

The Airbnb was at the top of one of the taller buildings of downtown. Out in the distance, over the rubble of the freeway overpasses, was a kind of silver shimmering curtain.

"How is she doing this?" I asked. I remembered that he'd gone with Mason to find this out. I hadn't heard yet what he'd found. "How is she keeping people inside? Is it that...mist out there?"

"That mist is a barrier, yeah. I don't know the exact how, but I know enough to assume that it is a form of dark, *very ancient* magic," he explained. "I'm assuming it's how Troy managed to stay impenetrable while under siege for eight years. It uses souls."

"Souls?" I said, startled. I turned from the window to face him.

"I don't know *whose*, but *lots* of them," he said, nodding. He was looking past me, out the window. "It makes sense now why she had a Soul Eater with her, seemingly bound to her. She was collecting souls for this enchantment. I just don't have even a guess as to *how* she did this."

He'd promised me he would reverse my condition. I'd thought he was being sentimental, but did he actually think...?

"You think my soul is out there? In that barrier?" I asked, my eyebrows knitting together.

"It's *possible*," he said, shrugging, but he didn't sound convinced. "It's possible it was consumed and is gone forever. It's possible it was harvested and is out there somewhere." He waved toward the window. "But it seems more likely that it was stolen from you, and Cassandra has it."

Yeah, that checks out. It wouldn't surprise me, with the way that Cassandra seemed a tiny bit obsessed with me—she'd cut her hair to match mine, somehow knowing that mine had been shorn. She was weirdly intrigued by me, even though I was nothing special, and weirdly jealous of Jeb. It made sense that she would wield my soul like a kind of trophy.

"I'll get it back if it is the last thing I do," he promised me, once again.

My mouth lifted slightly into a tiny smile at the cliché line. Soul or no soul, some things were still amusing.

"I'm flattered," I said, slightly sarcastic. "But that shouldn't be our only goal. Our goal should be to free this city, not just settle a score."

"I like focusing on the small goals first," he said, his mouth turning up into a small smile, too. "It seems to work out better that way. My current goal is to survive long enough to make some kind of a plan. Hopefully after that, everything will just fall into place as we go."

I nodded and moved back to the couch and took a seat. We were quiet for a moment. I was sure his mind was clicking away at ideas, but I didn't have that much going on in my head at that moment.

"You should get some sleep," he said. "We don't know what tomorrow will hold."

He was probably right. It was about three a.m. The Lapsi blood had me wired, though. I didn't know if I would be able to sleep, or if I even needed to.

"I don't know if I can while I'm like this," I said, shrugging.

"I don't know either. It's not a common practice," he admitted. "Couldn't hurt to try though. You're still mostly human."

I shrugged again. "What about you?" I asked. He didn't often sleep, because he wasn't human and he didn't need sleep to restore brain function or energy. But he did *sometimes*. At least I thought he did.

"I need to feed," he admitted, sightly regretful. He looked away. "I should feed, but I don't really want to. I don't want to add to the atrocities that are happening down there right now."

He's so oddly compassionate for someone without a soul, I thought as I watched his face from the side. I don't think it was real compassion—or at least it didn't run deep enough to be actual emotion—but more of an ingrained moral compass.

"You should feed anyway," I told him, shrugging. "So you're back to top strength. Like you said, we don't know what tomorrow will hold."

He nodded. While I went to the bedroom to lie down and try to sleep, he left to find someone down on the street to drink from. I removed the borrowed shirt and my jeans and crawled under the covers in just underwear.

I didn't think I'd be able to sleep at all, but somehow, I managed to fall asleep. I woke up a few hours later and realized Jeb was there, lying behind me. He was pressed against me, with an arm over my hip and his other arm under my pillow. I didn't move away or disturb him. I wasn't sure if he was actually asleep or just lying there. Sleepily, I put my hand beneath my pillow and took his hand in mine. A moment later, I was back asleep.

CHAPTER 28

JEB

I woke up when Hannah got out of bed, but I pretended I didn't. I'd surprised myself by falling asleep in the first place. I didn't need sleep often, but the mental exhaustion had returned by the time I came back to the suite, fully fed.

I stayed within the building to feed—within the floor even. I'd surprised the man down the hall—foolishly, I hadn't realized people would still be awake all night with everything happening, but I quickly put him to sleep and fed. I took less than I usually would have. With everything going on, I didn't want to sap too much strength from a human. They had it bad enough right now.

Hannah was fast asleep when I returned. Asleep, she looked peaceful and relaxed, not deadpan and cold like when she'd woken up without a soul. I crawled under the covers before quite realizing what I was doing. Then I curled up against her. I'd never *cuddled* anyone before, so it was odd that it came so naturally.

After an hour, she shifted in her sleep—or maybe she woke briefly. Her arm moved under her pillow and brushed my hand. After a pause, her hand was softly, sleepily entwined in mine. Her breathing softened and normalized again. I put my face into her hair and breathed in. The next thing I knew I was waking up to her movement.

Something had changed over the past several days. Was it love? I didn't know. I'd never felt anything but familial love: for my mother and for my sisters. I didn't think this was love the way it's usually written or shown in movies, but I wouldn't say it *wasn't* love.

We had a weird mutual dependance, but certainly she didn't realize how mutual it'd become. At first, it seemed one sided but faceted. I was protecting her because she was weak and helpless and because I'd dragged her into this, and I felt like I owed it to her. But now it was more.

Now, I needed her too. I'd developed a sense of purpose that I'd never had before. If I hadn't met her, where would I be? I'd have found out about Cassandra, but would I have pursued it any further? Or would I have left it alone and watched from a distance with figurative popcorn in hand? That sounded more likely.

Instead, Hannah happened, and she somehow made me into more of a doer than a watcher. This human I'd started to care about, who spurred me into action when I would have just stood aside. Who would use eternity to *dance*, and who wanted to enter a thankless, demanding career because she just wanted to *help*.

And then they took Hannah's soul: the thing that made her *her*. Gone. All gone. Just to taunt me. Or to punish her for refusing Cassandra.

I'd shielded and buried myself for years, convinced I was better alone. I was never cursed to be alone: I *chose* it instead. But now I couldn't see myself going back to that. I didn't want to watch from a distance anymore. I wasn't about to start a rock band and become famous or force a city to be my community, but *small* things. Starting with getting Hannah's soul back and dancing with her again. If that was love, it was love. A gentle, simple, caring, selfish *and* selfless love.

After spending about half an hour with my thoughts, I got up and out of the bed. My jeans were on the floor where I'd dropped them last night. And so were Hannah's. But the shirt I'd given her was gone. My jeans were a little loose without the belt, but that was still in the kitchen. I gave my hair one last hand-brush and then left the bedroom.

Hannah was sitting curled up on the far side of the couch. Her bare legs were tucked under her, and her toes were beneath a blanket she'd found. She'd tracked down some scissors, apparently, and evened out the long front pieces of her hair. It was all relatively the same length but still choppy. She had the TV on and was watching the news with the volume low. In her hands she clutched—of all things—a mug of what was definitely coffee. By all appearances, she could be on a relaxing vacation and not day one of a dystopian world.

She glanced my way as I entered the living room and held the mug of coffee aloft in a kind of salute.

"I thought it was too much wishful thinking as I looked in the kitchen. But I found coffee! No food though." She took a sip from the mug and looked back at the TV.

I approached the couch and took a seat on the opposite end.

"They've cut off the outside feeds," she said. The volume was almost muted, but it had subtitles on. "Instead, all the reports are from within the zone. They're telling us not to panic and to stay calm, that we'll be taken care of. And they're telling us where to find medical assistance and food. They're even reporting on the weather. As if anyone actually gives a fuck about whether it's raining right now."

I nodded but didn't say anything. I watched the reports for a while. Down on the streets, it looked like the apocalypse, with broken windows, burned out cars, and spray paint everywhere. But it looked like people were starting to clean up the mess of last night. Boards were in windows. Stations with water and grabbable food had been set up. Did the humans do that or the Lapsi?

"What a mess," I found myself saying aloud. "What an absolute mess."

"What are we going to do, Jeb?" she asked quietly.

"I still have no clue," I mumbled, rubbing my fingers into my left eye.

"We kill Cassandra. And we disrupt the barrier so people can escape," Hannah said, reiterating what we'd discussed last night.

"But we have no idea where Cassandra is holed up or how to find her," I said.

"You could use me," she said. My head perked up and turned toward her in bewilderment. "You could use me as bait again."

"That's not an option," I said firmly. I think she was attempting to tease me, but it hurt to imagine her being bait again. That'd been under different circumstances, and it had been before I cared.

"Fine, maybe not bait," she said, sipping from her coffee again. "I could be more of ... a lure."

"That's the same thing," I pointed out.

"Yes, but it *sounds* nicer," she said. My eyes darted to her, and she gave me a teasing grin. She was getting better at faking facial expressions.

"If anything, *I* should be the bait," I argued after a moment. "She seems to be driven in a lot of things by her obsession with me."

"No, she's intrigued by you," she corrected me. "But I'm the one she's obsessed with. You can't deny that."

I couldn't because it was true. The way she'd looked at Hannah while we were shopping. The way she'd asked Hannah to join her. The way she'd chopped her hair off to match Hannah's, *after* Hannah refused her. Cassandra was insane and dangerous.

I wished I knew how to exploit Cassandra's fascination with Hannah without risking Hannah's safety, because otherwise I had nothing. Cassandra was *insane*—calculating, gifted with foresight, and determined—but unpredictable. I wouldn't willingly send Hannah into her arms. I wouldn't do it.

"Fine," Hannah said after I didn't respond for a while.

We sat in silence, with the TV making barely any noise. She finished her coffee and got up to use the bathroom. When she returned to the living room, she'd put her jeans back on, and she'd taken my belt and fastened it around her natural waist, making the boxy shirt appear more like a fitted tunic. *I guess I'm not getting my belt back.* Not that it mattered in the slightest.

"Not to put too fine a point on it," she said after a few more minutes of quiet, "but I am going to need food at some point."

Crap. I ran a hand roughly over my neck. In everything, I'd forgotten that she needed things like water and food. *Stupid, shortsighted fool.*

"I'm fine for now," she assured me. "Really. Without a soul, I don't associate hunger with any emotion. It's just a physical feeling and it can be ignored. All I'm saying is that *eventually*, it'll be a concern. For now, I have coffee and water. And a strange desire for something metallic to suck on..."

"Okay," I said with a small huff. The metallic thing had to be a side effect of the Lapsi blood working through her system: a craving for blood but not a *need* for it.

I could forage from the neighbors in this building, but that seemed unethical at this moment. Resources were going to be scarce, people were scared. I'd seen how panic affects people when it came to food and toilet paper and water. It isn't pretty, and I didn't want to add to that.

The news said food stations were being put up, but venturing out into the open wasn't safe for us. But I couldn't see any way to get food that wasn't stealing or going out where the enemy could see us.

"You'd be surprised how hard it is to make a plan to take down a tyrant when you're weaponless and, generally, utterly fucked."

"I'm not surprised," she said with a hollow laugh. I hadn't realized I'd spoken aloud. "We're in the same boat here, remember?"

"I'm sorry." I didn't know why I felt guilty for saying it aloud. "I didn't think I was talking."

"I'm so offended, Jeb," she said in a sarcastic deadpan voice. A moment passed while neither of us spoke. "What about your weapons that you buried? We couldn't get there last night because everyone was around and panicking. Should we try again? See if it's a little deader out there."

I looked at her sharply at the dark, tasteless joke. She immediately apologized by wincing a little and dropping her gaze to her mug.

"We could make an outing of it," she continued, a little more subdued. "Go check if your weapons are retrievable and then grab some munchies. Sounds like a decent date in a hellscape to me."

I didn't see any other way, though I didn't like that she was treating it like a joke. I knew she was just trying to navigate where *personality* fits into soullessness, and she was an impressively adaptable human. She'd figure herself out soon.

We left the Airbnb around noon. I figured we'd given the city enough time to relatively recover from their shock—at least enough to not be bum-rushing places, anymore.

About two blocks from the Airbnb's building were a number of food stations lining the pavement outside a strip of restaurants that normally fed the office rats during the week. Though their windows were smashed and their doors hadn't opened, they were still operational, feeding the masses of stranded people because they had the supplies and perishables to use up.

While waiting in line at a stall, we gleaned from others that a grocery store a few blocks away was letting people in a few at a time, but not charging them. I assumed the "people" letting them in were Lapsi. We'd have to use that as an option, but we could wait until tomorrow, after I had more time to gather my wits.

We got Hannah's food and took a seat on a curb, away from everyone else. Hannah ate in silence while I kept my head on a swivel, ready to shift us back to the Airbnb at the smallest sign of Lapsi trouble.

Next, we headed over to the park at the edge of the zone. The barrier prevented me from shifting outside the zone, but I could shift anywhere within it that wasn't separately warded. But even though the world was aware of us now, shifting in broad daylight after a hostile takeover seemed like a way to incite more panic. As we neared the park, there were roadblocks and Lapsi in police uniforms, blocking the way forward. I diverted us down an alley and approached the park from a narrow service alley.

Before stepping back into the sunlight on the other side, I froze and backtracked, trying to shield Hannah from seeing what I'd seen.

Bodies. At least a dozen bodies were lined up on the sidewalk by the mouth of the alley which bordered the park. An ambulance was parked at the curb, with its back doors open. One Lapsus carried a body over his shoulder to the cab, and another stood by, having just deposited his load.

"Of all the things I thought I'd be doing on the first day of our revolution, body disposal was not among them," the first Lapsus grumbled as he hoisted the body into the ambulance. He had shaggy blond hair, worn long and dirty like Kurt Cobain's grunge following. "I thought the whole point of this plan was to step into the light and not worry about who sees us. So why do we have to clean up and *dispose* of the bodies from our triumph last night?"

"It's meant to reduce panic," the other Lapsus reminded him, with a tone that suggested his patience was wearing thin. This one was tall and lanky, with dark skin and a close-cropped afro. Something about the fact that he was still wearing his glasses hinted that he had been a banker or office IT manager in his past life. "It's easier to entice complacency and acceptance among the humans if there aren't bodies decomposing on the street."

"But look at this one. This one wasn't even one of our kills," Captain Grunge said, motioning to the body at his feet. "This one was bludgeoned with a brick. Why is it our responsibility to clean this up? And what the hell do we care about what humans *think*? They're cattle."

"But when cattle panic, they stampede," Ex-Banker quipped sensibly. "If they're fed and left relatively unharmed, they accept captivity."

"Let 'em stampede. I like it better when they run," Captain Grunge growled, but he bent down to lift another body.

Ex-Banker rolled his eyes and tilted his head toward the sky in his annoyance. He took off his glasses and looked at them incredulously and tossed them aside. He watched them bounce on the pavement, and when he glanced back up, his eyes found mine, and we both froze. I felt like a deer caught in headlights, but his expression didn't change. Instead he rolled his eyes again at me and smirked.

"You know what, I think I can take this from here," he said to Captain Grunge's back. He stepped closer to him, taking his hand from his pocket. "You're dismissed."

He rammed the silver knife into Captain Grunge's back and twisted for good measure. The silver pierced his heart and destroyed the magic flowing through him. He wasn't an old Lapsus, but he wasn't freshly made either, so rather than dusting, he collapsed into an almost dry but still juicy, grotesque skeleton.

Ex-Banker turned back to me, frowning, with the blade still in his hand. I slid as smoothly as I could to completely obscure Hannah from view and held my hands up innocently. He shrugged and shook his head, as if shaking himself free of any guilt at what he'd just done. He pocketed the knife and hefted his partner's rotten corpse, holding it away from him so it didn't further soil his clothes, and lobbed it into the ambulance's cab.

In that small, disturbing encounter, I realized Cassandra's plan moving forward. The menacing ones were expendable grunts. Cassandra gave them their night of fun, but she was going to eradicate the bad dogs for the sake of order, once they'd served their purpose.

While Ex-Banker was occupied, I rethought my no-shifting decision. I spun and pulled Hannah with me into a crouch, then shifted to the opposite side of the park from him and the ambulance.

It was a strange little sunken park that had three distinct zones. One side was a grassy field, and the middle was dominated by tall yellow grass, with a cement path through it. The third zone was an urban koi pond with the cement walkway fanning out on the far side into an industrial, artsy retaining wall. I'd hidden my grenades in the tall yellow grass, near the koi pond.

I couldn't decide if I felt relieved or scared when I realized my weapons were gone. I'd told Mason where they were, but I was still twenty percent sure that he was a dick, even if he acted like my ally and let me escape what I'd assumed was a trap.

"How do you think someone found them?" Hannah asked as I stood up.

I hadn't told her about Mason and escaping from the underground tunnel system. It hadn't crossed my mind until just then. I opened my mouth to tell her, but before I could—

"You have some serious balls coming back into this city," a voice snarled behind us. "But now you're trapped here with all your enemies."

My hand twitched toward my pocket.

"Ah-ah!" the Lapsi behind me said, stopping me. In my peripheral, a dark-skinned Lapsus had a gun pressed to the back of Hannah's head. "Don't you dare, unless you want him to blow her pretty little brains into this koi pond."

My hand moved away from my pocket.

"On your knees, both of you," another male voice said. Something hard jabbed into the back of my knee and it buckled.

Strong arms reached around me and pressed a police baton across my chest. Other hands fished in the pockets of my jacket and jeans, disarming me. My hands clenched, but I didn't attack. I refused to take my eyes off the gun pressed to Hannah's head. Her expression hadn't changed, even when they pushed her to her knees, though her eyes flicked to mine.

"Well, what is *this*?" One of the Lapsi held the round silver grenade in his hand, tossing it lightly and catching it. "You redesigned your little bomb, I see."

He grasped the grenade in his fist and slammed it into my jaw. Ordinarily a punch like that wouldn't hurt. But this was a Lapsus, not a human, and he clenched a hard, solid block of silver in his fist. This punch *hurt,* and something *crunched*. I barely held back a scream of pain and sagged forward against the police baton, my vision swimming.

But it cleared when I saw them force Hannah forward, all the way to the ground. They zip-tied her hands behind her back, and she grunted as they hoisted her to her knees by her bound arms.

"Oh, she's a beaut, isn't she?" one of the Lapsi cops handling her said. He came up behind her and put his arms around her, forcing his hands down her shirt. "No tits though!"

I lunged forward to kill him, but strong hands held my arms behind me, and the police baton across my chest barred my way.

Hannah tried to jerk out of the Lapsus's grip and shake his hands loose, but he moved a hand to her throat, squeezing threateningly. She grunted again against the pressure on her throat, but then she turned her head and spat at him. The wad of saliva hit him on the cheek, and he released her in disgust.

"Fucking bitch," he spat, wiping his face on his sleeve. He slapped Hannah across her cheek, and her head snapped to the side. She slumped to the ground, unable to catch herself on her hands. Blood spurted from her nose but stopped almost immediately, and the bright welt on her cheek faded in a matter of seconds.

"Well, what have we here?" the Lapsus she'd spat on said, leaning toward her, interested.

I growled and managed to rip one of my arms free. I swung at the nearest Lapsus, this one in plain clothes, and missed but managed to rip my other arm free. I gained my feet as the handsy Lapsus aimed something at me and fired.

Two threads shot toward me, embedding in my shoulder, and then everything convulsed.

I dropped to my knees as my body seized. My muscles were dead, but apparently they could still be electrified with volts. My jaw clenched against my scream, and my teeth chattered together so hard I thought they'd break.

"That's for my sergeant and my team you killed, you piece of shit." I somehow managed to hear one of the Lapsus through the convulsions.

Civilian taser pulses last only five seconds, but the charge they released into me had to be at least *twenty* seconds. I couldn't balance anymore. Over I went: face-first into the murky koi pond.

CHAPTER 29

HANNAH

I can honestly say I'd much rather be groped than tased. I never thought I would have to make that statement in my life, but there it is. Soul or no soul, if it came down to either being tased or having filthy hands force themselves down my shirt: grope away.

I was struggling to get into a somewhat sitting-up position—which is *difficult* when your hands are secured behind your back—when I saw the taser pulse into Jeb. And, yeah, he'd probably not like me to describe how he looked during those long seconds.

The pulse finally stopped when Jeb toppled gracelessly into the water. He'd gone limp, but he snapped to when he hit the water's surface. He put his hands to the bottom of the shallow pond and pushed himself up, water spraying off his head and shoulders as he shook with anger and post-tase fatigue.

"Get him out of there," the Lapsus with the taser—who'd just had his hands down my shirt—spat. He turned back to me then.

He leaned down to grab my arm and probably "help" me back to my knees, but I spat a curse word at him as I pushed myself farther from him and kicked out with a powerful leg. If my arms hadn't been bound, I could have done a cool acrobatic move called a kip-up, thanks to Capoeira practice. Instead, it was just a kick, but it angered him enough for him to growl.

To my right, they'd grabbed Jeb out of the water, and when he struggled in their grip, the dark-skinned, plain-clothed Lapsus struck him in his dark purple, swollen cheekbone. Jeb howled in pain and his knees buckled.

"Jesus Christ, just stop this and take us to Cassandra already!" I snapped viciously, stamping a sneakered foot on the ground. "She will be beyond *pissed* if you hurt us beyond repair."

"Oh, really, you think she *cares* about one pretty little blonde and one Lapsus traitor?" the Lapsus above me snarled mockingly.

"I know she'll care that she wasn't the one to kill us," I said unfalteringly. I hadn't meant to speak originally, but now I knew the exact card I needed to play. Jeb had paused in his struggle against his assailants to glare at me, but I ignored the reproach in his eyes and sneered up at Gropey McTaser-Hand. "Or, you know, go ahead, try it and see what happens."

Perhaps it was his fear of Cassandra's power or the cold stoicism of my expression that made him pause. I waited, deadpan, while he calculated.

Finally, he let out a string of curses and roughly pulled me to my feet by the arm. My shoulder dislocated with a soft pop, and pain blossomed down my arm, but it faded after a moment and my arm popped back by itself. Gropey paused, registering these sounds with suspicious eyes. I looked at him with innocent, ignorant eyes—or at least I think I did. Faking facial expressions was hard still.

They pulled Jeb roughly to his feet and shoved us shoulder to shoulder. His arm was soaking and cold, and the wetness spread through the arm of my—his—shirt. As they marched us out of and away from the park, I thought how grateful I was that I'd eaten and had coffee. It looked like it was about to be a very long day.

It's amazing how few things you can do when your arms are bound behind your back. For instance, keeping your balance when roughly shoved into a streetcar. My foot caught on the lip of the first step when they shoved me, and I toppled forward, all the way to my stomach. Thankfully, I managed to keep my face from hitting the floor, but there weren't many other victories to be had.

Jeb knelt and helped me back to my feet—and he did so gently, without popping anything out of its socket.

"I'm getting really fucking sick of being pushed around," I said quietly, grinding my teeth.

"I'm sorry," he said, just as quietly, setting me back on my feet.

"Hey, separate them!" The lead Lapsus barked as he stepped into the car. "This isn't a pleasure cruise here."

They ripped Jeb from my side and pulled him to the other end of the streetcar. I was shoved into one of the rear-facing seats. I lost my temper this time when I was pushed and kicked out at one of the uniformed cop's legs. This only gained me another slap across my cheek, though.

Across the car, a Lapsus fastened a thick silver chain around Jeb's neck.

"This will keep you from shifting away from us," the leader said with a sneer. "Now just sit tight and don't move."

"Did you steal these tricks and doodads from witches?" Jeb asked, his voice still a low growl, as if he was talking around a lot of pain. The side of his face where he'd been punched was mottled with a deep purple bruise. It hadn't healed. "Or do you have some on your side in this?"

"Witches?" One of the Lapsi spat like it was the biggest insult. "As if we'd stoop to working with *them*."

"No, you wouldn't believe us, but we're working with something much *older* and darker than mere witchcraft," the silent-until-then dark-skinned one said in a low, menacing voice.

"What? You mean Cassandra?" Jeb said with a slight snort. He eyed the leader of the cops rather than the dark-skinned one who'd spoken. "She's not older than witches: they've been around longer than Troy—longer than *Cain* the first murderer, even. Oh, but wait, why am I assuming you know this? You've been a Lapsus for all of, what, three months? Two?"

"Long enough to realize and appreciate real power," Leader growled.

Jeb laughed again, this time with real amusement behind it. "Yeah, okay, infant," he mocked. "Maybe wait until you hit your first hundred years before talking so brave, okay?"

The dark-skinned Lapsus snorted in amusement, though his scowl didn't change. Leader closed in on Jeb, grabbed his jaw, and pressed his thumb into the purple bruise. Jeb winced at first, but then a guttural, pained groan escaped his clenched teeth as he turned his head, trying to shake the Lapsus's hand off. Finally, he let go, and Jeb slumped back in his relief to be out of pain for the moment. A ragged hiss escaped through his teeth as he recovered.

"Can we get moving already?" Leader snapped. A door slammed at the front of the car, and the tram moved forward.

The car was relatively quiet now that Jeb was done taunting them, and I sat still, not wanting to provoke any more violence.

Hannah.

The voice sounded distinctly like Jeb's, but completely in my head. My gaze snapped up and looked across the length of the streetcar at him. He was looking at me, but it was clear his mouth hadn't moved.

Telepathy. Don't say anything. His voice came into my head again. I dropped my gaze from his to show I understood and wouldn't respond. *I'm in your head but not prying. Just think something, I'll hear it.*

You can read minds? I thought. I didn't think it as a specific response; it was more me talking to myself in my head.

Yes. I don't do it often. And never with you, he assured me, but I wasn't certain I believed him.

I promise, he said in response to my silent disbelief. *Look, this isn't a very sophisticated way of communicating, so try to keep your thoughts focused on replying to me. Don't think of anything crazy or absurd if you don't want me to be in on it.*

Soulless as I was, I was still human. And whenever a human is told not to think about X, they're going to think about X. So when Jeb told me not to think anything absurd, immediately, something absurd popped into my head. Looking across the way at Jeb, still sopping wet in his white henley and staring broodily at me, I suddenly pictured him on the cover of a steamy romance novel. Then, in the same instant, I imagined him in place of Colin Firth in *that scene* in the 1990s *Pride and Prejudice*. He brought it on himself.

Hannah. His voice came into my head, somehow loudly reproachful. *For the love of God...*

I'm sorry, I thought in response. *I'm focused now. I swear. I hope you have a plan because I haven't got a clue.*

Still working as I go, but...no. I have nothing, Jeb said. I could imagine him shaking his head, but I knew he didn't dare physically move. Neither did I. *Are you okay, though?*

I mentally shrugged, resigned. *What about you? Your face looks awful, and it isn't healing.*

Yeah, it's the silver. He punched me with it.

So silver didn't just kill them if stabbed in the right place. It also prevented healing. I brought up an image of kryptonite being used on Superman so Jeb could follow my train of thought.

Exactly right, Jeb said silently. *I'll be all right though. Don't worry about me.*

I'm sorry I forced your hand on this one, I thought carefully. He hadn't wanted to use me to get to Cassandra, but I'd put us here anyway. I looked out the window of the streetcar at the city passing by. We were heading east, toward the Willamette River.

We would have ended up getting snatched either way. I just wish I could have had more time to make a plan, Jeb communicated sadly. *Or seen more of Cassandra's Troy take shape.*

Cassandra's Troy. I often forgot that she was as old as the ancient legendary city. The way Troy fell had been so extravagant and ridiculous, though. I wondered how the story really went.

There was a wooden horse, but smaller. Inside it, they smuggled a dead horse into the city and dropped it down a well, poisoning the city's water. Most of the inhabitants of the city were dead by the time Troy officially fell, Jeb explained silently. *Unfortunately, we can't do something like that here. Lapsi don't drink water. It would only harm the humans, which isn't our aim.*

No, but we could still poison the soldiers in another way. I felt a small smile starting on my lips. I bit it down.

What do you mean? Jeb asked, still reading my thoughts.

He could poison their minds. From the violence they'd displayed in capturing us, it was safe to assume these Lapsi were the bad sort: the sort that would be eradicated before long. He and I both knew Cassandra intended to do away with them for the implementation of peace. If he let them in on that plan, they wouldn't be too happy. Clueing them in on the plan might sow enough discontent for them to completely turn on their queen.

I conveyed these thoughts in a number of images and ideas. At one point, I pulled my gaze from the window and glanced at him. I raised a mischievous eyebrow his way so he could understand my meaning extra well. His own mouth twitched sideways almost imperceptibly, acknowledging my thoughts with appreciation.

He looked away and studied the Lapsi around him with narrowed eyes. Somehow, I knew my thoughts were my own again and that Jeb had pulled his mind from mine. I felt simultaneously grateful to have my privacy back and lonely.

CHAPTER 30

JEB

I could have leapt across the streetcar and kissed the girl on the top of her messy blonde head, but I resisted. Instead, I pulled out of her mind and focused on my new mission. I studied the Lapsi around me for the first time since they'd attacked us. Not all were in police garb. There were four in total, with a fifth up front driving the streetcar. Three of the ones in the cab were uniformed. The fourth was in street clothes.

The lead Lapsus looked about twenty-five, young for a cop. He was blond with a buzz cut—poor thing. He'd never be able to adapt with the styles over the years. He was beefy, and I could tell he used to be on the fat side, with the eyes of a bullied kid that now got to be the bully.

His two lackeys also in uniform stood on either side of the tram, against the outer walls. They had probably been changed around the same time, and I gleaned that they followed The Bully's orders and not their own. If I convinced their leader, they'd follow suit. Yet was The Bully leading the whole group, or was he just the most mouthy?

My attention drifted to The Fourth next—the dark-skinned Lapsus who'd been mostly silent this whole time. He still stood at the far side of the cab by Hannah's side.

He was tall and black, with his afro-textured hair clipped close to his head. He wore dark jeans and a black collared shirt. The sleeves were rolled up to the elbow, revealing sleeves of tattoos—but *old* tattoos that suggested primitive tools and *tradition* rather than aesthetic. He was older than the cops by a lot, but I couldn't gauge how much older than *me* he was.

Normally, I'm wary of anyone older until I can get a proper read on them, and this brooding, watchful Lapsus was a hard one to read. He'd dragged me out of the water and struck my bad cheek to subdue me while I was still tase-dumb. Had he looked thrilled at hurting me, or had he kept the same stoic glare that he currently wore? I had no idea, but this unnecessary violence was the only insight I had into this man: that and his age. He was unpredictable and unreadable, but he was old enough to understand more of how the Lapsi world worked than the green cops. The cops would be easy to sway, but The Fourth was the key.

With the barest outline of a plan, I settled back into my seat and spread my legs wider, trying to exude an air of ease and confidence that I certainly didn't feel.

"You boys sure have fallen a long way from your oath to protect and serve. Tell me, who do you protect and serve now?" I said, finally deciding on my plan of attack.

The Bully's eyes narrowed, but his mouth remained pressed into a hard line. There was my answer, I noted. Now, I typically like cops. I respect their overall symbolic presence within a community. I appreciate their wanting to protect people and detain criminals. *But* there are a few—a certain personality type—that join the force for the wrong reasons: to feel powerful.

"I'm just curious, guys, really," I said conversationally. "You became cops to devote your lives to the safety of others. Then you were changed into these supremely powerful creatures. You can go anywhere, do anything—for eternity. Yet you stay in this city where you're trapped, still wearing a uniform and still following orders. Why?"

They were all glaring, annoyed that I kept talking, but at least I had their attention.

"Look, none of us are going anywhere," I continued. "So, tell me, what did she promise you?"

The two Pawns looked almost ashamed and diverted their eyes, and The Bully looked annoyed. The Fourth just eyed me, his face unreadable.

"All right, don't tell me. But I can guess," I said cheerfully. "Power, right? A land where you can kill with impunity? A land where you'll be above everyone else? Where humans are livestock and you are free to be a glutton or a terror? Or were you promised a community that you could still be a part of?"

I moved my eyes from The Bully and addressed The Fourth for the first time.

"And what about you? What were you promised?" I asked him. He didn't answer—I didn't expect him to. "They're young. They haven't had the experience of being exiles. They still understand what it's like to be part of a community, and they aren't going to be forced to *miss* it. But you—you know what it's like. And you don't seem like a social, model citizen, so what was the appeal for *you*? I bet it was the promise of carnage. Like being let loose in a candy store, unsupervised. Right?"

I paused for emphasis but continued after a beat. "Whatever you were promised—it doesn't matter. Think about this: Is this what you imagined? Is *this* what you were promised?"

"It's only the first day," one of the Pawns said. "Things are still taking shape."

"Sure, sure. You're probably right," I said, nodding enthusiastically. "Only, something's not adding up. Hear me out. You're under a dome and can't leave. *No one* can leave, and no one can come in. If you're allowed to kill with impunity, then resources become...limited. Don't they?"

All three cops exchanged a look, and The Fourth's eyes narrowed.

"She's letting you have your fun now, but for how long? And what about those other Lapsi that she's detaining here? Resources are scarce and nonrenewable. Those other Lapsi are just more mouths that need fed. Why would she do that?"

"She'll release them once they agree to comply and not get in the way," the other Pawn said.

"But it still doesn't add up, does it?" I said, gesturing vaguely with a hand. "More mouths to feed while still promising you all the run of the land. Yet Cassandra has said that her ultimate goal is peace and order."

All four sets of eyes raised to meet mine when I said this: each a different shade of disbelief. So, none of these lads heard her broadcast last night? Her mention of peace? Interesting. *Well, well, this worked out in my favor after all.*

"See? She promises an amusement park to the savage." I put out one hand in front of me, palm up. "And she promises a functioning, operational city with an economy to the...civilized." I held out my other hand, also palm up. I moved each individually, like the arms of a scale, leaning one way, then the other. "And since those two things contradict each other...it raises one major question." I put my hands back down into my lap. "Why did she bring *you* all in on the plan in the first place?"

Silence. All four Lapsi's eyes narrowed, not in anger, but in suspicion. I just hoped it wasn't suspicion of me. I steeled myself for another blow to my already broken face, just in case.

"From the lips of Cassandra herself," Hannah said, speaking up for the first time since we got moving. "'Every siege requires infantry. Soldiers that are ruthless but expendable.' That's you guys. Cassandra needed ruthless bad boys willing to get their hands dirty. But when she's established enough control, she'll put those dirty hands somewhere the sun doesn't shine."

I saw The Fourth's hands clench into fists. Given his unpredictability, I quickly plowed forward, bringing the focus back to me.

"She used your ruthlessness to her advantage. She wanted to take a city, but she wants to control that taken city. She promises you things in exchange for your help—but you probably didn't realize she actually demanded your *submission*. She promised you the power and freedom you want, and in turn you kept order up until last night. You cleaned up the streets, cut crime down, and dug her underground tunnels. And now she's making you clean up the mess of last night. Hiding bodies so the humans don't panic, keeping the power on so the humans don't freeze or scratch at the walls, keeping water running. All to keep them comfortable. They're the flock. She's the shepherd. You're the *wolves.*"

I paused just long enough to let that implication sink in, then continued.

"And she'll release those other Lapsi when it's time to put the wolves down. You'll be hunted. Trapped under this dome, you won't be able to hide for long." I leaned forward in my seat, staring directly into The Fourth's dark eyes. I knew, because he was older and clearly a malicious type, that he was used to roaming. He wouldn't like the idea of being trapped. "Do you feel trapped now, under this force field? Imagine what it will be like when you're trapped *and* hunted?"

The Fourth's eyes narrowed further, and I knew I'd gotten to him at least somewhat. I could see the inkling of fear in his eyes, like a rat starting to realize it's in a cage. I turned from him and looked again at The Bully. His face looked truly sour and wary, but he wasn't afraid yet. He was still riding the high of being made powerful and eternal, and the idea that eternity could *end* hadn't occurred to him yet. But he looked angry. Unlike The Fourth, I'd read The Bully well. His anger was at Cassandra's subterfuge and not at my rhetoric.

He has my weapons, I reminded myself. Mainly, he had the one grenade I had left. I leaned forward, looking at him, just as the streetcar pulled to a stop. There wasn't much time left to sow the seeds of revolt.

"That grenade you pulled off me," I said, fixing him with an intense look. "You know what that's made of?"

"Silver?" The Bully said, a note of uncertainty in his voice. Perhaps he didn't know for sure it was silver, but he could see my unhealed face. I'd assumed he could gather enough from context, but he wasn't proving to be the smartest of the lot.

I nodded. "If you want my advice, use that somewhere it could do a lot of damage."

"Like on a crowd of humans, right?" The Bully asked, raising an eyebrow incredulously at me.

I wanted to slap myself on the forehead in frustration.

"No, you shortsighted idiot," I blurted. Realizing it wasn't the best idea to insult someone I'd nicknamed *The Bully*, I continued quickly. "Don't destroy the livestock. Destroy the *fence*."

"We cannot," The Fourth said, speaking for the first time since we'd boarded the tram. "We cannot disrupt the fences as long as Cassandra is alive. It is an old magic, and she is connected to it. Her and the Soul Eater."

"You leave Cassandra to *us*," I said without blinking. I might have been only blustering, but I put extra emphasis on "us" so they wouldn't split us up.

The gropey Pawn went to Hannah and gripped her arm to get her to stand up from the seat. He nudged her toward the door, but he didn't push her. Progress.

"And the Soul Eater?" The Fourth said as the door slid open next to him.

"I find decapitation is a rather universal, albeit inelegant solution for killing most demonic beings," I said while I was pulled from my own seat. I gave The Fourth a wicked grin before a Pawn shoved me past him. It was how Adam had managed to kill the Soul Eater that attacked me and managed to release what was left of my soul from its slitted maw. "We'll kill Cassandra. You kill the Soul Eater if you see it."

Blinding sunlight greeted me as I stepped off the tram, disorienting me further. On the sidewalk by the stopped streetcar was an art installment that looked a bit like a circus tent. Across the street from us was a low parking garage with signs for the Moda Center. They ushered us in that direction, and we entered the parking garage. In the concrete stairwell, we were directed through a side door that led to an iron stairwell into a tunnel system that was familiar, thanks to last night's trip with Mason.

The other Lapsi were quiet, but I had a feeling they were conversing silently with each other. I only hoped I'd swayed them enough that they were planning a way to save themselves, rather than planning on how they were going to kill me. Or Hannah.

Hannah was silently following their directions, as I was. She'd adapted to her sense of balance with her hands behind her, and she stumbled a lot less. It also helped that no one was pushing her around anymore.

We were heading south now, down the tiled tunnel. It was hard to judge the distance we walked, but it was maybe the length of two city blocks before we paused at a wide, barred door, like a jail cell. Beyond it was a large holding cell made to be somewhat comfortable with a number of beds, a bookcase with books and DVDs, and a large TV on a wall. Aside from the barred door, none of this raised any immediate alarms. Until I focused on *who* was in this room.

There were maybe ten girls inside. All of medium height and slim build, with straight or slightly wavy blonde hair. All traits similar to *Hannah's*.

"This is a joke, right?" Hannah said, as she peered inside. True incredulity had crept into her voice, showing she was deeply disturbed. "This is a fucking joke, right?"

"Now it makes sense why they believed you when you said she wanted *you*," I said aloud. On one hand, it was amusing, but on the other, it was highly unsettling.

"It's...it's a *harem* of..." she said, horrified, though she sounded only perturbed. "Oh, fuck me!"

"I think that's the idea, yeah," I said, unable to resist. She glared at me.

The Bully moved behind Hannah and pulled a knife from his pocket—my knife. He cut the zip tie from her wrists just as one of the Pawns slid the barred door open. The Bully smoothly pushed Hannah inside, and the door slid shut again.

"Hey!" I snapped, lunging forward. But The Fourth stopped me by putting an arm around my neck from behind.

Hannah stumbled inside, but she managed to keep her balance. She turned back to the door, looking irritated but not surprised.

"I said *we*, damn it!" I growled. I was angry, but I kept my voice low in case we were overheard.

"She's human, fool. What good can she do?" The Fourth hissed in my ear, but loud enough that I think Hannah could hear him. "Besides, think of it like insurance. As long as you kill Cassandra, nothing is going to happen to her. If you don't kill Cassandra, then Cassandra will eventually find out that she's here."

Despite my anger, I couldn't argue with the logic. She was safer here as long as I succeeded. But I wasn't loving my odds. *We're so fucked.* I relaxed enough that The Fourth removed his arm from around my neck and took a step back.

"Shall we?" The Bully said, motioning impatiently down the hallway.

I paused, not wanting to leap when this bully said jump, but also not wanting to leave Hannah without saying a kind of goodbye. I turned back to the door and stared through the bars at her.

For what it's worth, I spoke telepathically to her. I didn't invade her thoughts like I had earlier. I didn't care if she responded or not. *To the best of my ability—as much as I'm able to...I love you.*

Her eyebrows twitched as her only reaction to my words, then they drew together almost imperceptibly. She didn't respond with anything at first, and The Bully was growing impatient. I only had about another second to commit her face entirely to memory—never mind that her face would always be burned into my retinas.

"Be careful," she said quietly. It wasn't a response, but I hadn't wanted one. Still, when she didn't need to say anything at all, she had. I felt like those words were loaded with something she didn't realize she felt. "And come back."

They pushed me past the door, and we continued on our way. I brooded for a while as we walked, but I couldn't do that for long. I needed a plan, or I was truly hung.

CHAPTER 31

JEB

*S*o *I don't mean to be a bother, but where exactly are we going now?* I asked The Fourth telepathically. The Bully was all bluster—like me—The Fourth was the true menace and leader of this pack.

You're going to where Cassandra is. We're under a stadium where they have concerts and basketball games. It's set up as an emergency center right now. You'll see. She's overseeing all of that, so that's where you're going, The Fourth explained silently.

And you don't think I need, you know, a weapon of any sort? You disarmed me, remember?

I hear decapitation is a rather universal, if inelegant, solution for killing most demonic beings, he sneered in my head, repeating my own words back to me.

Ah, yes, and you expect me to do that with my bare hands? I snapped in thought-speech. He was right, decapitation did technically work for killing Lapsi, but it was more gruesome and less elegant, and not to mention even *harder* to do when the target can disappear with a thought.

You'll figure something out, boy scout, The Fourth said, glancing back at me with a sneer. *Besides, she will have you searched the second she sees you. You'll just be disarmed, again.*

Won't it look strange if I walk in there unarmed? It'll suggest I was disarmed previously and taken here rather than wandered in here of my own volition, I argued coolly.

The Fourth's shoulders slumped slightly, as if he sighed in frustration. A moment later, he handed a knife back to me. I took it gratefully. The itch from the touch of silver was a welcome comfort.

Many thanks, I replied, and then I went silent. I hid the knife in an inner pocket I'd sewn into the waistband of my jeans, fumbling a little to get it inside—everything was still very damp.

We went up two flights of stairs, back up to ground level. At the top landing, we stopped, and they moved around me, so I was by the door, with them at the top of the stairs. It was clear they'd taken me as far as they would.

"This is the stadium. She's in the main arena," The Bully said.

"Fine. Thanks for practically nothing," I grumbled, ripping off the stupid necklace they'd made me wear. I almost threw it at them but bit back my irritation, in case they were still on the fence about what I'd said. To test it, I handed the chain back to the Bully and said, "Good luck with the Soul Eater."

"Good luck with the queen," The Bully said curtly, but the contempt in his tone for once didn't feel directed at me.

I glanced behind him at The Fourth, whose face didn't change, but he kept his eyes locked on mine and nodded once before they turned away and walked back down the stairs. I might have been reading too much into it, but something in that last exchange gave me a bit of hope—not much, but enough to relax my shoulders a fraction.

The door to the stairs opened into the lobby of the sports arena. There were sleeping bags, cots, and people lining the lobby. I must have looked quite the odd sight. I was a waterlogged rat traipsing through their refugee camp. My clothing was still dripping in some places and was covered in mud and sediment and who knew what else from the koi pond. They ignored me, though, and I ignored them as I made my way to the doors that led to the lower levels of the arena seating.

I found the way to the arena floor easily enough and paused at the last step before the hallway opened up onto the stadium floor, collecting myself. It was like an emergency refugee center had been set up within this space. There were cots and medical tables set up on the sides. The people in this space were all adults of various ages, but I didn't see a single child. I wondered about it at first but realized why. The attack had happened at midnight. These were the people who didn't live in this part of the city but had stayed late at the office, cleaned the buildings, drove cabs and Ubers, or were at the bars and clubs.

Cassandra was on a stage at the far end of the massive space. Her face was projected onto a large screen behind her as well as on the jumbotron overhead. She was delivering a speech to these displaced people. It was more of the peace-loving, comfort-promising jargon that I'd heard her spout in the news reports and the night I first met her.

I had no plan whatsoever. I was a dead man, but I'd thought that many times over the past week, and I was still here. I might have been a dead man, but I would take Cassandra down with me. No matter what.

After combing my damp hair back and out of my face, I stepped from under the cover of the hallway and walked calmly down the middle aisle of cots. There were Lapsi lining the stadium floor, keeping watch, and I scanned their faces for anyone familiar. Mainly, I was looking for Mason. I caught sight of a head with shoulder-length dark brown hair just as it disappeared down a causeway that might have been him, but I couldn't be sure.

I was almost all the way up the aisle before Cassandra finally noticed me. She paused in her speech and stared down at me, her eyes flashing and narrowing. She looked pissed, and it amused me more than I thought possible to see her so surprised and angry at me. Her livid expression was magnified twenty times on the screen behind her.

She recovered enough from her anger to move out from behind the microphone. She jumped down from the stage and landed with Lapsi grace on her feet. She approached me until she was about a foot from me. She still looked angry and disbelieving.

"I thought you said you didn't see me in your triumphant vision," I said boldly, recalling what she'd said to me that first night.

Her eyes flashed even more as her lividity grew, and her red lips were set into a hard, flat line. She didn't say anything though. I suspected she was communicating telepathically with Lapsi behind me. And the suspicion was confirmed when the two Lapsi grabbed my arms. The one on my right was—bafflingly—the redheaded Lapsi whose ass I'd followed at the start of all of this. Fleetingly, I remembered his name was Caleb or something similar.

"Follow me," she commanded the two Lapsi aloud. Her face became cool and in control. "My flock doesn't need to see anyone else die in front of them."

I was herded once again into the tunnels beneath the city. We walked behind Cassandra until we reached the widened hallway beneath the fallen freeway overpasses. I could see cracks in the ceiling from when it had fallen. We paused at last at a large alcove to the side. Through it was a kind of antechamber or foyer. She walked to a door on the side, opened it, and stepped inside. I was forced to follow her in, and the other Lapsi came too, still holding my arms.

This was obviously her bedroom, or one of many she probably had around the city—it was hard to imagine her wanting to permanently live in a tunnel system under the city. It was the most lavish master suite I'd ever seen, full of plush furniture and silken accents. She walked to the center of the room and spun slowly on her heel toward me.

"Search him."

I didn't know whether to protest the search or roll over and let them. It was possible they wouldn't find the knife hidden in my waistband, but nothing was a guarantee. The Lapsi roughly shouldered me out of my jacket before I could make up my mind and wriggle away from them.

"Oh, yes, good idea, boys," Cassandra said in a silky voice. She clapped in her excitement. "Might as well strip him. Make sure he's unarmed *and* keep him from dripping on everything. What happened to you, Jeb? Were you dragged through the river?"

"Koi pond," I corrected her. But then her order to have them strip me registered. I didn't like *that* idea one bit.

Caleb's hands were at my shirt, and the other Lapsus grabbed one of my beltloops—not used to stripping someone, apparently. But his hand brushed just near the hidden knife—my only protection—and I reacted. Snarling, I shoved him as hard as I could, but he didn't stumble easily, and he held his footing. He kicked at my knee, and my leg buckled under me. Caleb still had handfuls of my shirt in his fists. As I went to my knees, my shirt came up around my chest and face. The fabric dug into my cheek that was still throbbing and tender. I cried out and went limp as the pain blossomed in my face all over again. The shirt was off, but it was the least of my concerns as my face radiated with this fresh pain.

Caleb pinned me to the ground with a knee and reached for the waist of my jeans. He paused when his hand landed right on the hidden knife. He grinned maliciously as he pulled it out. I still fought to get his knee off my chest—to unbalance him—to do anything but lie there shirtless and unarmed.

I managed to unbalance him, but I suspected he let me out of pity or boredom. What threat was I now? I got unsteadily up to my knees, reeling from pain and anger.

"Frankly, Jeb, I would have been insulted if you hadn't brought a weapon," Cassandra cooed. Caleb handed over the knife, which she opened and turned in her hands idly. "But now you're anything but a threat. Now you're merely a toy."

"But you still can't account for the fact that I'm here," I spat. My chest was heaving, racked through with pain, and my nerves were fried from the stress of the past few hours. "How does that foresight work, exactly? Because I think you need to get it looked at."

"My foresight has saved my life for thousands of years," she said harshly. "And it would have saved my people if they'd only *listened* to me."

"But too bad you were born without a dick. So unlucky for you," I snarled back at her, purely to piss her off.

Her eyes flashed again. She stepped closer and put her hand gently against the bad side of my face. In my peripheral vision I kept track of the knife in her other hand. I needed to be *very* mindful of that knife so I could react when it moved and *maybe* not die if she struck. But also, her hand was on my injured face, and the threat of the throbbing, searing pain had me nearly quivering.

"That sure looks like it hurts, Jeb," she said softly. "I'd hate to cause you even more pain tonight. But, to be fair, you're ruining my moment, so you kind of have it coming."

"Fuck you," I said. Despite my reluctance to feel pain again, I couldn't help but be ornery.

She merely smiled. Flicking her hand, she sharply slapped the shattered cheekbone. I heard a sound between a snarl and a yelp escape me as pain exploded across my face again. I doubled over and caught myself on my hands. She backed away laughing, and all I could see were her sandaled feet. Nearly blind with pain, I lunged for them. I grabbed hold of one, but she shook it free of my grasp. Her foot went back and then came forward in a rough kick. Her foot connected with my cheekbone and *again* it felt like my head exploded, but much worse than before. I collapsed, groaning. If my stomach hadn't been dormant for 400 years, it would have seized and vomited its contents.

I heard Cassandra's silky laugh, but distantly. All I could see, hear, feel, and think was *pain*.

I don't know how much time passed before my vision cleared. I might have lost consciousness, or I might have merely been dazed. When I opened my eyes, I realized I was still facedown on a carpeted floor. My jeans were still damp, so not much time could have passed.

With a barely audible groan, I put my hands beneath me and pushed myself up to my hands and knees.

"That was fun, Jeb, but don't hurry getting up on my account. We can go another round once you're ready," Cassandra said from somewhere to my right and above. "But for now, we can just talk."

She was reclining on a lavish, cream-colored settee that had an expensive fur-like blanket draped over it. The two Lapsi were still in the room with us and stood a few feet away, glaring and alert. I cast my gaze around the room, taking everything in. If this were her bedroom, it might be where she'd keep Hannah's soul, if she had it.

"Talk about what, Cassandra?" I said irritably. "What is there to talk about? You've taken a city. I wasn't able to stop you. You've won. Congratulations."

"But I'm still just amazed that you *tried* to stop me. *You.*" She waved a hand languidly in the air. "If, when we first met, someone told me *you* would be the one trying to stop me, I would have laughed in their face. Then killed them for wasting my time with their joke."

I said nothing. I'd have laughed too, but I wasn't going to admit it.

"You should have killed me that night," I said, finally thinking of something to say. I was up on my knees now, my eyes level with hers, though we were feet apart. I doubted I could make any kind of lunge at her before the other Lapsi were on me.

"But then I'd have missed seeing your lovely transformation," she said cheerfully.

Into your little bitch? I thought with just a touch of self-pity. *Yes, quite the transformation.*

"And I think it was Hannah that did it," Cassandra said. She sat up on the settee and leaned toward me. "Sweet, beautiful Hannah."

I resisted the urge to roll my eyes. I really didn't need reminding that she was obsessed. I'd seen the room of Hannah lookalikes.

"Where is Hannah now, Jeb?" she asked sweetly. "Did you get her out of this city in time and then come back to kill little old me?"

You know I didn't, I nearly spat, but I held it in.

"No, I bet you didn't," she said, her smile slipping a little. She looked disappointed in me. "I bet she's here in my city. Is she scared?"

No, she doesn't exactly have any fears anymore, I thought, narrowing my eyes.

"Did she tell you I saw her last night? We got very close," she said, tilting her head and looking like she was thinking of a fond memory. "She is an *excellent* kisser. I wonder if you've discovered that yourself?"

"Yeah, and I heard she refused you," I said boldly. "You lowered yourself to her level, a mere *human*. And she told you to eat shit."

"Yes. Yes, she did," Cassandra said, with no small amount of bitterness and spite in her voice. "But she'll be back. She'll see I'm right."

"Did you have her attacked?"

"I did not," she said. Her face went serious. "I swear I didn't." Her face broke into that sweet smile again. "But the Lapsi that *did* brought me a lovely souvenir."

She does have it. She was keeping Hannah's soul on her, like a trophy. That gave me a little bit of hope. She was just one Lapsus, after all. Lapsi were hard to kill, but it wasn't impossible. I would tear her head off with my bare hands if it meant retrieving Hannah's soul. I didn't move my eyes, but I could see my knife on the side table by the settee. Within arm's reach of both of us.

"Where is it?" I asked in a low growl.

"Where is Hannah?" she returned, tilting her head.

"I think *you* have Hannah," I said. Everything that makes Hannah *Hannah* had been taken away.

"Mmmm, I do," she admitted with a crinkly-nosed grin. She was so pleased with herself. "And I love it *so* much. But I'll give it back. All she needs to do is ask me."

I scoffed loudly but couldn't think of a clever retort.

"Now, tell me, where is she? So I can return her belonging," she said. "And so I can offer her *belonging*."

"She'll still tell you to eat shit." I was done playing the game.

She reached toward me and put her fingers to my injured face. *Not again*. I gripped the edge of the settee hard, bracing myself.

"Then I'll just kill her," she said softly. Her fingers brushed my cheek gently. My face quivered involuntarily. "In front of you. That will be sweet and deliciously heartbreaking."

She moved her hand, ready to strike the shattered bone again, but I reacted faster this time. I lifted the settee and pivoted it, managing to overturn it almost all the way. She rolled off, without falling to the ground unfortunately. My maneuver knocked the side table over, and the knife hit the plush carpet with a barely audible thud, but she didn't lunge for it.

"Another round already, Jeb?" Cassandra said lightly. I could hear the chuckle in her voice.

She moved to kick me in the face again, but I caught her foot and pulled, twisting as I went. She tumbled to the ground but didn't stay down. She brought a knee to my chest, and I grunted from the impact. I rolled away, feinting another injury, but really, I rolled closer to the knife.

"Just tell me where Hannah is, and it'll all be over," she said as she righted herself onto her knees.

"Fuck you." I reached on the ground for something—anything really. My hand found a vase that had toppled off the side table. I lobbed it as hard as I could in Cassandra's direction. She blocked it with a forearm, and broken pottery sprayed everywhere.

"Where is she?" she said again, her voice getting higher the angrier she got.

"Fuck off!" I yelled, getting to my knees again. This time she was the one to throw something at me. I didn't get my arm up fast enough to block it, and the crystal ashtray glanced off my wrist and struck my cheek.

Pain again. That beautiful, billowing explosion of pain, starting in my cheekbone, ricocheting through my teeth and all the way to my shoulders. I toppled again but caught myself on my elbows. The room was spinning, but one thing was in focus. The knife on the ground. I could reach it if I extended my arm.

Without marking where Cassandra was in relation to the knife, I took the chance and reached for it. But then something stabbed right through the back of my hand, pinning it to the floor. It wasn't the silver knife but a steel fireplace poker. Fleetingly, I noted that my hand would heal, but not until it was no longer *impaled*.

Then, after a second, the pain finally registered. A guttural, primal cry of pain ripped from my lungs. My body tensed and started to curl in on itself, though I was still crouched on all fours. Then, as my vision cleared through some of the pain, Cassandra crouched before me, holding the knife to the vulnerable flesh of my throat.

"Where is she?" she asked when she knew I was paying attention to her again.

"Go to hell." Leftover spittle from my guttural cry flew from my mouth. Most of it landed on the blood-soaked carpet, but satisfyingly, some hit her cheek.

I was beaten, and I was ready for this to just be fucking over. She repositioned the knife, this time just over my heart, the point brushing my exposed pectoral.

"Cassandra," a voice from the doorway said as she flexed her hand, ready to plunge the knife in. "Another blonde was brought in around the same time that *he* showed up."

My vision was swimming, but I saw her red rosebud lips turn up into a smile. When she lowered the knife and stood, I collapsed forward onto the carpet.

"Bring her to me," Cassandra said.

CHAPTER 32

HANNAH

Cassandra was insane. She was absolutely, undeniably unhinged and batshit insane.

I knew she was evil and cunning and warped going in, but then I was put into the *room of Hannahs.*

I'd thought Jeb foolish for believing she had my soul, but now I was convinced he was right. She was probably masturbating with it while she killed a woman who happened to have my same hair color and blood type, all while I sat in this room of Hannahs.

Insane.

I fumed at the images as the group of bullies ushered Jeb away, leaving me in a room of my lookalikes, to sit and wait for madness or death. Most likely both.

He'll be back, I told myself with a mental shrug. *Or he'll die. And then I'll die.* It should have surprised me that there was no emotion behind this reassurance—if you could call it that. But being soulless sucked the surprise out of most things.

The large cell was a glorified adult playroom. Not *adult*, like S&M, make-you-blush kind of adult. Just, adult in the sense that there were books and movies and gym equipment and things, rather than push-toys and stuffed animals.

I walked farther into the room to explore. Some women were curled up on beds or holding each other crying, and others were poking listlessly through magazines. At first, the hugging girls looked to me as I passed, wondering if I would comfort them or if I needed a hug. But something about my soullessness must've been detectable, because they looked away after glancing my way once. That was perfectly fine with me. I planned to give everyone in here a wide berth.

I sat on a couch for a little bit. One of the girls had put the TV on and it was playing an atrocious season of *America's Next Top Model*. I didn't even know that show still had a following.

While the show played, I stared at the wall, thinking. But when that got too boring, I went exploring around the room some more. I hadn't noticed right away, but there were Lapsi in the room with us. Mostly male, but one or two female, standing along the walls at intervals. I counted six as I idly scanned the room.

In the back corner, there were racks of clothing for various occasions. I wondered if Cassandra thought we would want to play dress-up to pass the time. But I remembered that most of these girls had probably been out at the bars or clubs in this area. This was offering them more comfortable clothes to change into.

Deranged, insane, but thoughtful, I thought pessimistically.

I looked at my own clothes. My jeans were dirty from the explosion and torn in both knees from being pushed to the ground so many times in the past twenty-four hours. The shirt was Jeb's and so big I had tied it with his belt to make it into a kind of tunic. I could do with a change of clothes.

I pulled out a pair of warm leggings, a simple tank top, sports bra, and a zipper hoodie, like the one I lost at the party the previous night. I didn't bother hiding behind anything to change. Let people watch, who even cared?

Once I was in comfortable clothes, I walked over to the little gym area. I didn't care for the equipment, but there was a large enough open space around it where I could stretch out my limbs and maybe do some dancing to loosen my muscles and pass the time.

I stretched and did some basic barre, using the treadmill's guard rails as support. Once warmed up, I started to freestyle some basic contemporary blended moves. I couldn't get into it though. I tried a dance I knew well—not my mantra dance, but another I'd done before.

My limbs flexed and arced through the motions, but it all felt mechanical and lifeless. I tried to draw up something from within me. Anything, really. I remembered how dancing *felt* before, but it was like grasping at the seeds of a dandelion as they blew away.

It hurt in an empty way: not being able to tap into the thing I'd always loved and that had always brought me peace. I hadn't really missed my soul until I tried dancing without it.

I stopped and sat on the floor, staring at nothing. After a moment or two, I folded my legs and brought a knee to my chest. I stretched my muscles out and focused on breathing.

I finished stretching and stood up, almost too late to realize that one of the Lapsi had walked up. He was nearly on top of me. I jerked backward but stopped as I recognized him.

Mason.

Wasn't he an ally? I remembered Jeb was distrustful of him.

I was opening my mouth to say his name, but his eyes flashed at me. Somehow in that single look, I gathered that I should stay silent or we were both dead.

He grabbed my shoulder and turned me, pushing me roughly into the wall. I braced myself against the wall with my hands, so my face didn't hit it.

Don't fight me, his voice said in my mind.

It was a dumb thing to say because it made me *really* want to fight him. My muscles coiled, ready to buck backward, but he leaned more of his weight into my shoulder blades.

I *am on your side*, he said telepathically, punctuating his words as if he were gritting his teeth. He kicked my feet apart and pressed himself against my back.

Ah, yes. Because this feels trustworthy all right, I thought sarcastically.

His hand reached around me and slipped beneath the top hem of my tank top. My hands clenched into fists against the wall and my body tensed for a fight. But then I froze. There was something cold and solid between his hand and my skin. He was planting something on me.

I'm sorry, he apologized as he slipped beneath my bra and inserted whatever it was beneath my breast. *Not a lot of places to hide a knife on you. You had to wear pants without pockets, didn't you?*

Yeah, well, options are limited for women in the pockets department. It's so they can sell us purses. I grumbled silently, but I didn't think he was reading my thoughts. He extracted his hand slowly and grabbed my arm.

I don't want to be rough with you, so if you could play along, it would be helpful. You're doing good so far.

He pulled my arm and made to drag me away. He didn't pull roughly, though, but I tottered and stumbled after him to make it look like he did.

Good.

"Your presence is requested elsewhere," he said aloud, and he play-dragged me from the room. The barred door slid open as he approached and closed again once we were on the other side.

Someday you'll have to tell me how you fooled me into thinking you were Lapsi. That was good.

He kept both hands firmly wrapped around my upper arm as we walked. I couldn't respond telepathically, but his quip didn't warrant a response, anyway.

"Where is Jeb?" I asked aloud. I figured that was a safe enough question to be overheard.

I don't know, he responded silently. *I left to come here when he appeared. I knew Cassandra would want to see you, so I opted to be the delivery boy. I have a hunch he's in the same place we're going. Just...brace yourself. He might be dead.*

It was probably a one in five chance that he was still alive, I guessed. It wasn't surprising, so should I be feeling something?

And he said he loves you, a small voice chided me. It was the little voice from deep down that told me what I *should* be feeling, even though I couldn't feel.

If he's dead, it's up to you to kill Cassandra. She won't be expecting it from you, I almost guarantee it, Mason continued.

"I don't think I can kill anyone," I said aloud, as quietly as I could. But my mind flipped back to last night. The dead man at the party. The human death I'd caused. I felt no shame now, or even guilt. *I guess that's one bright side of losing my soul.*

Well, you're going to have to try. We're running out of options. He was unsympathetic. *I took Jeb's weapons and rigged them to several soul pillars. But they won't do any good unless Cassandra's killed.*

I didn't know what a soul pillar was, but I could guess. And apparently Jeb had told this Lapsus where to find his weapons. I relaxed a fraction as this dawned on me. Jeb trusted him, which meant I could too.

"No promises. But I'll try," I murmured quietly.

We turned into a smaller hallway that looked like an unfinished foyer. A Lapsus stood guard outside a door at the end of the foyer. Mason tugged roughly on my arm, renewing the role of jailer. I exaggeratedly stumbled as he dragged me forward.

Sorry in advance, but I'm going to have to be violent, Mason warned me silently. *Good luck.*

The Lapsus guard opened the door for Mason and stood aside. I had only a second to brace myself before he shoved me, hard, through the door. I careened gracelessly into the room, stumbling forward several feet before tripping on the thick carpet. I fell awkwardly on my right leg and heard myself cry out involuntarily. *God damn it, Mason,* I wanted to yell, but I held it in. I threw a glare back at him, but he'd already slammed the door closed.

The room was a lavish, creamy, fur-accented master bedroom. Or at least it was lavish fairly recently. A fancy reclining couch was overturned a few feet from me. Broken pottery and crystal littered the plush cream carpet. A trail of mud led away from the door—Jeb's, I was sure. And his soiled shirt and jacket were tossed on the carpet near me. Blood stained the cream-colored carpet in several places.

Two male Lapsi I didn't recognize stood shoulder to shoulder, hovering over a prone Jeb, who crouched in a child's pose on the carpet. He was shirtless, and his head rested facedown on a section of blood-soaked carpet. His hand was speared through by a steel fireplace poker, which pinned it into the carpet.

Jeb is having a very, very bad day, I couldn't help thinking as I took him in. Face broken, tased, dunked into a koi pond, and now stabbed through the hand. I couldn't tell if he was alive or dead.

Beyond them, Cassandra was seated on the foot of the king-sized bed. Her legs were crossed primly at the knee, and she rested back on her hands. She hadn't reacted visibly to my abrupt entrance, but now her rosebud lips broke into a wide, beautiful smile, and she stood up from the bed.

I had no idea how I was going to attempt to kill her. Because that's all it would be—an attempt. She was stronger than I was. She was cunning. She could see the future. She was *insane*. Both Jeb and I were doomed. I at least wanted to go down fighting, but I was armed only with a knife. I didn't doubt that it was silver and could kill her: Mason wouldn't have given me something that couldn't kill her. But the execution would be the tricky part.

And the knife was annoyingly hidden in my bra—not easily accessible. At least she wouldn't find it: there was no way I was going to let her fondle my chest. I was so *done* with people touching me without my consent for one lifetime.

"There you are at last, my love," Cassandra said, bending down as she stood over me.

She was gorgeous as ever in a dark green satin dress. It was sleeveless, low cut, with gold chains as straps, and it draped fluidly over her bosom. She'd abandoned the empire waist today, and this time her dress was ruched at the hip and folds of fabric spilled from her hip to below her knees. Her hair looked disheveled, but mostly intact in a half-updo. As in the reports, her fiery red curls were now only about an inch past her delicate collarbones.

She held a hand out to me, which I reluctantly took, and helped me to my feet—already the pain from my awkward landing was gone—and led me farther into the room. I took extra care in keeping just the right amount of distance between us. I wouldn't let her close enough to touch intimate areas of myself, yet I had to stay close enough to stab her.

"You okay, Jeb?" I asked him as Cassandra led me around his prone form. He lifted his head from the carpet—so he wasn't dead—but he didn't look all the way up at me. Aside from the blood-stained tips, his brown hair was mostly dry now and hanging everywhere.

"He's just fine," Cassandra said cheerily.

She released me and roughly pulled the poker from his hand. He groaned almost meekly when his hand was freed, and he brought it up to his chest. Still looking at the floor, he started to push himself onto his good hand and knees.

Cassandra swung the poker, almost casually, at Jeb before his head was fully raised. The hard steel connected with the broken side of his face. I wouldn't call the sound he made a scream, but more of a blind, guttural shriek of agony.

His whole body jerked backward, and he collapsed onto the carpet where he writhed. The hole in his hand was almost completely healed as he buried it into his hair. He started to curl into a ball as involuntary weak whimpers escaped him. I wanted to look away; it wasn't fair of me to watch him while he was like this, but Cassandra was watching for my reaction.

I stared impassively at Jeb and then looked away to give the same impassive "so what" expression to Cassandra. Deep down, I was seething. Truly, I wanted to bash her skull in for hurting him. For making *anyone* hurt like that. His audible agony shook something *deep* in me, and I could recognize it now: it was *rage*. But it was so deep that none of it had any chance of reaching my face this millennia.

"My, I admire this change in you." Cassandra put a hand to the side of my face, cupping some of my hair at the same time. "So impassive, so unmoved, so calm. What a change a soul makes."

"And yet I thought you liked me innocent and fragile. But I suppose I have you to thank for this?" I reached up and moved her hand away from my face and let go. I did it gently, hoping not to agitate her.

"Actually, no." She shrugged. "But Jeb thought the same thing. Do you really think me so monstrous?"

You harvested souls for your city wall, and you store them in what Mason referred to as "soul pillars," I thought incredulously but held my tongue.

"But even if I didn't cause it, I can still admire the artful result." She was still staring dreamily at my face. "It really is quite the improvement. It's what always intrigued me about Jeb. Maybe now that you no longer have that pesky soul, you'll come over to my side and join me."

"Is that what you think?" I blurted, unable to stem the derisive laughter bubbling up in my chest. "Is that what you've *foreseen*? Me, standing by your side while you rule over your stolen city?"

"No, I haven't seen that specifically, but I hope to," she admitted. Her eye twitched, no doubt in response to my mocking tone.

"But have you seen me in any kind of context in your version of the future?" I asked flatly.

"No. I've seen my success up to this point. But I have not been shown anything past that yet," she admitted.

"So, you can still lose, then, can't you?" I asked, too bold for my own good.

Any remains of humor disappeared from her face. Lightning quick, she backhanded me across the cheek. My head snapped to the side, and my teeth rattled in my head. Without a second's hesitation, I brought my own hand up and slapped her, open-palmed, across her face.

It made a satisfying clap and she jerked back, more in shock than in pain. But it was satisfying, nonetheless. I heard

Jeb snicker, but I didn't take my eyes from Cassandra. In my peripheral, I could see he was kneeling now, recovered from the last blow. But the two Lapsi were holding him back.

"You petulant child," Cassandra hissed. She had a hand to her cheek still. I savored the surprise still on her face like it was a square of bitter dark chocolate. "You openly mock me and deride me when I have clearly *won*! I have this city, and it will only expand from here. But not only will I have control, I will be *loved* by Lapsi and by humans. I've shown humans nothing but compassion and kindness. I disrupted their lives and their comfort as little as possible. They will remember that when they come to accept the new atmosphere of this community! They will love me!"

"Sure, you kept the power on. You assured supply chains wouldn't be disrupted. You made sure we wouldn't run out of food or supplies. But that's all you did." I knew I was poking a bear again, but I was determined to fight her tooth and nail. "Humans cooked for the humans that couldn't go home. Humans helped humans. It's our nature. You spent thousands of years being denied community, and suddenly you can have belonging, but you know nothing about *running* a community.

"Rather than start one yourself from the ground, you decided to *take* one. That was your first mistake. Your second is underestimating our desire for freedom. You think you can win complacency by assuring comfort? A cage is still a cage!"

"If they aren't happy with the comforts I've provided, that's fine," she said quietly. "Then their souls are forfeit and will be used to expand our city. They lose the right to be nothing more than cattle."

"That's your solution?" I demanded, bewildered. "Take our souls to make us complacent? Look at me. Look at Jeb. We're soulless, but we still have no intention of bowing down in complacency!"

"Jeb isn't soulless, sweet child," she said, looking at me almost pityingly. "He still has part of his."

She said this as if it was supposed to rattle me, but it didn't. Sure, that tiny voice in my head was telling me that he *could* actually love me, and he hadn't just blurted something he thought he *should* say when the chips were down. But that tiny voice had no place in this life or death situation. I ground it beneath my mind's figurative boot heel for the time being.

"Even if he isn't, I am," I plowed on. "And I'm not accepting captivity. Humans won't accept it. Take it from someone who knows: you take our souls, you take away our fear of consequences. You take away our fear of death. *And* you take away our desire to procreate and *actively* raise the next generation. Maternal and paternal instinct? Gone. How will your little community thrive, then?"

I savored every single change in her expression as she conjured up a response to my brazen mockery of her dream. I watched the obsessive love she had for this weird concept of *Hannah* die in her eyes, like an ember extinguishing. I hoped she was realizing that *that* Hannah didn't exist. The Hannah she believed would join her *could never* exist. The Hannah she wanted to tear away from Jeb was merely a construct, and instead I was merely—as she put it—a petulant child who wouldn't see things her way.

"This is the last time I ask," she said quietly. "Will you be with me?"

"No. Never," I said without any hesitation, and also without any spite or mocking.

Her face closed off then. Her mouth pursed in displeasure, but that was all before she reached behind my neck and pulled me to her. Before I could gasp or steady myself, her sharp fangs tore the tender flesh of my throat, and her lips fastened over the cut.

But there was no pain. In fact, it was the opposite. A loud ecstatic moan escaped my lips, and my eyes closed as waves of pleasure rolled over me. It felt so good to *feel*, even if it was purely a physical, orgasmic kind of pleasure. The waves gradually receded, but there was still no pain, even as my physical strength waned.

Way, way off in the distance, I could hear Jeb. I recognized his cries from last night—though that felt like a lifetime ago. The primal, soul-racking rage was roaring out of him as he...he what? Was he fighting something?

I tried to focus on his rage through the wondrous floating feeling all around me. The rage intrigued me. I'd been feeling something similar just moments ago, hadn't I? Why had I been feeling rage? What was even going on?

Slowly, my mind grasped at something—something important. Then, I realized I was also physically grasping at something. Something within my shirt. No, deeper. Something under everything, pressed against me. Something small. It had been cold at first, but it'd warmed from the heat of my skin. The heat that was slowly leaving me...along with my strength.

I realized suddenly that that little voice in me was still yelling. It wasn't any louder, but I could sense its insistence. It wasn't just a voice, though, it was a will. And it was trying to guide my hand into grasping something. Maybe I should help it. It was so little, after all.

My fingers closed around the knife and pulled it from my shirt. My mind snapped awake, but my muscles refused to follow any further instructions. Too weak. What was even in my hand, again?

Knife.

Knife. Knife. Knife.

I flipped open the knife and, with the last of my reserved strength from the Lapsi blood I'd ingested, I thrust the blade as hard as I could into Cassandra.

She gasped and released me. With nothing to support me anymore, down I went into darkness.

CHAPTER 33

JEB

When Cassandra bit down and started drinking, all I saw was red. I had to get to her. I had to save her, but I had to get through the other two Lapsi first.

I don't remember a lot of the next two minutes, but I remember being showered in blood, and I remember, vaguely, tearing at the Lapsus—Caleb, I think, not that it matters—with my bare hands.

The second Lapsi turned tail and ran as Caleb fell backward, headless. One less Lapsus to fight. The red cleared from my vision, and I gained some semblance of rational thought just as the blade flashed between Hannah and Cassandra.

They both fell when Cassandra released her. I didn't lunge in time to catch Hannah. She was limp and sank slowly to the ground. Her head bounced lightly on the thick carpet. I scrambled over to her and pulled her head into my lap. The skin of her throat had already healed—Lapsi saliva did that naturally after a bite. She had a rapid, fluttering pulse, but it was a pulse.

Cassandra sputtered messily behind me. I'd expected her to dust, but she was still alive. She was on her back on the carpet, the knife still in her abdomen. Her body was convulsing, and she was gripping the knife in her belly with weak, blood-drenched hands, trying and failing to pull it out.

I quickly, but carefully, set Hannah's head back on the carpet and crawled the two feet to Cassandra. I shoved her hands out of the way and gripped the knife in my hand, keeping it lodged in her belly. Hannah had missed her heart but buried it impressively deep into her stomach. She wasn't dead, but she'd bleed out and whither soon enough.

"You weren't *shown* this, were you?" I snarled. The savagery in my voice surprised me, but I didn't care.

"I saw success," she said, almost dreamily, choking weakly on Hannah's blood that was still coating her mouth.

"You saw the *attempt*. The initial, passive shock. That isn't success." I'd had enough fun taunting her. I needed something from her before she died. "*Where is it?*"

"Where is what?" she said. It was amazing that she could still mock me, even though she was dying. I narrowed my eyes.

"You know what. Her soul. Where are you keeping it?"

"Fuck you," she spat.

I tightened my grip on the knife in her stomach and forced it downward, toward her belly button, opening her up further. She screamed in agony and writhed to get away from me, but it was impossible. I stopped cutting her.

"Where is it?" I growled even louder as I gave her a reprieve from the pain.

"It's close to my heart," she hissed bitterly and spitefully.

I saw the chain around her neck. It was almost imperceptible through the blood. It disappeared down the front of her dress. I wrapped my other hand around the chain and pulled, hard. It wasn't a slender, fragile chain, but it broke when I gave it enough of a pull. Then I jerked the knife out of her belly and plunged it right back down, this time into her heart. I gave the knife a twist for good measure, and her body disintegrated into blood-soaked sediment.

I had only a few seconds to savor the feeling of relief for the job well done. I'd joked about killing a Lapsus with my bare hands, and I had. Just a different Lapsus than I'd originally intended. But the queen was dead. And that was all that mattered.

Then the ground trembled. Not just the ground but *everything*. I heard distant explosions, and then everything was shaking.

I dragged myself back over to Hannah and put both hands on either side of her face, willing her to wake up. But I knew she wouldn't. She'd lost too much blood. She had a pulse, but her body was focusing too much on damage control for her to regain consciousness.

I knew what others would tell me to do in this moment. They'd tell me to change her. And I wanted to. Trust me, I wanted to. I wanted her with me, and for her to have an eternity to dance. But I wanted it to be on her terms, not mine. I had to get her somewhere safe.

A pressure wave ripped the walls of the room apart.

I dove on top of her, tucking her completely under me, and took the entire force of the room caving in on top of us.

I lived through the cave-in, and with pure determination, I dug us out.

We were two stories down from the surface above, but thankfully—miraculously—all two stories hadn't collapsed on top of us. I dug us out of the rubble and carried Hannah out the rest of the way.

I climbed out of the tunnels right at the collapsed freeways. And when I clambered over the boulders of cement and bent, hazardous rebar, with Hannah cradled in my arms, I was met with men and guns on the other side.

That wasn't surprising. The city had been taken by a hostile force, so of course there would be guns in my face. No one fired, though, because of the unconscious, defenseless woman in my arms.

I stepped over the last of the cement debris and went to my knees, cradling Hannah. Men approached, but all I cared about was getting Hannah to a hospital. I followed as they put her into an ambulance. The hospital was less than a mile away; she would be fine. As the ambulance pulled away, I surrendered to the men with guns.

I didn't have to. The barrier was gone. The souls had been released like pressurized steam, fracturing the ground as the gas-like vapors escaped, and none of the wards survived the destruction. I could have easily shifted away. But instead, I allowed myself to be hauled away and allowed these men to think I was detainable.

Because I figured someone had to talk to the men outside. All the other Lapsi, I was sure, would scurry back into mystery and obscurity, but I wouldn't. Humans had just been shown our ugly side, and I wanted to talk to a few of them, so a few knew we weren't all monsters.

First, I demanded a shirt or a sweatshirt. I didn't want to talk official talk while shirtless. They supplied me with the most basic, formless, gray T-shirt from a bin. They also let me wipe all the blood from my face, shoulders, and hands so I no longer looked like an ax murderer. They took DNA samples before letting me do this. I told them it was pointless—Caleb's and Cassandra's blood was guaranteed to not be in any system, and they were dead now.

Next, I demanded to be taken to the highest authority with the most widespread influence. That, apparently, turned out to be Homeland Security. This was, after all, a terrorist attack of sorts on home soil. DHS was brought in to work with local responders and task forces in all of Oregon. I didn't mind talking to Homeland Security. I didn't mind being treated like a low-grade terrorist, even though I was the one who'd stopped the damn thing. And I didn't mind that one of the Homeland Security agents in the back of the room was a witch. I had nothing against witches, and most recognized my name from their history—another story for another time.

I was just glad I wasn't taken to Area 51. Not just because it was a *long* drive from Oregon to New Mexico, but because Area 51 is run by witches. Yes, you read that right, but I won't elaborate, and no, this isn't one of my conspiracy theories. Needless to say, if I was taken to Area 51, I wouldn't be able to effortlessly escape.

I have no qualms admitting that I wasn't the best person to shoulder this task. I wasn't a diplomat, and I wasn't a talker. I'd spent the past fifty years hiding and disassociating from the world. My exposure to culture and world events was purely through shows, movies, and podcasts—and unsolved mystery documentaries.

I grew crankier and crankier as the interrogation dragged on. I didn't mean to be a dick, but my soullessness came out more than I would have normally allowed as my fuse shortened.

But I *think* I managed to get the point across that this was an *extreme* case and unlikely to happen again. Most of my kind were still grappling with this new concept of belonging or wanting to belong. We'd all go back into the shadows most likely. Some might rent out an entire apartment building and live there, together, and some might join bowling leagues or trivia nights. But, like before, humans would never even know.

Cassandra was extreme, and she was insane. She'd gathered all the extreme vampires that wanted chaos around her, with the intention of eradicating them once order was established. But we never saw that happen. It was only a day, after all.

Those extreme Lapsi were out there still, but I imagined they would all go back underground for a bit—until they felt the world needed a new Zodiac Killer. But I didn't tell them that part.

By the end of it—what I decided was the end of it—I think I got my points across. We'd always been, and we'd always be. We blend. We adapt. We survive. Our impact is minimal. Cassandra was dead. Aside from the damage she did to the city, everything was finished. *I* was finished. I was hungry, in pain, and I was fucking tired. The bones in my face were broken, and nothing but time was going to heal them.

I was adamant about finding Hannah in the hospital, and I wouldn't be detained longer than I wanted to be. The DHS witch was the one to escort me away. He intended to drive me back to Portland, but there was no need; it was just a formality.

"I suppose we'll be hunted again," I said as we left the discrete, uncrowded building I'd been taken to for interrogation. "Because of all of this."

"Not overtly. Not by us as a race," the witch said, shrugging. He pulled out a cigarette and lit it. He was maybe in his late forties, but he looked great. He didn't have an ounce of unnecessary fat on him, and his dark Mediterranean hair wasn't going anywhere soon. He kept his cigarettes in a fancy silver case, and as it flashed out of sight, I caught the name *Christian* engraved on its lid. "But there may be some that take it upon themselves..."

He let his sentence trail off, but it wasn't hard to get his meaning. Some might take it upon themselves to track down all those who were involved. I hoped they mostly targeted the bad ones, the ruthless malicious ones, and not the ones, like Riley, who just happened to be detained by Cassandra. But I didn't know their tactics.

"Yeah, I don't blame them," I said with a shrug. "A lot of bad happened here that needs to be answered for. This was...this was awful. It doesn't make my kind look good at all." I rubbed my neck awkwardly.

"No, no, it doesn't," he agreed, taking a long drag from his cigarette.

"And what about the rest of the world? What's going to happen? Is there going to be some kind of Roswell or Arizona Lights cover-up?" I knew—I just *knew*—this whole thing would show up on some conspiracy theory or unsolved mystery documentary. Even with the widespread carnage and evidence, this would fall into obscurity. It was human nature.

"I can't say." He shrugged. He looked at me a little slyly. Because he didn't know, and also, because he was DHS, he *couldn't* say. "But I have no doubt that there's going to be quite the resurgence in supernatural young adult romance novels and movies in the coming years."

"Oh, I guarantee it," I agreed with a little chuckle. My nerves were so frayed that I had no problem finding amusement in the absurdity.

"This was a mess, but the sentiment behind it all isn't condemnable," the Homeland witch said as he took his last drag on his cigarette and deposited it in the ash tray. "I'm only one witch in millions, so I don't speak for everyone. But personally, I can't say I hate the idea of Lapsi having a kind of community. Maybe one that isn't taken by force, that establishes itself slowly, naturally, and noninvasively."

"Oh, really?" I ran a hand through my hair but regretted it immediately. It was a crusty mess from the dried blood.

"That's how civilization started in the first place, isn't it?" He put his hands in his pockets. "I'm talking before power struggles, before territorial skirmishes and wars. Back in hunter-gatherer days. Civilization happened naturally and organically and purely for the need of belonging and protecting each other."

"Yeah, I guess." I leaned against the wall. "But it's difficult to be noninvasive and develop naturally when everything on the planet is already so established. But it sounds...nice."

It did sound nice. A town or village of Lapsi—maybe even codependent with humans. Something permanent.

Some tiny seed had been planted in my brain. It was a lot to think about, but not right then.

I shoved my hands in my pockets. My fingers brushed the glass vial pendant, and I remembered I had it in the first place. I needed to make one more stop before the hospital, I decided.

I said a brief goodbye to the Homeland witch—a little more abruptly than was polite, but I blame the exhaustion—and I shifted away, leaving Oregon in the dust.

It was well after one or two in the morning when I arrived on the porch and started pounding on the door. But the door opened to my insistent knocking almost immediately.

"Jeb!" Libby exclaimed as she opened the door wide. "Oh my god, you're alive!"

I was surprised at how welcoming she was to me, considering my haggard appearance. But I must have looked better than I did when I'd nearly broken her door down a week earlier. At least I wasn't starving this time, just exhausted.

I knew she wasn't holding her arms out for a hug—because why would she be? But I put myself into her arms anyway and deflated. My shoulders sagged, and my head fell onto her shoulder. I was just *so tired*. All I wanted to do was rest, but I had something else to do first.

CHAPTER 34

HANNAH

I woke to the smell of medicine and sterilizing products, and the sound of buzzing and beeping machines.

Based on those clues, I knew what to expect when opening my eyes: the boring beige décor of a Legacy Emanuel Medical Center's hospital room. I'd been inside this hospital several times for nursing school clinicals. At first, I hoped none of my fellow classmates had seen me, but the cards and balloons that littered the otherwise boring room squashed that hope.

Jeb was seated by the bed, his head resting on his arm. His other hand rested in mine, awkwardly around the pulse oximeter on my index finger. I gave his hand a brief squeeze to alert him that I was awake, and he raised his head with a start. His expression showed muted relief.

"You finally got me to a hospital," I said by way of greeting. I lifted one side of my mouth and winked.

"Yeah, this time the hospital was a little more handy than a witch." He returned my smirk with a wary smile. "They can heal wounds, but they can't do a blood transfusion."

"But he still brought a witch, anyway, as backup," Libby said, announcing her presence. She was seated in a hospital-issued pleather chair in the corner of the room. She smiled her warm smile at me and waved. "Welcome back to the land of the living!"

"Thanks," I said automatically.

My fake smile faltered as we all fell silent. I thought about the last bit I remembered. Cassandra had bled me to the point of death, and it was foggy, but I *thought* I stabbed her in the end. After that is dark, but my surroundings assured me that everything worked out. Jeb was alive—showered and in clean clothes too—so I'd been out for at least a few hours. Probably more, I suspected.

"Your dad's here too," Jeb informed me.

That explained his polished appearance and casually styled hair. He wanted to make a good impression on my dad.

"He must have been really worried," I said, deadpan. I didn't like that I couldn't draw up any feelings about my father. He was my dad, after all, and I should want to see him, but I was still soulless. I couldn't conjure up feelings of love or bring myself to have any *wants*.

"Your mom was too. She showed up earlier," Jeb said. He hadn't let go of my hand yet.

"I hope you told her to go to hell for me," I said automatically. Apparently, my contempt for my mother was still intact, despite losing my soul. I just *knew* that, like everything else, she'd blame this on quitting ballet.

"No, but I think your dad did," Jeb said. He looked like he was trying to hold back a grin, and that was enough to stir up some genuine amusement from my depths.

"I brought Sophie with me too," Libby added cheerfully. She scooted the chair out of the corner of the room so she was closer to the bed. "Your dad has her right now. That girl...she can charm the birds out of the trees..." She shook her head in exasperated disapproval and smiled again. "She's going to be so happy to see you."

I struggled to find something polite or fake-enthusiastic to say. I could recall the emotions, but bringing them to my face was so damn hard. I didn't want to offend, but I just...felt nothing.

"It's okay," Libby assured me, gently. "You don't feel anything yet, but you will."

"I will?" I was still soulless, and they don't regenerate. If she was making a joke, it wasn't funny.

Jeb sat back and, from the pocket of his flannel, withdrew a metal-accented glass vial pendant about the size of my thumb. He held it out to me, but I hesitated to take it. I bit my lip against the smirk, remembering the thought I had earlier about Cassandra masturbating with it.

"I hope you washed it," I said, still smiling with amusement.

"Well, it was covered in blood, so yeah, I did," he said, his brow furrowing.

I wasn't about to let him in on the joke. Instead, I put my hand out and he placed the vial into my hand. Inside it was a swirling silver mist. I'd never seen a soul before, and I hadn't had any idea what I *thought* a soul would look like. But here it was.

It felt comfortably warm to the touch, and not from Jeb's body heat. This was *my* heat. *My* warmth. I held it gingerly in my open palm, not closing my fingers around it.

"So do we just...crack it like a glowstick?" I asked after staring at it for a moment.

"More or less," Libby said, smiling. "I'm here to help guide it back into you, but since it's yours, and it hasn't been separated from you for that long, it shouldn't really need guidance."

I just stared at the beautiful thing in the palm of my hand. I tried to conjure up how I felt about it, even though I knew I couldn't feel anything. I liked the idea of being whole again and functional. But I was functional like this too. *More* functional, almost, just not whole. While soulless, the only thing I looked forward to feeling was physical, intimate pleasure, and that was so brief and inconsistent.

"Just a word of caution, though, before we do this," Libby said, breaking my train of thought. "Reuniting with your soul might be a little rough. You'll suddenly be reconnected with your emotions and will have to process...everything you've seen over the past few days."

"The poor girl has her work cut out for her," I mused aloud, a smirk spreading on my lips. I'd experienced so much in a short amount of time. So much violence. So many groping hands. And so much death. Two of which were at *my* hands.

But maybe she'd be fine. Perhaps when I merged back with my soul, the separate traits would remain somewhat separate. Maybe souled-Hannah would learn to brush things off a little easier. Maybe she wouldn't fall back on her empathy as much. Having less empathy wasn't necessarily a good thing, but it was a helpful survival tactic. It was all about balance.

"All right," I said finally. "Let's do it."

I rapped the glass vial sharply against the edge of the side table, like an egg. The glass split and the shimmering mist released through the cracks like steam under pressure.

"One more waffle left. Claim it, or Sophie gets it," Colt said, lowering the plate down onto the table.

"Colt," Libby said reproachfully. "She is eighteen months old. She can't have more than one waffle. Her little stomach is too small."

"More incentive for Hannah to take it, then. Or else little Sophie might burst," Colt said, pinching Sophie playfully in her side. Sophie released a throaty giggle.

"But then she'll be a chubby little baby and even more adorable," I said, chuckling involuntarily at the irresistible sound of Sophie's giggling. "But, fine, I'll take it." I stabbed the last waffle and put it on my plate. I hadn't calorie counted since I left the ballet academy, and I wasn't about to start again now.

"I still don't understand waffles," Jeb said, narrowing his eyes skeptically as I reached for the syrup. "They're the same batter as flapjacks. So why not just make flapjacks? They don't require a separate appliance to make them."

"They're appealing because the little cavities in the waffles hold more syrup than a flat surface," I chided him. "And we call them pancakes now. You're showing your age."

He sat back heavily in his chair and didn't say anything. Colt wiped Sophie's hands off with a dish cloth and lifted her from her highchair. As soon as her feet touched the tile floor, she took off running out of the room, trilling loudly. Libby followed her into the living room, and Colt brought the highchair over to the sink to clean it. Jeb and I were alone at the table.

I turned in my chair and brought my legs up and draped them over his lap. He uncrossed his arms and rested his hands on my shins, casually.

A week had passed since waking in the hospital and reuniting with my soul. I'd had a long conversation with my dad about what Lapsi were and that they weren't all monsters. He didn't need any convincing accepting their existence—it was hard to deny it when you lived in the city where the proof had been broadcast. I hadn't exactly told him that Jeb was a Lapsus, but I would soon. And I'd assured my classmates that I was alive and made up some elaborate lie for my roommate about why and how I disappeared without a phone *and* got trapped within the seized city a week later.

Because Portland was still reeling from the destruction of a major portion of its central transportation system, school hadn't resumed. The general populous was still in a state of shock, though I wasn't paying any attention to the yarns people were spinning. I'd lived it, I'd been there, I'd almost died, and while I didn't kill the big bad bitch, I took her down like a badass.

Instead, I'd spent the past week shifting with Jeb between his apartment, my dad's house, and Libby's house. I was untethered from the reality of normal life, and I was reluctant to return to it. And while I still hadn't fully adjusted to having a soul again, life felt nearly perfect.

And I swear, the food tasted better. These were only Eggo frozen cinnamon waffles, but they tasted like the best waffles on the planet.

"I love you, Hannah," Jeb said softly, pulling me out of my thoughts and immediately sending me spiraling into different ones.

We'd spent a lot of time together over the past week, but he hadn't said those words since Portland. We hadn't even kissed or acknowledged that we'd almost had sex a week ago: we'd just been enjoying each other's company. I'd put my legs across his moments ago, but that was just something I *did*. I used to do it to my fellow dancers at the academy.

The last time he'd said he loved me was when he thought he wasn't going to see me again. Was he going somewhere?

"Don't tell me that's something you only say when you're saying goodbye," I said after staring at him for a moment.

"What?" His eyebrows drew together, and his hands tensed on my calves. "No. It's something I say only when I mean it."

"I thought you couldn't love," I said softly. I didn't know what else to say.

"I didn't think I could," he agreed. "But something's changed. I don't want to...I don't want to live without you."

And that was really saying something. I'd seen his apartment; I'd seen his habits. He put enormous effort into the wall that faces his door to make people take one look inside and leave him alone forever. He was practiced at avoiding people and at being unapproachable in a *harmless* way. This was a man perfectly content to be alone forever, but now he wanted me there with him.

And did I love him?

Undeniably, *yes*. Not in a high school, hands sweating, hormones raging, die-without-you pining kind of way. Something deeper.

He was gruff and hard to know, but he *danced*, and all of his rare genuine smiles were directed only at me. He'd stopped himself from having sex with me even though I was willing because he wanted it to *matter* to me. No matter how much I told him I'd been genuine in my wants and needs in that moment, he still stood by the fact that it would have been wrong.

Regardless of how frustrating it'd been in those moments, it was probably when I realized I loved him. I'd been soulless at the time, blue-balled, and angry, but I'd known, somehow. Or maybe I'm just inserting my souled self into that memory. Either way, he gets major points and respect for how he respects *me*.

And I didn't want to imagine a life without him in it, either.

I leaned forward, into his chest. I put my hand on the back of his head and brought his face to mine. The kiss lasted for a long moment but didn't deepen into anything passionate—we weren't exactly alone in the house. He pulled back and pressed his forehead to mine.

"But being with me is complicated," he said in a soft murmur.

"Because of the whole 'you're an immortal and I am not' thing?" I teased. I glanced to the kitchen sink and realized Colt had left us alone. Good man.

"Yes, that thing."

"Well, we have an option, as you know," I said with a nonchalant shrug. I didn't have to say it, but I did anyway. "You could..."

"I don't..." He averted his eyes. "I don't want that for you. I don't want that to be the only option."

"Why not?"

"I want you to have a life," he said. "I want you to experience a normal life with normal, dull experiences."

"Well, you're not selling that normal life very well by calling it 'dull.'" I rolled my eyes.

"I see you with Sophie. You want a family. You want children."

"I can do this thing...what's it called, exactly?" I tapped my chin thoughtfully. "Oh, right. *Adopt*."

"And your dad. You still have your dad."

"My *dad*? My dad is *awesome*," I said simply, emphatically. "He didn't blink when I told him I was bi. He stood by me when I quit dance, and he divorced my mom because she wouldn't stop verbally abusing me over it. He is the most *accepting*, chill, supportive person I know. He knows about Lapsi, and guess what? He's *okay* with their existence."

"But..."

"If you change me. *If.* He will grow old knowing I'm fine," I assured him gently. He looked away at the table beside us. I reached for his head with both hands and turned it—ever so gently, because his face was still broken—healing, but still broken—toward mine again. "I want it. I want life with you. But it doesn't have to be immediately. I have things to get in order first. So you can warm to the idea for a bit."

"What kind of things to get in order?" His brown eyes stared into mine, and I so wanted to kiss him.

"Well, for starters," I said, sitting back, "probably start a trust for myself, that I will pass on to my heir, and then her heir...because that's apparently how you grow money for eternity."

"I can help with that," he said, nodding. A small smile was growing on his face.

"Second is grow my hair out a little bit longer. If I want to be a ballerina any time in the coming centuries, it's a little hard to get into a regulation ballerina bun at its current length."

"And what else?"

"And *eat*. Ever since my soul was returned, food tastes *amazing*. And I'm not ready to give that up yet." I twirled my sticky fork in the air as I said this. "And one more thing."

"What's that?" he said, grinning. I could almost hear his thoughts just then: *How very human.*

"I should probably finish school," I said seriously. "Finish school. Graduate. And *then* 'die,' so I never have to pay back any of my student debt."

He chuckled softly and nodded in acceptance. "Okay. I can agree to that."

I touched his face again and turned it gently back to me. "I love you, too, Jeb," I said quietly, putting my forehead to his.

He put his arms around me and drew me even closer to him. We were still connected at the lips when he shifted us away from Boston and to somewhere more private.

FALLEN SOULS

The End

ACKNOWLEDGMENTS

Well, dear reader, here we are again, and I owe you another million thank yous! You will always be the first entity that I thank. Without you, there would be no point in this. I write for you, and only a small fraction of it is really for me.

Second, and this is going to sound weird, but I want to thank Hannah, Jeb, and all the characters of this book, as well as the book itself. This wonderful, ambitious book pulled me out of the longest writing slump of my life, and saved me from a looming depression spiral. Hanah and Jeb saved my life, and I wouldn't be here if this idea hadn't locked onto my brain, and sent me into a writing frenzy like nothing I've ever experienced.

And none of the books would be out in the world if it weren't for this book. It forced me to rewrite the two books I was least proud of. And, two years later, the books I never intended to be the FIRST books I published are out in the word, ushering this lifesaving baby into the limelight.

So, yeah...I kind of...dedicate this book to itself. It's that important. Maybe not to you, but definitely to me.

Next, special thanks go to my beautiful beta readers, who I always worry will tear me apart, but they really do remind me that I can do this, that I should be proud.

To my parents for believing in me, and always telling me how proud they are of me. To my husband, who just stands back and lets me do my thing, especially when I'm in writing mania.

Thank you Julia, who I texted FIRST when I had the idea for this story, and who rode the brainstorming rollercoaster with me, whether she knew it or not.

And finally, thank you Hozier, James Arther, Lewis Capaldi, and Dean Lewis, who were the vibes I floated on while writing this book. Your voices will always make me think of Jeb and Hannah.

Please Review

Please tell me and others what you thought of this book? Thank you so much for reading my story. Your eyes on the page mean the world to me. If you feel comfortable doing so, I implore you to leave a rating and review for this book on any of the e-commerce or booky platforms. Reviews (whether good, bad, or neutral) are invaluable to authors. They help us see where we need to improve, and help us get our books into more hands.

Don't miss out!

Visit the website below and you can sign up to receive emails whenever Amelia Rose publishes a new book. There's no charge and no obligation.

https://books2read.com/r/B-A-LGDZ-GQRAD

BOOKS 2 READ

Connecting independent readers to independent writers.

About the Author

Amelia Rose has a BA in English and Classical Humanities, but barely remembers any Latin. She lives in Ohio with her husband, and fills every moment of her free time with writing, drawing, making beaded jewelry, or constructing cardboard sculptures. She loves dancing shamelessly to all kinds of music, obsessing over musicals, devouring horror movies—the gorier the better—and going to concerts. She never passes up the chance to ride a rollercoaster or get kisses from a dog.

Fallen Idols is Amelia's debut novel, and the first in an ever expanding series called *The Fallen Favorites*. Follow her on Instagram @Nontalkativewriter for updates, promotions, and artwork.